ANGELICA ELING

UNCHARTED *Waters*

A Waverly Cove Romance

For everyone who has had to change direction when life took an
unexpected turn, and for the harbors we find in unexpected
places.

Dear Reader,

The story you're about to read is a romance, but it's also an honest exploration of women's health struggles that are too often over-looked in fiction. While Gemma and Liam's journey toward love is at the heart of this novel, their path includes realistic portrayals of endometriosis, fertility challenges, and the complexities of navigating our healthcare system as a woman.

This book contains content that may be emotionally triggering for some readers, including:

- Detailed experiences with chronic pain
- Medical gaslighting
- Discussions of infertility

Please be gentle with yourself as you read. While this story ulti-mately celebrates resilience, it doesn't shy away from the very real difficulties that millions of women face in seeking proper medical care. If you need resources or support for endometriosis or other reproductive health conditions, please contact the organi-zations in the author's note at the end of the book.

Thank you for joining Gemma on her journey. Your willingness to engage with these important topics helps break the silence surrounding women's health.

With gratitude,

Angelica

Chapter 1

Gemma

Four hours driving from Boston and I still wasn't ready to arrive.

My hands gripped the steering wheel tighter as Waverly Cove emerged around the bend, knuckles white against the black leather. The town spread below like a postcard: Whitewashed clapboard buildings sat nestled amongst granite outcroppings, as if they'd grown there. September sun caught weathered buoys and turned them amber and crimson across the restless harbor.

It looked exactly as I'd left it, which somehow made everything worse.

I pulled into the scenic overlook and shifted into park. My phone sat silent on the passenger seat, no last-minute emergencies from clients who didn't know I'd stopped being their planner three weeks ago. The cramping pulsed low in my abdomen. Manageable if I didn't move too fast, concerning if I acknowledged how long it had been building.

Tourists in catalog-fresh fleece milled around the wooden

sign boasting about Waverly Cove's illustrious history as a 19th-century fishing village. A family posed with matching day packs. A couple in brand-new hiking boots took selfies with the harbor in the background. People who could afford to discover charming coastal towns in peak foliage season without calculating whether the gas money should have gone toward medical bills instead.

I cracked the window. Salt air rushed in, mixed with that particular fall smell of decomposing seaweed, wood smoke, and something sharp and organic I'd never been able to name. Across the cove, harbor seals dotted the rocks at low tide. The eastern headland rose dark against afternoon light, the historic lighthouse a white exclamation point at its summit.

Nan's cottage sat just below that lighthouse.

The memory surfaced without permission. Seven years old, flour dusting the kitchen counter in clouds. Nan's weathered hands guiding mine as we crimped pie crust edges. *Press here, fold there, don't worry about perfect.* Her cottage had smelled like woodsmoke and vanilla, and she'd never once asked why I was quiet or tried to fix my careful need for order. She just handed me measuring cups and let me organize her spice cabinet by height.

Last year, before everything imploded, I'd planned to visit. Add it to the list of things I'd meant to do.

The cramping intensified. A familiar tightening that meant I had maybe twenty minutes before I needed a bathroom and pain medication. The pattern had started in Portsmouth as dull background noise. By Augusta it demanded attention. Now it edged toward urgent.

I'd already stopped twice. Once at a rest area where a well-meaning elderly woman asked if I was pregnant, her eyes dropping to my hand pressed against my lower abdomen. *No, just my uterus trying to kill me, thanks for asking.* Once at a gas station where I'd given myself a pep talk in a fluorescent-lit bathroom between waves of nausea, mascara smudged under both eyes.

My phone buzzed. Kate's third text in twenty minutes.

KATE

Alex made his famous curry. Not too spicy, promise! Fair warning: the children have prepared what they're calling a 'welcome ceremony.' Interpretive dance and glitter may be involved.

I laughed despite everything. The sound felt foreign in the car's silence.

GEMMA

Running 15 minutes late. Got lost.

True, if you counted the three traffic lights where I'd doubled over the wheel. Or that bathroom break that lasted twenty minutes.

KATE

Might be easier to navigate if you visited more than once a decade, Prescott.

She had a point. Kate and Nan had extended invitations for years. Christmas, summer barbecues, Maya's dance recitals, Noah's science fair triumphs. I'd perfected the art of declining: cite the current crisis, promise next time would be different, repeat as needed.

Until there was no next time to promise. Until my business

partner suggested I take "some time" and I realized time was a polite way of saying *before we push you out entirely.*

I dry-swallowed the pill I'd been avoiding, bitter coating dissolving against my tongue. The prescription bottle rattled in my purse like dice in a cup. A sound I'd grown to hate. The medication would blunt the worst of the cramping within thirty minutes, but it came with a price. Cotton-wrapped thoughts. Distance from my own body. That floaty sensation that made everything feel slightly unreal.

A small price to pay for being able to sit through dinner without excusing myself to cry in the bathroom.

I needed time. Time to return to my home away from home for the first time since I lost Nan two years ago. Time to decide whether to let a surgeon cut into me or keep pretending everything was manageable. Time to figure out what came next after my carefully constructed life imploded in front of Boston's social elite.

Boston Public Library. Last year.

The Livingston-Price wedding. The culmination of nearly eighteen months of planning, and my biggest commission of the season. I'd been adjusting centerpieces when the pain struck. Not the usual cramping I'd learned to work around, but a twist that brought me to my knees. Cold marble pressed against my palms. Peonies and garden roses scattered around me, five hundred dollars a centerpiece. The future Mrs. Livingston-Price's Louboutins two inches from my face.

Her voice, sharp with alarm: "Someone call an ambulance!"

The florist's hand on my shoulder. The caterer's whispered speculation. Everyone staring.

Take some time, my business partner had suggested over lattes the next day. Her voice was overly casual while her mani-

cured nails tapped against her cup. Each click measured, deliberate, counting down to the bombshell.

Get the surgery. I'll handle things.

And if I don't?

I've been thinking of bringing Eva Coronado in. Temporarily.

Right. Temporarily. Like a medical leave that becomes permanent when everyone realizes the company runs smoother without its constantly canceling, frequently hospitalized co-founder.

I gripped the steering wheel until my knuckles ached. I could turn around. Drive back to Boston. Pretend I wasn't running away from a life that no longer fit.

Except being in Boston meant watching Eva learn my client lists and charm my vendors. It meant my business partner's tight-lipped concern and unstated disappointment. It meant my immaculate South End condo, where every surface reflected back my failure to build the life I'd so carefully planned.

At least in Waverly Cove, I could fail quietly.

I put the car in drive.

As I drove through town, I cataloged changes that I had missed from the overlook. The old bait shop had transformed into Compass Rose Brewery with chalkboard signs advertising locally sourced ales. The corner market now boasted organic everything and kombucha on tap.

But underneath the trendy rebranding, Waverly Cove remained stubbornly New England. Granite bones and salt air and history you couldn't airbrush away.

Kate's Victorian belonged in a magazine spread. Slate-blue siding, crimson door, wraparound porch with original gingerbread trim. Only the children's chalk masterpieces decorating the driveway and the basketball hoop above the garage suggested actual family life happened here.

I parked behind Kate's car, a station wagon with bike racks and those stick-figure family decals I'd always found aggressively wholesome, and sat for a moment. The pain medication had kicked in, creating that familiar distance between me and my anxiety. Everything was slightly muffled.

But it couldn't quite silence Dr. Whitman's voice from three weeks ago, crisp and clinical: *Stage IV endometriosis. Extensive adhesions. High risk of permanent damage without surgical intervention.*

The car door swung open.

"You were overthinking so hard I could see it from the kitchen window." Kate appeared in paint-splattered jeans and a flannel shirt that had seen better decades. Her dark hair escaped what might once have been a ponytail. Paint flecks dotted her fingernails, cerulean blue and burnt umber. The lines around her eyes had deepened since I'd last seen her, but they only emphasized her smile. "Get out of this car before I call the twins to perform their welcome dance right here in the driveway."

My Kate stood there. The one person who'd never given up on me. No matter how many times I'd let work consume me or forgotten to call back. No matter how many times I'd promised to visit and then manufactured an excuse.

Her expression softened. She reached through the open door to take my hand, fingers weaving together the way they used to when we were eight and facing down Mean Sally Morrison behind the playground.

"I know." Kate squeezed my fingers. "But you're here now."

The front door burst open to reveal two whirlwinds wearing matching mischievous grins.

"SHE'S HERE! SHE'S HERE!"

A little girl with Kate's dark eyes launched herself toward us, wielding a silver wand topped with a star hanging on for dear life. Glitter sparkled in her hair and across her cheeks like rogue fairy dust. Behind her, a boy clutched a clipboard with a serious expression, glasses askew.

Kate raised one finger to her lips without looking at her daughter. "Maya, volume control."

Her grin suggested this was a losing battle she'd stopped fighting.

"Noah! Status report?"

Noah adjusted his glasses with grave purpose, consulting his clipboard. "The welcome committee and refreshments are ready."

I suppressed a laugh. "Very thorough."

"Uncle Liam says proper preparation prevents poor performance." His chest puffed slightly. "Also, Daddy made Maine-shaped sugar cookies."

"WELCOME TO MAINE, THE PINE TREE STATE!" Maya threw her arms wide and nearly took out a potted fern with her wand, sending glitter cascading to the porch floor.

The house smelled like bread and curry. Cumin and cardamom. When was the last time I'd cooked anything more elaborate than microwave oatmeal in my eight-thousand-dollar kitchen?

"We prepared a whole show," Noah informed me solemnly, tugging my hand with sticky fingers. "Maya made costumes. Sort of."

"She made costumes." I let him lead me into a living room that somehow balanced design with child-proof practicality.

Hardwood floors gleamed with the patina of family life. Colorful storage bins overflowed with creative chaos. Family photos covered every flat surface in frames ranging from elegant silver to hand-decorated construction paper. A half-finished thousand-piece puzzle of the Maine coastline had taken over the coffee table.

"Gem?" Kate's voice sounded distant, muffled by the gauzy sensation the medication created. "You okay?"

"Just tired." I plastered on the smile that had closed a hundred wedding contracts, the one that said *everything's under control* even when centerpieces were on fire. "After the twins' welcome ceremony, maybe I can crash?"

Kate had known me too long to buy the professional smile, but she nodded anyway. "I'll show you to your room after their performance. You can take a nap before dinner."

"It's not just a performance." Maya planted her hands on her hips. She had draped a blue bedsheet around her shoulders like a cape. "It's a full historical and cultural exploration of Waverly Cove. With dance."

"Interpretive dance," Noah clarified with the air of someone who'd recently learned this important distinction.

"It's now a condensed history," Kate assured me, "since Aunt Gemma drove all the way from Boston today."

Her casual "Aunt Gemma" loosened muscles I didn't realize I'd clenched since pulling into the driveway.

"I've been looking forward to this all day." I lowered myself carefully onto the couch. The soft cushions embraced me like a hug, fabric worn smooth from years of family movie nights. The medication had blunted the worst of the cramping but left my limbs heavy and disconnected.

"I'm ready when you are."

Maya beamed and pressed a button on a tiny speaker, filling the room with what sounded like whale songs remixed with a synthesizer.

"Welcome, traveler, to our journey through time." She extended her arms and swayed like seaweed in a current, her voice carrying the confidence of a seasoned performer. "Before humans walked this shore, the mighty ocean carved our destiny from stone and storm..."

I caught Kate's eye over the children's heads as Noah began what I could only assume was his interpretation of colonial-era net fishing, complete with dramatic swooshing noises and the occasional "splash!" His glasses slipped down his nose with each enthusiastic casting motion.

Maya spun in circles while Noah demonstrated the proper technique for hauling imaginary lobster traps, their feet padding across the hardwood floor.

The knots between my shoulder blades unraveled.

For the first time since my body had betrayed me, I could see past survival mode. Past the constant calculation of whether I could make it through the next hour, the next meeting, the next event without collapsing.

Yes, I thought. This was where I needed to be. Not to recover. Not to decide. Just to exist for a while without apologizing for it.

Chapter 2

Liam

The pinot noir bottle was cold against my palm as I stood on Kate's doorstep. Colder still was the evening air. September in Maine didn't mess around. The temperature had dropped fifteen degrees since sunset. My neck muscles had knotted themselves into their usual pattern of tension after a day of stubborn cases and insurance denials.

Kate's texts from earlier were still fresh in my mind.

KATE

Still on for tonight? Just a casual family dinner. Nothing special.

Oh, and my friend from Boston is staying with us for a while. Gemma Prescott?

Anyway, 6:30. Don't be late. Bring wine.

Seven years back in Waverly Cove had taught me to recognize my little sister's matchmaking radar when it locked onto a target. She was about as subtle as a lighthouse in fog.

The door swung open before I could even knock.

"Uncle Liam!" Maya's voice cut through my exhaustion. She launched herself at my legs, plastic tiara askew on her dark curls. "You're here for the special dinner!"

I lifted her, eyebrow raised. "Special dinner? Your mom said it was just plain old Tuesday family dinner."

"Nope!" Maya shook her head emphatically, sending the tiara dangling. "Mama said it's special 'cause Aunt Gemma is here, and you're gonna like her 'cause she's pretty and smart and makes scary spreadsheets!"

Noah appeared, clutching his emotional security clipboard. "You're four minutes and thirty-seven seconds late, Uncle Liam." He made a careful check mark, tongue between his teeth in concentration. "Mom said you'd be early or really late, dependin' on whether Mrs. Espy brought photo albums."

"Bingo." I grinned. "Complete with running commentary on every appetizer served aboard the Enchantment of the Seas."

Kate emerged from the kitchen, a dish towel dangling from her back pocket. "Wine. Good. You remembered." She lunged for the bottle.

"Don't get grabby," I warned. "And don't think I don't see what you're doing, Katherine Elizabeth."

"I have absolutely no idea what you mean, William Robert." Her wide-eyed innocence hadn't fooled me since she was four. "I simply invited my oldest friend to stay while she recovers from some health challenges."

A shadow flickered beneath her enthusiasm. "She's had a rough time lately, Liam." Her voice dropped. "She needs friends more than complications. So just... be yourself? Not the whole brooding, emotionally unavailable thing you do so well?"

Alex appeared in the doorway, saving me from this unfair but accurate character assassination. "Liam! Glad you could escape the clinic." His handshake was firm, callused palm rough against mine.

"Barely." I followed him into the kitchen as Kate and the kids headed upstairs to summon Gemma for dinner.

"Beer?" He retrieved one from the fridge.

"God, yes."

I kept my voice casual. "So, Kate's friend. Gemma. I'm supposed to remember her from childhood, but I'm drawing a blank."

Alex's mouth quirked. "Kate's best friend from elementary school. Spent summers here with her grandmother, Nan Prescott. She's an event planner from Boston. Apparently quite successful."

"And she's staying here because...?"

"Health issues." Alex hesitated, glanced toward the stairs and lowered his voice. "Not my place to share details, but I filled some prescriptions for her yesterday. Pretty heavy duty pain meds."

The pharmacist in him had said more than he'd intended. The PT in me ran through possibilities. Chronic pain. Significant enough for high-dose medication. Recent enough that she was taking time off to adjust to the treatment.

"And here they are." Alex looked past me.

A woman entered the room with Kate hovering behind her like an anxious stage mom.

My first impression was of someone who'd mastered professional presentation. Thick auburn hair secured in an effortless-looking twist, jewel-toned blouse that worked for both office and dinner. The kind of polished competence that came from years of managing high-stakes events and difficult clients.

My second impression was the careful calculation in her every movement. She paused at the threshold, a micro-hesitation most people wouldn't catch. Her weight shifted slightly to her left side. She assessed the room layout before committing to enter, like someone navigating around invisible obstacles.

Pain compensation patterns. My PT brain cataloged them automatically.

My third impression, the one that bypassed clinical assessment entirely, was that she was beautiful in a way that made you forget whatever witty thing you'd planned to say.

"Gemma, you remember my brother Liam?" Kate's eyes darted between us with painful obviousness. "Liam, this is Gemma Prescott."

Gemma offered a polite, professional smile. Green eyes that shifted to gold near the pupils, gauging me with clear wariness. She'd been briefed on Kate's intentions and wasn't thrilled about it.

"Nice to see you again." She extended her hand. Her voice had a slight roughness to it, like sea glass worn smooth. "Though I'm not sure 'remember' is accurate. You were already off conquering college when I was still following Kate around like a devoted puppy."

Her handshake was firm, the professional grip of someone who'd learned to project confidence. But I caught the details my training had wired me to notice: the slight tremor in her fingers, quickly controlled. The way her grip strength started strong but faded fractionally, like sustained muscle engagement cost her. How she held her spine perfectly straight, compensating for core instability or protecting against movement that might trigger pain.

All of this processed in the three seconds of a handshake.

"The infamous Gemma." I kept my tone light, ignoring the

way my pulse had kicked up. "Kate mentioned quarry jumping and Mrs. Henderson's berry bushes?"

The smile that broke across her face changed everything. Genuine delight replaced professional courtesy, transforming her features. "In our defense, Mrs. Henderson told us to help ourselves. We interpreted that with creative license."

"She meant the basket on her porch, not every bush in her garden." Kate laughed.

Kate seated me directly across from Gemma at dinner. A placement so obviously engineered that Alex offered an apologetic half-shrug from his end of the table.

"Do you work primarily with athletes?" Gemma asked as we settled in. "Kate mentioned you took over your father's practice."

"Expanded it, actually. Dad focused mainly on sports injuries. I added chronic pain management and women's health services."

The tension in her eyes eased fractionally. Recognition there. Relief, even.

"Liam's being modest." Kate interjected. "He completely revolutionized the practice. They get referrals from Portland specialists now, even Boston doctors."

"That's impressive." Gemma's interest seemed genuine, not just polite conversation. "Chronic pain seems so poorly understood in traditional medicine. Most doctors just throw medications at symptoms."

Her words carried lived experience. She pressed her fingers against her lower abdomen. An unconscious gesture, the kind patients made when pain was present but manageable.

"Exactly. Traditional medicine excels at emergency intervention but often fails at chronic dysfunction. We focus on integrated approaches: PT, pain psychology, nutrition, medication management when appropriate."

As we moved through topics—her event planning successes, my expansion of Dad's practice, the twins' latest creative projects—Gemma's guardedness eased. Her wit emerged in unexpected observations about small-town tourism and the fine art of managing mother-of-the-bride meltdowns.

But I couldn't ignore how she shifted position every few minutes, subtle weight redistributions that most people wouldn't notice. The way she braced herself before laughing, protecting against the spike of pain that movement might trigger. How she held her fork in a modified grip that reduced wrist strain.

Professional assessment warred with personal interest. I wanted to know what was causing her pain, wanted to help. But more than that, I wanted to hear her laugh again without seeing her brace for the cost.

Complication. Definitely a complication.

"Aunt Gemma, are you sick?" Maya asked abruptly, with a child's ability to slice through adult pretense. "Mama says we hafta be quiet in the mornings because you don't feel good."

Gemma froze, fork halfway to her lips. She set it down carefully and straightened her spine, a deliberate recalibration of composure.

"I have a condition that makes me uncomfortable sometimes." Her voice held remarkable steadiness. "Kind of like when you have a really bad stomachache, but for grown-up reasons."

"Can Uncle Liam help?" Noah's clinical interest was evident. "He fixes people who hurt."

The question settled into the room. Gemma's composed

expression faltered. Her jaw tightened, then relaxed, like she was making a decision about how much truth to offer.

"Some things are more complicated than a broken bone."

"Like when my Transformer got stuck between robot and car." Noah nodded seriously. "Daddy tried to fix it with his best tools, but it still doesn't work the same."

The comparison startled a genuine laugh from Gemma. The first unguarded sound I'd heard all evening. Worth the flash of discomfort that crossed her face immediately after.

Kate suggested the twins show Gemma their artwork while adults handled cleanup. As Gemma followed the children, she paused before standing, gathering herself with calculated effort. The kind of preparation that spoke to experience with her body's limitations.

"Well?" Kate materialized beside me at the sink. "What do you think of her?"

I glanced across the room. Gemma knelt to examine Maya's finger painting at eye level despite obvious discomfort. The movement clearly cost her. A brief pause, her hand bracing against the wall for support. But she did it anyway, focusing completely on Maya's animated explanation about purple elephants and rainbow oceans.

"I think she's dealing with a serious medical condition and trying very hard not to let it define her."

Kate's matchmaking enthusiasm faded. "She was quieter than usual tonight. Bad day?"

"From what I can see, yes." I kept my voice clinical even as attraction tangled with professional concern. "But diagnosing across a dinner table isn't appropriate."

Kate bit her lip, glanced at her friend. "She's struggling more than she admits. I've been trying to convince her to establish care here while she's staying. Her Boston doctors are excellent, but she needs ongoing support, not just telehealth appointments."

I knew where this was heading. "Kate—"

"I know, I know." She raised her hands. "Professional boundaries. But Lisa specializes in exactly what Gemma's dealing with. Couldn't you at least mention it?"

I considered this, watching Gemma patiently explain something to Noah while Maya added enthusiastic commentary. Her careful attention to the children despite her own discomfort showed something essential about her character. Generosity of spirit, even when it cost her.

"I could mention Lisa's services as a professional resource. But that would be the extent of any involvement."

Kate's shoulders dropped, tension leaving her face. "That would be perfect. Lisa's approach could really help her."

"Let me talk to Lisa first. See if she has availability, what her initial recommendations might be. Then I can mention it casually, without pressure."

Kate's innocent expression fooled no one. "Would I pressure?"

"Is the harbor surrounded by land?"

Alex called us into the living room for dessert, ending our consultation. As we rejoined the group, Gemma had settled on the couch with Maya tucked against her side, sharing a picture book. The domestic scene pulled at something I'd deliberately ignored for a long time. The possibility of this kind of connection, this kind of quiet domestic contentment.

"Uncle Liam, Aunt Gemma doesn't know about your magic

house!" Maya announced as I took a seat in the adjacent armchair. "The one with secret passages!"

"It doesn't have secret passages, Maya." I corrected gently. "Just the widow's walk and built-in cabinets that seem mysterious to you. And someone else built it over a century ago. I just brought it back to life."

"You did?" Gemma leaned forward slightly, voice brightening. "Restored a historic house?"

"I worked construction summers in high school and college." I accepted coffee from Kate. "Bought the old captain's house in Harbor Heights a few years ago. It needed work."

"There he goes being modest again." Kate's meaningful look was visible from orbit. "He practically rebuilt it from the foundation up. Preserved all the original features while adding modern conveniences. It's the perfect family home now."

The emphasis on "family home" landed like a foghorn. Gemma's quick glance in my direction probably wondered if I shared my sister's transparent agenda.

"I enjoy working with my hands. Physical therapy is rewarding, but sometimes you need more immediate results. Something you can see transform day by day."

"I understand that completely." Gemma shifted for comfort. "Event planning is similar. You create something tangible, and then it's done. Finished. Unlike chronic problems that just... persist."

The personal note in her voice suggested she wasn't just talking about wedding venues.

Before I could respond, Maya let out an enormous yawn. Alex clapped his hands once. "Bedtime, you two."

"But Aunt Gemma hasn't seen our rock collection!" Noah's protest came with crossed arms.

"Or heard my new song!" Maya added, suddenly alert.

"Tomorrow." Kate's voice was firm. "Aunt Gemma will be here for weeks. Plenty of time for geology and performances."

As Alex herded the twins upstairs, silence filled the living room, thick and obvious. Kate glanced between Gemma and me with painful transparency, then remembered "something important" she needed to discuss with Alex upstairs.

"Your sister has many talents." Gemma shifted again, seeking a more comfortable position. "Subtlety isn't among them."

"Kate approaches matchmaking like a military campaign planned by someone who's never been in the military."

"I should apologize. She lured you here under false pretenses."

"No apology necessary. At least this time she introduced me to someone interesting."

Her cheeks flushed. "That's the kindest acknowledgment of unwilling participation in a setup I've ever heard."

I paused, then decided to risk it. "Speaking of which, our practice has expanded since you were here last. Dr. Lisa Patel joined us last year. She specializes in integrated pain management. Many of her patients have reported significant improvements."

Gemma stiffened. "Kate shouldn't have discussed my medical situation."

"She didn't share details." I kept my voice reassuring. "Just mentioned Lisa might help. Professional courtesy, nothing more. I won't bring it up again."

Her shoulders eased. "I appreciate the information. I'll keep it in mind."

The conversation shifted to safer territory. We debated whether the Daily Knead made superior blueberry muffins or sourdough bread, discovered a shared appreciation for mystery novels with complicated plots, argued good-naturedly about whether hiking or kayaking offered better coastal views.

When Kate returned, she failed to conceal her satisfaction at finding us deep in conversation. "I hate to interrupt serious culinary analysis, but it's getting late."

"I should head home anyway." I stood. "Early morning means earlier paperwork."

"It was nice seeing you again." Gemma's smile was warm despite her exhaustion. "And for the record, the Daily Knead's sourdough is superior."

"Fighting words in blueberry muffin country. But I might reconsider with proper evidence."

I paused at the door. "The offer about Lisa is sincere. No pressure, just a professional resource that might help."

Gemma considered me, measuring intentions against what I suspected was experience with medical professionals promising things they couldn't deliver.

"Thank you. I might take you up on that. I wasn't planning to stay long, but I'm realizing I might need more support than I initially thought."

I recognized that tone from countless patients learning to ask for help after years of fierce independence.

"Thanks for handling Kate's romantic campaign with such diplomatic grace."

"The pleasure was mine." I meant it more than I'd expected.

Driving home along the coastal road, my thoughts circled back to Gemma Prescott. Medical instincts tangled with personal interest in a way I hadn't experienced since residency. The professional side cataloged her symptoms: chronic pelvic pain, possibly gynecological based on hand placement and Alex's mention of heavy pain medication. Something she'd been managing for a while, given how practiced her compensations were.

The personal side kept replaying her unguarded laugh, the intelligence that sparked when discussing projects that engaged her, the way she'd prioritized the twins' enthusiasm over her own comfort.

I pulled into my driveway, the restored captain's house dark except for the porch light on its automatic timer. I'd have to be careful about boundaries if she sought treatment at our practice. Refer her to Lisa, maintain professional distance, ignore the way she'd leaned forward when interested in a topic.

Yet I couldn't dismiss the memory of her smile, genuine and unguarded. The quick wit that surfaced once she relaxed. Small gestures that revealed character beneath the composed professional surface.

Kate's matchmaking attempts had always been easy to deflect before. This time felt different. Maybe it was how she'd knelt for Maya despite the obvious pain, or the way her fingers worried the hem of her shirt between confident declarations. The recognition in her eyes when I'd mentioned chronic pain management, like she'd finally found someone who might understand.

Standing in my restored doorway, I had to admit the truth: I looked forward to seeing Gemma Prescott again.

That was either the beginning of something good or a complication I wasn't prepared to handle.

Probably both.

Chapter 3

Gemma

Kate ambushed me over breakfast in what was clearly a premeditated attack.

"Lisa has an opening today." She held the phone, already dialing.

I opened my mouth to protest.

"And don't even think about telling me you're fine. You were creeping around at two AM like some kind of heating pad-seeking ghost."

Fair point.

Westfield Physical Therapy lived in a converted Cape Cod building that tried hard not to look like a medical office. Blue-green shutters, colorful flower boxes, the whole charm offensive. It still smelled like a doctor's office, though. Antiseptic with a hint of lavender air freshener.

The reception area had warm lighting, comfortable furniture, and plants that looked actually alive. Someone who understood that white walls were the devil's invention had designed this space. An older woman whose placard identified her as Margaret sat behind the desk, with tidy gray hair and watchful eyes that probably didn't miss much.

"Gemma Prescott?" Margaret didn't wait for confirmation before continuing. "Kate's been talking about you for weeks." She smiled like she meant it. "Nancy Prescott's granddaughter, right? I still have one of her watercolors. That woman could make a lobster trap look elegant."

"She had a gift for that," I said, surprised by the catch in my voice.

Margaret slid the paperwork across the counter. "Dr. Patel will be ready shortly. Tea? Coffee? Something stronger?" She winked. "Kidding about the stronger part. Mostly."

I declined and settled by the window with the clipboard. I'd completed these forms so many times I could do it blindfolded. A depressing superpower if ever there was one.

My pen moved through practiced motions while I recounted my sordid history. Previous treatments: birth control pills (failed), depo shots (failed), Lupron (brief success, then spectacular failure), dietary elimination (ongoing, mixed results), various pain protocols (jury still out).

Halfway through the pain scale questions, voices approached from the treatment area. I recognized Liam's warm baritone. He emerged with an elderly woman who moved like she was carrying glass in a cardboard box.

"Dorothy, I'm serious about the twenty-pound lifting limit." His tone managed to be both authoritative and affectionate.

"Oh, Liam." She patted his arm. "I've been hauling lobster traps since you were in diapers. A little shoulder tweak won't kill me."

"It might if you decide to reorganize your entire garden shed this weekend."

The exchange had the ease of long familiarity. A jarring contrast to my specialists back in Boston, who treated me like an interesting case study. Polite, professional, and about as personal as a tax return.

He walked Dorothy to the door, and I found myself watching despite my best intentions. The light from the windows caught him in profile. He was tall enough that he had to duck slightly through the doorway, his rower's build evident even in the professional khakis and navy polo that bore the clinic's logo. He moved with an easy confidence that came from someone comfortable in his own body, which made sense for a physical therapist.

When he turned back toward me, I understood why Kate had been so smug about this setup. Dark hair showed just the faintest touch of silver at the temples, which only made him more attractive instead of less. He had a clean-shaven, strong jaw. And when his gaze found mine across the room, those brown eyes held an awareness that made my stomach flip in a way that had nothing to do with pain.

Be professional, Gemma. He's Kate's brother. And you're here as a patient.

None of those very sensible thoughts stopped me from noticing the way his forearms looked as Dorothy patted his arm one final time as she departed.

Liam's gaze found mine across the room. He approached with measured steps.

"Morning, Gemma. Kate up to her usual tricks?"

"If by tricks you mean psychological warfare disguised as sisterly concern, then yes." I attempted what Kate called my "normal person" smile. "Is there a support group for this?"

"For what?"

"Westfield persistence."

His mouth quirked. "Community center's booked solid. Mondays for blind date victims, Tuesdays for the babysitters they trapped."

"What about people strong-armed into medical appointments?"

"Thursdays. Bring snacks. It's an extensive program."

I relaxed despite myself. Amazing how someone making you laugh could undo hours of tension.

"I'll pencil that in."

He glanced at his watch. "Lisa's finishing up with her current patient. Fair warning: she's going to want to listen instead of handing you a prescription and a pat on the head."

"Revolutionary."

"I know. We're rebels that way."

He seemed about to say more when a woman in a matching polo appeared in the doorway. She was quite petite, with dark hair that had given up on staying styled, and the confident bearing of someone who knew exactly what she was doing.

"Gemma?"

"That's your cue," Liam said. "You're in good hands. Lisa's the closest thing to magic we've got around here."

As I stood, my body reminded me why I was there in the first place. I had to grip the chair arm while my pelvis sent up an urgent memo about the sudden movement.

Liam tracked the motion. Observation mode.

"I'll check in with Lisa later," he said as I gathered my things. "Professional consultation only. Your business stays your business."

"I'd appreciate that."

Dr. Patel guided me down a hallway lined with coastal

photography and plants that someone actually watered. The carpet was thick enough that my footsteps disappeared instead of echoing off institutional linoleum.

Her treatment room had soft lighting and a pair of chairs that looked like they belonged in someone's home. Someone had painted the walls soothing gray. A large abstract painting of the harbor that I had a sneaking suspicion Kate had painted covered most of one wall. Only the padded table gave any indication that this was a medical facility and not an overly minimalist living room.

"I'm Lisa Patel." She introduced herself as she settled into the chair across from me, leather creaking as she adjusted, pen poised over her notepad. "And before you ask, yes, I'd prefer that you call me Lisa. Life's too short for unnecessary formality."

"Kate's been thorough in her communications about my situation." I immediately wished I'd found a more diplomatic way to say my best friend has a big mouth.

"Kate cares about you. That's obvious." Lisa's expression stayed steady. "But I'd rather hear your version. Medical records tell one story. You tell another."

The invitation caught me off guard. When was the last time a doctor asked for my narrative instead of writing it for me?

My shoulders relaxed. "Let's see. The greatest hits of my medical mystery tour." I settled back into the cushions. "Started at fifteen with what every female in my family called 'just part of being a woman.' You know, that special time when you're expected to suffer and accept that your womb is a monthly hostage situation."

Lisa made notes but kept her eyes on me. She was listening, not just waiting for her turn to talk.

"College was fun. Picture this: straight-A student hunched over a toilet in the campus health center, vomiting from pain, while a nurse explains I need to 'learn to cope with normal discomfort.'"

"How many doctors before someone took you seriously?"

"Let's see." I counted on my fingers without meaning to. I'd never actually tallied it before. "Seven. Seven different doctors before anyone listened. Eight, if you count the nutritionist who suggested yoga and positive thinking." My voice carried an edge I couldn't suppress. "The diagnosis came courtesy of a spectacular collapse at a client's high-society wedding. Nothing says 'professional event planner' like face-planting in front of two hundred guests."

"And the diagnosis?"

"Stage four endometriosis. Extensive adhesions, multiple endometriomas, the works." Medical speak for my body waging war on itself for sixteen years while doctors told me it was normal. "Basically, my reproductive system became an over-achiever in all the wrong ways."

I paused, swallowing against the sudden tightness in my throat. "My Boston team is pushing for excision surgery. Possibly an oophorectomy, if the adhesions are as bad as they appeared on the scans. It all depends on what they find when they go exploring."

Lisa absorbed this without offering platitudes about my age or suggestions to "just relax and try getting pregnant." Points in her favor.

"That's a significant decision you're facing." Her voice held understanding without pity. "In the meantime, my approach focuses on improving function through targeted therapy. Instead of just dulling the pain, we work on changing how your body responds to the chronic inflammation and tension. Would you be open to a hands-on assessment?"

I nodded, curiosity overriding my usual medical appointment wariness.

The next forty-five minutes were like learning a language I didn't know existed. Lisa's examination was thorough without being invasive, her explanations clear without being condescending.

"Feel this." She placed my hand on my hip flexor. The muscle beneath my palm vibrated with tension I hadn't known I was carrying. "Your body's trying to protect you. But chronic guarding creates more problems than it solves."

She applied light pressure. Warmth cascaded down my leg and up into my lower back. The knot softened under her touch, and my whole pelvis seemed to exhale.

"That's... actually helping."

"These exercises help retrain your nervous system." She demonstrated a technique that looked deceptively simple. "Think of it as teaching your muscles they don't have to work overtime anymore."

For the first time in years, someone recognized that living with chronic pain wasn't just about enduring. It was about recovering yourself, one small victory at a time.

"So this could actually improve how I function? Not just make things marginally less terrible?"

"Exactly." Lisa's smile reached her eyes. "Research shows targeted pelvic PT can improve quality of life, whether or not you pursue surgery."

Not a cure, not a miracle. But something real and achievable.

A soft knock interrupted us. Lisa stepped outside, returning with an expression like she was fighting a smile.

"Dr. Westfield would like to consult on your case, if you're comfortable with that. Strictly professional."

"That's fine. He can know about my rebellious reproductive system."

Amusement flickered in Lisa's eyes. "I'll make sure he understands the professional nature of the consultation."

We finished reviewing exercises and scheduled follow-ups. When Lisa walked me back to reception, my steps landed with more certainty than they had an hour ago. I wasn't hugging the wall anymore, wasn't scanning for the nearest escape route.

At the front desk, Margaret chatted with an elegant older woman who radiated the kind of authority that suggested she'd once been someone very important.

"Perfect timing," Lisa said. "Gemma, meet Elena Orocho. Elena educated most of Waverly Cove's youth before retiring."

"English teacher for twenty years, then principal for the last decade," Margaret added with obvious affection.

Elena extended a manicured hand, her grip firm and assessing. "Those eyes are unmistakable. You must be Nancy's granddaughter. Your grandmother saw potential in everyone."

"She saw the best in people," I agreed.

"A career in education teaches you to read people quickly." Elena's gaze moved between Lisa and me with open curiosity. "So what brings you to our local miracle worker? Sports injury? Stress-related issues?"

The probe made my professional mask snap into place. "Just managing some ongoing health matters."

"Ah yes, stress affects everything at our age." She gestured eloquently. "Sometimes we push ourselves too hard, especially successful women like yourself."

The assumption that my condition stemmed from lifestyle choices hit wrong. Before I could craft a cutting response, Lisa intervened.

"Actually, chronic pain often has complex genetic and phys-
iological components. It's not always related to stress levels."

Elena had the grace to look chagrined. "Of course, you're
right. I didn't mean to suggest..."

"No offense taken," I lied smoothly. "It's a common miscon-
ception."

"Speaking of which," Lisa said, touching my arm lightly,
"remember what we discussed about the home exercises. Call if
you have questions."

"Thank you. I will."

Outside, the morning fog had lifted to reveal Waverly Cove
in crisp fall detail. I paused on the steps, inhaling salt air mixed
with wood smoke from someone's chimney.

I had exercises to try. A timeline that wasn't just "wait and
see." Actual steps to take, for the first time in months.

"How did it go?"

The voice made me jump. Liam stood nearby, coffee cup in
hand. His question sounded casual, but his eyes narrowed with
focus.

"Is it that obvious I needed a check-in?" I straightened automatically, defaulting to my everything-is-fine posture.

"Only to someone who spends their days watching how
people move when they hurt." He nodded toward the cafe
across the street. "I've got thirty minutes before my next patient.
Coffee? I could bore you with updates on Waverly Cove's new
pier regulations. Guaranteed distraction through municipal
tedium."

I blinked at the unexpected invitation. "Tempting as that
sounds, I'm expected at Casa Chen for volcano construction
duty."

"Ah, the famous underwater diorama project." His face

stayed straight, but humor lit his eyes. "Noah's been planning this for weeks. Engineering precision meets artistic vision."

"They mentioned something about a very specific glitter-to-baking soda ratio."

"That sounds like Noah. He's probably created a color-coded timeline."

"Naturally. Maya's contribution will be 'more glitter everywhere.'"

His laugh transformed his entire face, revealing humor his professional demeanor usually kept hidden. "You've clearly figured out the way to Miss Maya's heart. More glitter, indeed."

The silence was easier than last night. More comfortable.

"I should rescue Kate from whatever chaos the twins have created," I said.

"Godspeed. If anyone can survive the Chen volcanic creation process, it's someone who plans events for a living."

"We'll see if my crisis management skills transfer to elementary school science projects."

"I have faith in your abilities." The way he said it sent warmth curling low in my belly.

"See you around, Gemma."

"See you around, Liam."

His gaze followed me down the walkway. When I glanced back, he raised his cup and held my gaze a beat longer than necessary.

Great. One more complication added to my list.

Chapter 4

Liam

The Saturday after Kate's matchmaking attempt, Henderson's Hardware hummed with weekend warriors. Ambitious to-do lists, neighbors catching up on gossip, and a guy buying his third leaf blower of the season. I dodged through them all, headed for the plumbing section.

My own bathroom renovation had hit a wall when I discovered that vintage plumbing and modern fixtures went together about as well as Maya and vegetables. The pipes from 1962 had opinions about my design choices.

"Liam Westfield!" Ben's voice boomed over the whirr of the ceiling fan display. He'd been running this place since before Home Depot was even a concept. "Settle a debate about foundation repair before winter hits."

I gave him the nod that meant 'I respect your expertise, but please don't trap me in a twenty-minute lecture on mortar composition' and kept moving.

I stopped short as I registered familiar auburn hair and shoulders held rigid with frustration.

"There must be someone who can assess what needs to be done." Gemma's voice carried a layer of professional politeness stretched thin over mounting irritation.

She faced off with Todd, Ben's nephew. The kid had inherited his uncle's hardware knowledge but none of his people skills.

"Ma'am, like I said, everyone's booked through November." Todd managed to make 'ma'am' sound condescending. "Summer people always think they can just—"

"I'm not summer people." The interruption sliced through the tension. "My grandmother lived here year-round for forty years."

Professional boundaries meant staying out of this. Not my patient, not my business.

But Gemma was Kate's person, which made her family. Watching her get the runaround made my jaw clench.

My boots echoed on concrete as I approached. "Problem here?"

Gemma's face changed when she recognized me. Surprise, then careful neutrality.

"Just discovering the local contracting situation."

"End of season rush," I explained, turning to Todd with a smile that suggested cooperation would benefit everyone. "Gemma's restoring the Prescott cottage. Nancy's place? You remember her watercolors in the town hall. I "told her that Henderson's was the place to go to take care of everything she needs."

The lie came easy. In Waverly Cove, you needed a local to vouch for you or you'd wait until Christmas for a callback.

Todd looked marginally more impressed, though he still had the helpfulness of a wet blanket.

"What kind of work are you looking for?"

"Mostly cosmetic." She'd shifted into what I suspected was her client-facing tone. Smooth, professional, revealing nothing. "Painting, fixing windows, updating the bathroom. The usual wear and tear."

I nodded. Classic Maine architecture meant classic Maine problems. Surprises behind every wall. The cottage would need more than cosmetic work if it had been sitting empty since Nancy passed.

"Have you had anyone assess the structure yet?"

"That's what I'm trying to arrange." For just a moment, her professional mask slipped. Frustration bled through the careful facade.

Todd suggested some DIY guides and offered to put her on the cancellation list. When he wandered off to help someone else, I moved closer.

Close enough to smell coffee on her breath and see how her hands trembled slightly. Whether it was from caffeine or stress, it was hard to say.

"Waverly Cove takes some calibration," I said. "Locals test you until they can figure out where you fit. It's like hazing, but slower and more polite."

"And where do I fall in this social hierarchy?" The dry humor caught me off guard.

"'Nan Prescott's granddaughter' buys you a lot. She was beloved. 'Kate's oldest friend' helps too. But you're still new until you've survived a winter or sat through a town meeting. Preferably both."

That earned me a laugh, and I returned it with one of my own.

"I'll add 'achieve full citizenship' to my renovation list, right after 'figure out why the kitchen window won't open.'"

My offer came out before I'd thought it through. Before I

could calculate whether this crossed some invisible line between helping Kate's friend and personal interest.

"I could swing by today and take a look. At the cottage. Help you figure out what needs contractors versus what you could handle yourself."

Her smile faded. Wariness replaced the humor. She'd learned to be careful about accepting help, that much was clear.

"I don't want to take up your whole Saturday."

"You'd be doing me a favor." I meant it. "I was procrastinating on my own project anyway. Organizing my sock drawer started to look appealing."

She hesitated. Running some calculation between practical need and personal boundaries. I recognized the pattern from patients who'd learned that accepting help came with strings attached.

"If you're sure," she finally conceded. "I'd appreciate another perspective."

"I'm no contractor, but I know who to call for what. Consider it competitive intelligence gathering. I get to see how the other half renovates."

While Gemma paid for a DIY guide that was clearly more diplomacy than actual need, I grabbed my forgotten plumbing supplies. My mind shifted to structural assessment. Integrity, systems functionality, what was cosmetic versus what was critical.

Safe, technical territory.

Then Ben's voice boomed across the store like a foghorn. "If it isn't Gemma Prescott! Heard you were back in town. Shame about your condition."

Ice settled in my gut.

Gemma's posture snapped rigid, her knuckles going white around that useless guide.

"Mr. Henderson." Her voice could've frozen water. "How lovely to see you again."

I reached the register fast, launching into a conversation about her Boston event planning business that redirected Ben's attention from medical gossip to proximity to minor celebrity status. Not subtle, but effective.

Small mercies.

"Ready to head over?" I asked when we'd escaped.

<hr>

The fall air hit like a cold shower after the store's stuffy atmosphere. Gemma exhaled slowly. "Thank you." Her shoulders dropped from their defensive position. "For all of that."

"Waverly Cove specialty. Equal parts genuine concern and pathological nosiness, with boundaries that shift based on how long you've lived here and whether your mother makes good pie."

She tucked the guide into her bag, movements radiating suppressed irritation. "Kate warned me, but I'd forgotten how intense the information networks are. In Boston, you could have a medical emergency in broad daylight and people would step over you while avoiding eye contact."

"Here, someone would call the ambulance, hold your hand, and have the entire town informed of your diagnosis before the sirens faded." I paused. "But they'd also bring casseroles."

Her laugh made the whole awkward encounter worth it.

"A generous interpretation of community care."

As we walked toward our vehicles, details I had no business cataloging. The efficient way she moved. How she tested the car door handle before pulling it open, that micro-pause before stepping off the curb. Her body's protective patterns, the compensations I'd seen in the first dinner.

I climbed into my truck. In the rearview, she settled into her sedan with deliberate movements. Still guarding, still careful.

Professional boundaries, I reminded myself. Helping Kate's friend. Nothing complicated.

But as I pulled onto Harbor Street with her car following at a careful distance, curiosity had shifted beyond structural integrity. Watching her navigate Todd's condescension and Ben's nosiness with that blend of professionalism and sardonic humor had been more interesting than anything in my own stalled renovation.

The cottage was only ten minutes away. Ten minutes to shore up those guardrails. To remember why getting personally involved with someone who might need treatment at our practice was a complication I couldn't afford.

Just helping Kate's friend.

The lie got easier every time, but harder to believe.

Chapter 5

Liam

I'd kayaked past the Prescott cottage a hundred times, wondering what it looked like up close. Now I knew: worse than I'd expected. The cedar shakes had gone soft in places, porch steps rotted through on the left side, and the windows were so crusted with salt you could barely see inside. The blue paint on the door and porch swing had faded to something closer to gray. Whatever garden Nancy Prescott had once tended had surrendered to rugosa roses and beach grass, though even abandoned it had a kind of wild beauty to it.

But Gemma stood at the bottom of those questionable steps looking at the place like it was perfect.

She tested the first board before stepping on it, then the second. Deliberate and cautious. Most people would've just charged up those steps without thinking. Smart woman.

"It's smaller than I remembered." She stood in the doorway with one hand on the frame, her shoulders pulling inward. "But the view's exactly the same."

"Your grandmother used to say she had the best view in

Waverly Cove," I said. "Drove the real estate agents crazy when she wouldn't sell."

"You knew Nan well?"

"Everyone knew Nancy. She taught art at the high school." Her voice echoed in my head during gait assessment lessons. *Don't just look, Liam. See.* "Used to quote Einstein. 'Imagination is more important than knowledge.'"

Gemma's expression softened, the composed mask she'd worn since arriving dissolving into something warmer. "That sounds exactly like her."

"She was right." I gestured toward the interior. "Shall we?"

The cottage was quiet in a way that felt intentional, like it had waited to be inhabited again. Nancy's books still lined the shelves, organized by a system only she understood. Shells and sea glass caught the afternoon light from their places on windowsills and shelves. Everything positioned for the view.

Dust coated every surface.

I cataloged structural needs while tracking how Gemma moved through the space. The way she tested a chair back before trusting it with her weight, how she trailed her fingers along surfaces like she was relearning the place. The floorboards creaked under our feet, the only sound in the stillness. No buffer of receptionist chatter or family noise. Just us and the work that needed doing.

"Nan replaced the roof right before she died," Gemma said, following my gaze to a water stain on the ceiling. When she pointed up, her shoulder brushed my arm.

I moved back, trying to maintain professional distance. Then failed at it about thirty seconds later when the light caught the copper in her hair and I forgot what I'd been about to say about water damage.

"The bedroom needs work too," she announced, leading me

down the narrow hallway. "The windows stick, and I think the floor's settling."

The bedroom swallowed us in accumulated stillness. Dust coated every surface. Nancy's last morning frozen in place. An open book perched on the nightstand, reading glasses beside it, slippers by the bed. It felt intrusive to be here, like we were disturbing a shrine to her final hours.

Gemma braced herself against the window frame and pushed. Nothing happened.

"Painted shut," I said. "Here, let me."

I positioned myself behind her, my hands covering hers on the latch. The placement put me close enough to feel the warmth radiating from her skin. Lavender, maybe. Or honeysuckle. The window gave way with a crack and ocean air rushed in, cool and clean.

"Thanks." She didn't immediately step away, and neither did I.

We stood there for a moment, the salty breeze moving between us, her shoulders rising and falling beneath my hands. Then she cleared her throat and moved toward the hallway. "The bathroom's going to be worse. See for yourself."

The bathroom belonged in a museum or a dumpster, hard to say which. The clawfoot tub looked original, probably from when the cottage was built. An avocado green toilet that should've died in the seventies crouched next to it like it was ashamed of itself. Pink tiles climbed halfway up the walls, and a pedestal sink with a crack running through it like a fault line stood beneath a medicine cabinet mirror that had lost most of its silvering.

When Gemma turned on the faucet, the pipes groaned like they were auditioning for a horror movie. Water came out rust-colored at first, then cleared. She moved back from the initial sputter and bumped into me in the narrow space. Her hand found my forearm for balance.

"Sorry."

"No problem." My voice came out hoarse.

I knelt to check the floor near the tub, as much to give myself some distance as to assess the actual damage. The cold tiles radiated through my jeans. "Moisture issue here, but it looks contained. Probably a slow leak over time rather than anything catastrophic."

"So 'frustrating in new and creative ways' rather than disaster."

I looked up. She was smiling, and tension in my chest released. "Pretty much."

I stood and checked the sink fixtures, watching her reflection in the cracked mirror. She'd shifted her weight to one side, hand pressed to her lower back in that way meant to look casual but wasn't working. The pain was there whether she wanted to acknowledge it or not.

"Can I tell you something?" Her composed mask slipped as excitement crept into her voice. "I've wanted to renovate this bathroom since I was sixteen. That tub is the original from 1901. My grandmother refused to replace it even when everyone told her to get something more modern."

I looked at the tub with new appreciation. Real cast iron under that porcelain. "They don't make them like this anymore."

"Exactly." Her hands started moving as she spoke, sketching shapes in the air and gesturing toward corners and walls. The studied line of her shoulders relaxed and she moved closer to the space, proprietary and passionate. "I want to make it the centerpiece. That toilet has to go, obviously. And these tiles. Look at this tiny vanity. Have you seen how much stuff women need these days? This bathroom is screaming for storage and actual lighting you can see by."

I'd maintained deliberate distance since she'd arrived in Waverly Cove. Clipboard barriers and timed visits, deflecting personal questions back to structural assessments. Fear masquerading as professionalism. But watching her talk about honoring the past while reclaiming the space for herself, I leaned forward instead of maintaining that studied distance.

This wasn't just about practical renovation. This was about rebuilding something she'd lost and was reclaiming.

"You could refinish the tub," I suggested, calculating what it would take. "Keep the history, update everything around it."

She went still, her sketching hands freezing mid-gesture. "You think that would work?"

Then a wince tightened the corners of her eyes and color drained from her cheeks.

I closed the distance between us. "You okay?"

"Just..." She attempted a smile. "Standing too long. It's been a while since I've done this much walking around."

Without asking permission, I guided her to sit on the edge of the tub. "Better?"

She nodded, drawing her knees toward her chest. One hand still pressed to her spine, the other gripping the tub's rim. "I hate this. Feeling like my body calls all the shots."

"Your body's been through trauma. Healing isn't linear." I resisted the urge to touch her hand, to offer more comfort than words. "What helps usually?"

"Heat. Rest. Time." She laughed, shaky and bitter. "None of which are conducive to home renovation schedules."

"They can be." My mind worked through possibilities, seeing the space not as it was but as it could be. "We can design around what you need. Take the shower, for instance." I moved to the far wall, gesturing to where the new fixtures would go. "Grab bars here and here, but integrated into the design so they look intentional rather than medical. Built-in bench, adjustable shower head at multiple heights."

"That sounds expensive."

"Let me show you what I mean." I turned her to face the wall, guiding her hands to press against the cool tile. "Put your hands here, like you're steadying yourself."

I positioned myself behind her, my arms coming around to show the placement. The position put us close enough that she could lean back against my chest if she wanted to. I found myself hoping she would and hoping she wouldn't in equal measure.

"Grab bar here," I said, my voice closer to her ear than I'd intended. "At this height, this angle. It's not about limitation. It's about creating a space that works with your body rather than against it."

Her breathing quickened. Her shoulders rose and fell beneath my hands. "That sounds thoughtful."

"It's practical," I said, though we both knew it was more than that. "When you're designing a space, you design it for the person who'll live there. All of who they are."

She turned in my arms then, and suddenly we were face to face. Too close. Not close enough. Her eyes searched mine, a question in her eyes she didn't voice.

"You'd do that? Design around my... complications?" She gestured vaguely at herself.

"They're not complications, Gemma. They're just you."

This is where I should have moved back. Maintained the professional distance I'd constructed so deliberately since Kate first mentioned her friend was coming home. Instead, the words came out: "I could help you with the renovation. If you'll let me."

The offer settled between us, carrying far more than simple neighborly assistance.

"That's generous, but I couldn't impose that much. You don't even know me."

"Kate would never forgive me if I let her best friend tackle this alone," I said, which was true but not the whole truth. Not even close. "Besides, I enjoy renovation projects. It's a different kind of problem-solving than my day job."

I could have told her how I'd noticed the careful way she moved when she thought no one was watching. Could have admitted that I wanted to be part of whatever she was building here, that I'd been thinking about this cottage and her plans for it more than was strictly professional. But my throat closed around confessions that would change everything between us before we'd barely begun.

Gemma searched my face, her green eyes thoughtful and unguarded in a way they hadn't been since our first meeting. "You're serious."

"I am. Full disclosure though: between work and this, we're looking at weekends and evenings. I'll get estimates from local contractors for the major plumbing and electrical work. But the finishing touches, the design elements... we could handle those together."

She hesitated. Wanting the help but needing to prove she could do this alone. That fierce independence was central to who she was.

"I should at least pay you. A consultation fee, at minimum."

"Tell you what. My sister Abby is expecting her first baby in a few months. Use your event planner skills to help Kate organize her shower, and we'll call it even."

Her hand found her stomach, fingers unconsciously pressing against the fabric of her shirt. Her spine straightened and her chin lifted as her lips curved into the smile I'd seen her use with difficult conversations. Polite, efficient, emotionally bulletproof. "That seems uneven. What else can I do?"

"Renovation projects run on caffeine and snacks. The superior quality of both is non-negotiable."

That drew a laugh from her, the kind that warmed the cottage's cool interior. "When you put it that way, how can I refuse?"

We moved to the kitchen, where the vintage Formica table became our planning center. I sketched layouts while Gemma took meticulous notes on her tablet, her detailed color-coded system suggesting she'd never met a project she couldn't organize into submission. When she leaned over to see my sketches, her hair brushed my shoulder. When I pointed to fixture placements, our hands bumped over the paper, the brief contact making my pulse skip.

The cottage's silence amplified everything. The scratch of pencil on paper, the tap of her stylus on the tablet, the way her breathing deepened when she concentrated on something.

"So demolition first," I explained, drawing out the sequence. "Address any hidden surprises, update the plumbing, install the fixtures, then finish with the tile work."

"Timeline?"

"A few months, working evenings and weekends. Less if I can call in some favors with local contractors. More if the house decides to share any of its secrets with us."

Gemma nodded, her pen moving across the tablet as she recorded every note with the precision that had once orchestrated million-dollar corporate events. "I appreciate this more than I can say. Tackling all of this alone would have been..." She let out a shaky breath. "It would have been overwhelming."

The admission hung between us, honest and vulnerable in a way I suspected didn't come easily to her.

"Partnership makes most things more manageable," I said. "And renovation definitely benefits from two sets of hands."

"Partnership," she repeated, holding out her hand across the table with a smile that lit up her whole face.

I took her hand. Her grip was strong and her palm warm against mine. We held on a beat longer than necessary, long enough for me to feel her pulse against my thumb, before she pulled back first.

"Partners," I agreed, holding her gaze.

We spent the next hour compiling materials lists and discussing details, the conversation flowing easily between renovation specifics and more personal territory. I learned she had strong opinions about lighting placement, had never met an organizational system she couldn't improve, and got excited about storage solutions in a way that both charmed and intimidated me.

When she shifted in her chair and winced, I automatically scanned the room for better seating options. My PT brain never fully turned off.

"We should probably wrap up for today," I suggested. "You've got enough to put together a proper materials order."

Her shoulders sagged, the composed posture she'd maintained throughout our planning session relaxing. She rubbed her temple with two fingers, a gesture that spoke louder than any complaint.

"Next Saturday for demolition day?"

"Sounds like a plan. Gives us a week to get materials delivered."

"Perfect. I'll clear everything out beforehand."

I stood and moved toward the front door. She navigated around furniture with more space than strictly necessary and let me pass first through doorways. Small adaptations she'd probably integrated so thoroughly into her movement patterns that she didn't even notice them anymore. I pretended not to notice either.

"The cottage has wonderful bones," I said. "Even needing work."

"Nan always said a house should hold you, not just shelter you."

"Smart woman." The words carried more weight than I'd intended. "It's why I could never live in those modern glass boxes everyone's building now. I need a place with some character."

"Even if that character comes with plumbing challenges and drafty windows?"

"Especially then. Perfect is boring. Give me interesting any day."

I hadn't intended the double meaning, but I didn't take it back either.

"I should go," I said finally. "You need to rest up before game night at Kate's tomorrow."

"Should I be worried?"

"Only if you're not prepared for the twins to challenge you to some game that makes no sense to adults."

"Intimidating but manageable." Her smile held a trace of nervousness.

"Thank you," she said, her voice softer than before. "For

today. For all of this. You've made something that felt impossible seem possible."

"That's what neighbors do in Waverly Cove." Her face changed in the afternoon light streaming through the salt-crusted windows, belief replacing doubt. We both knew this was more than neighborly.

Already planning weekend trips to the hardware store, mentally rearranging my schedule to accommodate longer work-days here. The drive home would give me time to think ratio-nally about all the reasons this was a bad idea, but right now, standing in the golden light with sawdust in our future and transformation ahead, I couldn't make myself care about any of them.

Just doing a favor for Kate's best friend, I told myself as I headed to my truck. Simple, practical, neighborly, and defined.

But driving away, glancing in the rearview mirror to see Gemma still standing on the cottage porch watching me go, I knew nothing about my connection with Gemma Prescott would remain simple for long.

More concerning still, I wasn't sure I wanted it to.

Chapter 6

Gemma

I woke up before my alarm. Again. Only to be greeted by the cracked plaster ceiling of Kate's guest room whose pattern I'd been mapping for two weeks.

A familiar weight settled across my lower back as I shifted. Not the sharp, demanding pain that sometimes announced itself with dramatics, but a dull, persistent ache. Background noise. I tested the sensation with cautious movements, cataloging. Reading my body's morning report like checking the weather before planning the day.

Manageable. I could work with manageable.

My phone lit up as I finished braiding my hair.

The message gave me space to decline without explanation. Without medical justification. When was the last time someone had offered me that?

James Westfield's involvement meant more witnesses to my learning curve. Still, I couldn't turn down volunteer labor.

The cottage seemed different in morning light. Less abandoned, more expectant.

The Daily Knead had provided diplomatic currency in the form of baked goods. The box's weight suggested generosity beyond my request, accompanied by insider intelligence: Liam's weakness for wild blueberry muffins, James's preference for cinnamon scones.

Such casual intimacy, knowing someone's breakfast preferences. My parents approached food like any other scholarly problem. Efficient, nutritionally sound, emotionally neutral. My Boston acquaintances knew my professional preferences, my client-facing choices.

But who knew what I reached for when seeking comfort rather than fuel?

Gravel crunched under tires, interrupting my musing. First James's massive truck, then Liam's more reasonably sized vehicle following close behind.

"Morning," James called, gravitating toward the bakery box with unerring recognition. "Di hook you up?"

"She may have been generous when I mentioned who'd be here."

James grabbed a scone. Crumbs scattered onto his work boots. "Diane doesn't give everyone the family discount and extra treats. She's an excellent judge of character."

Liam appeared carrying a tool bag that spoke of more construction knowledge than I'd accumulated in my entire adult life. Sawdust coated his flannel sleeves from some earlier project.

"Don't let him fool you. His wife gives discounts to every child, dog, and out-of-towner who walks through her door. It's why their profit margins are terrible."

"She's building relationships, not just a business." James brushed crumbs from his chin. "That's more valuable than the bottom line."

Their banter absorbed some of my earlier anxiety. Almost.

I pulled out my tablet. "I've made some notes about the demolition sequence. We can start with bathroom cabinets, then kitchen if time permits. I've sorted supplies by room and created a disposal plan for—"

Identical raised eyebrows stopped me.

"What?" My palms dampened against the tablet's leather cover.

"Nothing," Liam said quickly. "That's very organized."

"It's bathroom demolition, not one of your fancy shindigs," James added, though his tone carried amusement. "But I appreciate someone who comes prepared."

"Force of habit." The words tumbled out too fast, defensive.

"Demolition requires sledgehammers and pry bars," James said, hefting a tool that looked borrowed from medieval warfare. "Which, coincidentally, I brought plenty of."

Demolition proved to be a lesson in translating precision into power.

My first attempt at tile removal resulted in nothing but a sore shoulder and wounded pride.

"Here." Liam closed the distance between us. "It's about leverage, not strength."

His hands covered mine on the pry bar, callused fingers guiding my grip lower, angling the tool differently. "Try again. Physics, not force."

Under his guidance, the tiles surrendered with a satisfying crack. The sound of something giving way, finally.

"There you go."

An hour later, we'd fallen into a rhythm. James worked on the kitchen cabinets while Liam and I tackled the bathroom tile. The afternoon passed with the scrape of tools against ceramic, the thud of debris hitting the drop cloth, the occasional direction or encouragement.

"You're getting the hang of this," he said during a water break.

"I had a good teacher," I managed, then turned back to the wall before he could see how my pulse had kicked up.

But his reflection caught in the window. His hands stilled on his tools when I stretched overhead. Twelve inches separated us in the narrow bathroom. He adjusted his stance when I moved closer, hyperaware.

"Alright, you two," James called from the kitchen. "I'm heading out. I promised the crew I'd help with a boat engine issue."

"You're leaving?" Liam's voice carried studied neutrality that didn't quite mask disappointment.

"You've got this handled. Besides," James grinned, shouldering his tool bag, "three's a crowd for precision work."

The knowing look he shot us before leaving made my neck flush.

Alone, the cottage's silence amplified everything. The scrape of my pry bar. The whisper of fabric when he moved. My breath catching when Liam's shoulder brushed mine in the narrow space.

"You can take a break," he said without looking over. "You've been going at this for two hours straight."

"I'm fine."

"Gemma." His voice carried quiet authority. "Rest. The tiles aren't going anywhere."

"I said I'm fine."

But even as I spoke, my hand cramped around the tool handle.

In three strides, he was beside me, fingers gentle as he worked the tool from my grip. "You're shaking."

He was right. My hands trembled, fine tremors running from fingertips to wrists.

"I don't enjoy being treated like I'm fragile."

"I'm not treating you like you're fragile. I'm treating you like someone who's been swinging a demolition tool for two hours without a break." His thumb traced across my knuckles, easing the tension there. "There's a difference."

The simple touch sent warmth up my arm.

"I'm not good at accepting help."

"I've noticed." His voice was quiet. "But you could try. Just for today."

While Liam tackled the stubborn corner tiles, I moved to the living room bookshelves. Book organization gave me permission to stop pretending I wasn't aware of every measured breath he took when we moved around each other.

Behind a row of mysteries, leather binding caught my eye. It was patinaed with age, distinct from the paperbacks surrounding it.

Not a book. My grandmother's handwriting filled the pages.

Renovation plans.

Page after page of architectural drawings, material lists, color schemes. Her flowing script annotating each sketch with notes and dreams.

Clawfoot tub - original to house - refinish don't replace! read one annotation beside a bathroom sketch nearly identical to what Liam and I had discussed.

Kitchen windows - expand eastern exposure for morning light.

Living room built-ins - restore original glass doors.

I sank into the window seat, swallowing against a sudden tightness in my throat.

The final entry bore a date just months before she died: *Considering tin ceiling for bathroom restoration. Ask Gemma's opinion when she visits this summer.*

A client crisis had kept me away that summer. One of a dozen excuses I'd manufactured over the years, each one seemingly justified at the time.

My chest constricted. Salt burned behind my eyes. The first tear dropped onto the yellowed page before I could stop it.

"Find anything interesting?" Liam's voice startled me.

I looked up too quickly to hide how my hands shook holding the notebook, or how my lower lip trembled.

"My grandmother's renovation plans," I whispered. "She wanted to restore the clawfoot tub too. She was going to ask my opinion when I visited, but I never..."

The words broke in my throat. More tears came, hot and fast, blurring the careful drawings.

Without hesitation, Liam crossed the room and sat beside me on the window seat. The small space pressed our thighs together, warm and solid.

"She knew you'd come back," he said quietly, taking the notebook from my hands and setting it carefully aside. "Look at this planning. She prepared this place for you."

"I should have visited more. Should have been here when she..."

"Hey." His finger touched my chin, lifting my face to meet his eyes. "You're here now. You're making her dreams real."

His thumb brushed across my cheek, wiping away tears with such gentleness it made my chest ache.

"Liam," I whispered, not sure what I asked for.

His eyes searched my face, dark and intent. When his gaze dropped to my lips, the space between us felt charged.

He leaned closer. I tilted toward him.

The notebook slipped forgotten to the floor as his hand cupped my face, thumb tracing my cheekbone with reverent slowness.

"Gemma," he breathed.

"Yes," I whispered.

His lips met mine, gentle and warm. I tasted salt from my

tears and coffee from this morning. My hand found his chest, his heartbeat fast and strong under my palm. His fingers slid into my hair, cradling my head.

The world narrowed to this. His mouth on mine, careful and sure. The calluses on his palm against my cheek. The way he held me like I was precious.

Then pain seized my lower back. Sharp, sudden, vicious.

I jerked away from him, gasping.

"Gemma?" His voice sharpened with concern. "What's wrong?"

"Back," I managed through gritted teeth. "Cramping."

His hands hovered, ready to help without assuming. "Tell me what you need."

The cramping intensified, radiating down my legs. I couldn't suppress a soft sound of distress.

"Heating pad," I gasped. "Bedroom. Medication in the kitchen."

He moved fast, returning in moments with both.

I fumbled with the pill bottle, hands shaking too hard to open it.

"Here." He took the bottle and shook out the dose. "Water?"

I nodded, accepting both with grateful, trembling hands. The medication left a bitter coating on my tongue, but my shoulders dropped a fraction as I counted down the twenty minutes until it would kick in.

"I'm sorry," I whispered as the heating pad warmed against my back. "This is embarrassing."

"Stop." His voice was firm but gentle. "You have nothing to apologize for."

"We were kissing and then I..." My face burned. I couldn't meet his eyes.

"We were kissing," he said. "And then your body reminded you it needs care. That's not your fault."

My throat constricted with unexpected relief.

"Will you stay?" I asked quietly. "Until the medication works?"

"As long as you need."

As the heat eased the worst of the cramping, I studied his profile. The line of his jaw. The patience in his posture as he sat beside me without touching, giving me space while staying close.

"That was my first kiss since the diagnosis," I admitted.

He turned to look at me fully. "It was perfect. Right up until it wasn't."

"And that doesn't bother you? That my body might interrupt any moment we—"

"No." His voice was quiet but certain. "It doesn't bother me."

His words lodged in my chest, warm and solid as the heating pad against my spine.

My grandmother's notebook lay open on the floor, pages filled with dreams and plans she'd never finished. But I was here now. Making those dreams real, just as Liam had said.

The weight I'd carried for so long released. Air moved through my lungs deeper than it had in months.

This cottage shifted from necessity to possibility. A future rather than just survival.

And perhaps that future might include the man sitting beside me, patient and steady as the tide.

"When are you coming back?" The question slipped out before I could stop it. "To help with the cottage."

His smile was soft, reaching his eyes. "Tomorrow. And the day after." He held my gaze. "You'll be seeing a lot more of me before this renovation is done."

Not just the renovation, I thought. But I wasn't quite brave enough to say it yet.

Chapter 7

Liam

The early afternoon light cut across my office. I'd tried to review Mr. Gallant's file three times, but kept replaying yesterday's demolition instead. The moment when our hands had overlapped on the pry bar. The way she'd caught her breath and looked away.

"Someone's elsewhere today," Lisa said from my doorway.

I closed the file. "Mr. Gallant's presenting some interesting compensatory patterns."

"Mmhmm." Lisa stepped inside and closed the door. "And this sudden fascination with knee pathology wouldn't have anything to do with Kate's friend, would it? The one you're using vacation days to help with carpentry?"

Heat climbed my neck. "Just helping a friend navigate small town contractors. The cottage needs a lot of work."

"I'm sure it does." She leaned against my desk, arms crossed. "Liam, I've known you for three years. I've seen you manage complex cases without breaking a sweat. But yesterday, after Gemma's session, you reorganized your desk twice and asked me three questions about exercises you've been prescribing since the Obama administration."

I had no defense for that. I'd prided myself on maintaining clear boundaries, on giving each patient my undivided attention. Yet Gemma Prescott had walked into my practice and my professionalism crumbled.

"She's dealing with a lot," I said.

"She is," Lisa agreed. "And she needs someone in her corner who understands that her pain isn't a puzzle to be solved, but a reality to be lived with. Someone who won't try to fix her or pity her or treat her like she's made of glass."

Molly came to mind, my ex. Her well-meaning attempts to "motivate" my father during his recovery. The cheerful insistence that if he just tried harder, pushed through the discomfort, he'd regain full function. The impatience she'd barely concealed when limitations couldn't be overcome through determination.

I'd learned how easily compassion could turn into condescension.

My phone vibrated on my desk.

GEMMA

Material delivery just arrived. They're asking about placement and I'm nodding like I know what they're talking about. Help?

I smiled.

LIAM

Tell them bathroom materials need to stay dry. Kitchen items can handle weather under tarps.

I'll call between patients to double-check everything.

The admission without shame was brave. How many of us confessed when we were out of our depth?

I set the phone down. My smile lingered too long. Across from me, Lisa watched.

"Your next patient is in Room 2," she said, rising. "And Liam? Whatever's developing here, be careful with it. And with yourself."

After Mr. Gallant, my phone showed two missed calls from Gemma. The voicemail was brief: "Hi, it's me. Everything's fine, just... could you call when you get a chance? Thanks."

Her tone came too light. Breathlessness edged her words, that catch that suggested pain underneath.

"What happened?"

"Nothing dramatic. Just a miscommunication about which materials needed immediate unpacking. I may have moved more boxes than planned, but everything's sorted and covered for tomorrow."

I glanced at the clock: 2:30. My last appointment wasn't until four. "I could swing by now, make sure everything's secure before the rain."

"Oh, you don't need to..." She stopped herself. "Actually, that would be great. If you're sure you have time."

The gratitude in her voice told me everything.

When I reached the cottage, Gemma sat on the front steps, covered in drywall dust. Materials surrounded her, organized like a museum display. Bathroom fixtures stacked on the porch. Lumber sorted by length in the side yard. Smaller items arranged by necessity.

The organization didn't surprise me. She'd coordinated elaborate events for demanding couples. But her posture did. How she shifted when she thought I wasn't looking. The coaching herself through standing when she spotted my truck.

"Impressive logistics," I said, climbing out. "Though I'm guessing you weren't planning to reorganize a lumber yard's worth of materials solo."

She smiled. "The delivery team had a creative interpretation of 'organized placement.' I may have gotten carried away fixing it."

"Show me what needs securing."

I didn't ask about pain levels or offer medical advice. Some things were better acknowledged through action.

As we tied down tarps and anchored materials against the weather, her method revealed itself. Everything positioned within easy reach of the cottage. Heavy items where I'd placed them. Smaller necessities moved closer to the door, creating workflows for the weekend's work.

"You've been thinking about the renovation sequence," I said, watching her hand me a bungee cord.

"Force of habit." Our fingers brushed. She paused. "I see everything as a timeline with dependencies and bottlenecks. Give me a project, and I'll give you a color-coded schedule with backup plans for the backup plans."

"That'll be useful for the rebuilding phase. Though I should warn you that contractors around here aren't known for project management. More like controlled chaos with occasional productivity."

"I've worked with worse. You'd be amazed how many couples want a Tuscan vineyard wedding in Massachusetts in December. Those events teach you creative problem-solving and miracle-working."

A glimpse into her professional world. The impossible requests. The diplomatic navigation of other people's dreams and budgets. I wanted to hear more about those stories, about the life she'd built before endometriosis forced her to rebuild.

We worked in comfortable silence, securing materials as the first drops fell. When we finished, Gemma invited me in for coffee, and I accepted before I'd fully considered what staying might mean.

The cottage interior showed meticulous preparation. Plastic sheets covered furniture. Painter's tape marked demolition boundaries. Everything removable was catalogued and stored in labeled boxes.

"You've been busy," I said, accepting the mug she offered.

"I have." She cradled her own mug. "It helps, having everything in its place before the chaos starts."

In the kitchen's afternoon light, tightness rimmed her eyes that hadn't been there at our first meeting. The morning's manual labor had cost her, but she wasn't offering details.

"Can I ask you something?" I settled against the counter, close enough to talk without crowding. "And you can tell me it's none of my business."

Her posture sharpened. "Okay."

"Yesterday, you mentioned this cottage being temporary. But looking at all this planning, this investment..." I gestured to the evidence around us. "It doesn't seem temporary."

Her professional mask slipped. "I don't know what this is," she confessed. "I came here to figure out next steps. But the more time I spend here, the less Boston feels like home. And that terrifies me, because I've spent my entire adulthood building a life there."

She abandoned her mug on the counter. "What about you? You obviously didn't grow up planning to run a small-town PT practice."

"I had a similar moment when I came back." Outside, a fishing boat's engine puttered past. "Medical school, residency, fellowship. Fifteen years of training for a life that was supposed to happen in Boston or New York." I laughed, bitter. "Coming home meant trading everything I'd worked for to fix shoulders and knees in the town I'd spent decades trying to escape."

"But you stayed."

"I stayed." I took a sip, buying time. "Not because it was easy, but because I realized I'd been measuring success by other people's definitions. My father's reputation, my professors' expectations, my..." I stopped.

"Your ex-girlfriend's plans?" Gemma's perceptiveness caught me off guard.

I looked up. "Kate talks too much."

"Kate worries about you." The words came out measured. "She mentioned that someone left Waverly Cove because it wasn't enough for them."

Wind rattled the windows. "Trust me, I understand that feeling from every angle."

The admission hung there. Neither of us was ready to unpack it.

Outside, the rain intensified, drumming against the aging windows.

"I should probably head back." But I leaned against her counter, coffee mug between my hands. Through the window, my truck sat in what felt like a different time zone. "Last appointment at four."

"Of course." But Gemma didn't move either.

We stood in her grandmother's kitchen, navigating the terrain between professional courtesy and personal confession.

Finally, she spoke. "Liam? Thank you for the suggestions you've made about accessibility features. Most people either pretend my limitations don't exist or assume they define everything about me. You've acknowledged reality without making it the entire story."

I set down my mug, needing something to do with my hands. "During my father's recovery from his heart attack, I learned the difference between helping someone and trying to save them. Helping means seeing people as they are and supporting their goals. Saving is imposing your vision of what they should be."

"And which one are you doing here?"

The question was direct, not accusatory. Like someone checking the foundation before deciding whether to build.

I considered this. My answer mattered more than either of us was acknowledging. "Helping, I hope. Though I'll admit my motivations aren't just professional anymore."

Her eyes widened. My pulse kicked up in response.

Rain continued its rhythm against the glass.

When Gemma finally spoke, her voice was quieter. "I appreciate the honesty. And for what it's worth, I'm not sure mine are either."

We looked at each other across the small kitchen. The attraction I'd been acknowledging alone found its echo in her expression, in the way she held my gaze a beat longer than necessary.

I paused at the door. "Gemma? This weekend, when we start construction... it's going to be a marathon, not a sprint. James and I will be here early, but we're planning for steady progress over several months, not miraculous transformation in a few days."

Her shoulders dropped. "I'll try to remember that pacing applies to more than just my PT sessions."

<hr>

Driving back to the clinic, my truck's heater fogged the windows faster than the defroster could clear them. Harbor Street was empty. Smart people stayed inside when storms hit this hard.

But I drove anyway, reluctant to put distance between myself and the cottage.

My phone sat on the passenger seat. I hoped it might announce another call or text from Gemma.

When had I started looking for her name on my screen? When had ordinary afternoons started feeling incomplete without her voice in them?

A few weeks ago, I had tidy compartments. Work. Family. The slow renovation of my own house. Occasional dinners with whoever Kate deemed in need of social intervention.

Simple. Predictable. Safe.

Now I thought about my parents' invitation to dinner

tomorrow and wondered if I should mention it to Gemma. The thought had crossed my mind as we'd stood in her kitchen. How natural it would feel to say, "Come with me." How much I wanted to see her laugh at the twins' enthusiasm, watch her navigate Diane's maternal attention, observe how she'd fit into the easy chaos of family dinner.

But I'd held back. It was too soon. Or maybe I was over-thinking what should be a simple invitation between friends.

Except nothing about what I felt for Gemma Prescott felt simple anymore.

Maybe next time. Maybe when the timing felt right, when I could work up the nerve to risk shifting this relationship into something neither of us could take back.

The foundation was there. I just needed to decide whether I was ready to build on it.

Chapter 8

Gemma

October settled over Waverly Cove like a painter's fever dream. Scarlet maples bled against the harbor's steel blue. I arrived ten minutes early for my second appointment with Lisa Patel, the crisp air cutting through the brain fog that had been my constant companion for weeks.

My leather planner sat open on my lap, pages covered in color-coded charts. If I couldn't control my body's spiral, I could at least document it.

"How are we feeling since last week?" Lisa settled into her chair, pen poised over my chart.

I flipped through the rainbow pages like I was presenting evidence. "Morning stretches helped, especially before long days of standing. The hip flexor work you showed me is magic, but my lower back keeps cramping when I move too quickly."

"Pain levels?"

"Manageable most days. Though yesterday I had to explain to a vendor why I was conducting our meeting from the floor of my kitchen."

Lisa's laugh was unfiltered by clinical training. "At least you're maintaining your sense of humor."

A gentle knock interrupted us. Lisa opened the door to reveal Liam in his navy polo and khakis. His presence changed the room's energy.

"Sorry to interrupt. Margaret mentioned you needed the Smythe files."

"Right, I left them up front." Lisa moved toward the door to take the folder.

Liam's gaze landed on me. I forgot whatever I'd been about to say. His pupils dilated. My next breath came shorter than the last.

"How are the sessions going?" he asked, voice carefully neutral.

"They've been very helpful," I admitted, surprised it was true. "Lisa's teaching me that my body responds to kindness instead of just caffeine and spite."

His mouth curved. "Lisa's the best we've got."

"Actually," Lisa said, returning with her file, "your timing is perfect. I was about to demonstrate a myofascial release technique. Could you assist with the initial positioning?"

My shoulders stiffened. "Is that necessary?"

"It's completely external, fully clothed," Lisa explained. "But having experienced hands for the first demonstration helps establish proper pressure and placement."

Liam stepped back without hesitation, hands already dropping to his sides. "I can leave if you'd prefer. No pressure."

No injured ego. No pressing for explanations.

"No, if it'll help, I'm willing to try." I paused. "Just remember I know where you live now, so if this goes badly, revenge is an option."

What followed was Lisa guiding Liam's hand placement

along my hip and lower back. Despite my wariness, his touch conveyed competence without crossing boundaries I hadn't even realized I'd drawn. The technique brought immediate relief to knots I'd been carrying for weeks.

"The goal is interrupting the pain-tension cycle," Lisa explained as Liam's thumbs worked in small, precise circles. "Your body develops protective patterns, but sometimes those patterns become part of the problem."

I focused on breathing through the release, acutely aware of the heat from Liam's hands, the careful way he adjusted pressure based on my body's responses.

Not clinical. Something else entirely.

"Better?" he asked quietly, his voice rough.

"Much." My voice sounded breathier than I'd care to admit.

Lisa showed the sequence once more, but I was hyperaware of every place Liam's hands had been. When he finally stepped back, my skin cooled where his hands had been.

"I can show Kate how to help with this at home," he offered, professional mask sliding back into place. "As a clinical consultation."

I paid partial attention to everything else Lisa said, too distracted by the lingering scent of Liam's soap and the way my pulse hammered against my wrists.

Liam was waiting by my car when I emerged from the clinic, leaning against the passenger door. Salt air ruffled his dark hair. He'd changed out of his clinic uniform into jeans and a navy pullover that made him look less like the medical professional who'd just had his hands on my back and more like the man who'd spent weekends wielding power tools in my cottage bathroom.

"Hi," he said, straightening as I approached. The afternoon light caught the stubble along his jaw. "How did the rest of your appointment go?"

"Fine. Good. Lisa's very thorough."

"She is." The corner of his mouth quirked. "Listen, I wanted to ask you something."

Oh good. Overthinking time. Some people can have normal conversations. I am not one of those people.

"My parents are having the whole family over for dinner tonight." The words tumbled out faster than his usual measured pace. "Nothing formal, just the usual Westfield Friday night chaos. I thought you might like to join us."

Of all the things I'd been preparing for, an invitation to meet his entire family ranked somewhere near the bottom of my readiness list.

"Tonight?" I repeated, buying time. My hands wanted to fidget with something. Anything. I shoved them deep in my pockets.

"I know it's last minute." Liam ran a hand through his hair, leaving it mussed. "And I know family dinners can be overwhelming, especially Westfield family dinners. We're loud and we interrupt each other and my sister Sophie will probably try to diagnose your childhood trauma based on how you hold your fork."

I almost smiled. "Little Sophie?"

"Not so little anymore. She's a social worker now. Everything is psychology to her." He shifted his weight. "But I'd really like you to be there. If you're interested."

"What time?" I heard myself ask.

Liam's face brightened. "Six thirty. I can pick you up, or you can follow me over, or Kate's probably going anyway if you'd rather ride with her..."

"I'll follow you," I said, because riding with Kate would involve twenty minutes of pointed questions.

"Great. Perfect." His smile was soft and sure. "Fair warning though: there will be children. Lots of children. And my mother might try to feed you until you physically cannot consume another bite of food."

"Noted," I said. "I'll prepare accordingly."

What had I agreed to?

The Westfield family home looked like a postcard. White clapboard siding weathered to warm gray, wraparound porch with hanging ferns, windows glowing amber against the approaching dusk. Enough cars crowded the circular driveway to suggest either a family gathering or a very friendly home invasion.

I sat in my car for a moment after parking, watching Liam walk toward the front door. Through those windows, I could just make out moving figures and organized chaos.

This is what normal families do, I reminded myself. They gather for dinner. Mine had academic conferences and scheduled phone calls to discuss research findings. The Prescotts were more comfortable with intellectual discourse than emotional intimacy.

I was still giving myself this pep talk when Liam appeared at my window, breath forming small clouds.

"You okay?" he asked.

"Fine," I said, rolling down the window. "Just... mentally preparing."

"For the record," he said, "they already love you. But if it gets overwhelming, just catch my eye and I'll make our excuses."

Exit strategy planning. The mark of a thoughtful human being.

"Ready?"

No, I thought. But I nodded anyway.

The front door opened before we reached it, revealing Jo Westfield. She looked just as I remembered, with more silver in her dark hair and deeper laugh lines around her eyes. She had the same warm smile that had welcomed a lonely eight-year-old during those long-ago summers.

"Gemma!" she said, extending both hands to take mine. "Look at you, all grown up. It's been far too long, sweetheart."

"Mrs. Westfield," I managed. "Thank you for having me."

"Jo, please. And you're always welcome here." She squeezed my hands before releasing them. "Come in, come in. Don't mind the noise. Dinners around here tend toward controlled chaos."

The living room looked like organized chaos. Children occupied every horizontal surface, adults navigated around small bodies, and conversations flowed in overlapping streams. The air was warm and rich with the scents of roasted meat and garlic bread, underlaid with whatever dessert waited for after the meal.

Robert Westfield appeared behind his wife, his weathered face lighting with recognition. "Gemma Prescott. I should have known you'd grow up to be as lovely as your grandmother." He wrapped me in a hug that reminded me of summer evenings on their porch, when he'd listen patiently to Kate's and my elaborate plans.

"Mr. Westfield," I said into his shoulder, which still smelled like wood shavings and saltwater. "It's so good to see you again."

"Bob," he corrected. "You're not eight years old anymore."

A petite woman with dark curls approached, bouncing a toddler on her hip. "Sophie!" I called, recognizing the determined expression that hadn't changed since she was ten.

Sophie's face lit up. "Gemma! I was hoping you'd be here tonight." She hugged me one-armed while maintaining her grip on the squirming toddler. "How are you handling being back in Waverly Cove? That's a major life transition."

"Still processing," I admitted. "But it feels right."

"That's Taylor," Sophie said, pointing out the blonde woman with kind eyes and full arm sleeve tattoos. "My wife. Taylor, this is Gemma, Kate's legendary summer partner in crime."

"Pleasure," Taylor said, extending a hand. "I've heard stories. Something about berry bushes?"

"We'll never live that down," I protested, then caught sight of James across the room. He raised his beer in acknowledgment. His wife, Diane, emerged from the kitchen, carrying a platter that smelled like heaven.

"Gemma! Welcome back, sweetheart." She balanced the food expertly while gesturing with her free hand.

"And that's Abby," Liam said, gesturing toward the heavily pregnant woman making emphatic points to James while rubbing her lower back. "Though you probably remember her as the little sister who always wanted to tag along."

I laughed, remembering a determined seven-year-old with pigtails. "Abby Westfield. All grown up."

"Morales now," called a man wading through tiny humans. "I'm Miguel, the lucky guy who convinced her to marry me. We're both teachers at the elementary school."

Before I could process the family roll call, a small whirlwind in butterfly wings launched herself at my legs.

"AUNTIE GEMMA!" Maya's voice probably carried to the

next county. "You're HERE! With Uncle Liam! This is VERY important information!"

"Hi, Maya," I laughed, steadying myself. "Nice wings."

"They're MAGICAL," she announced, spinning. "Noah says they're not scientifically accurate, but Noah doesn't understand about MAGIC."

Noah appeared at a more reasonable volume, adjusting his glasses. "Hi, Aunt Gemma. Are you Uncle Liam's girlfriend now?"

The surrounding conversation dimmed as the adults pretended not to listen.

I glanced at Liam, who was watching me with an expression that suggested he was as curious about my answer as his nephew.

"We're friends," I said carefully.

"But do you LIKE him?" Maya pressed. "Because if you like him, then you could get MARRIED and then you'd be our aunt for REAL and not just pretend!"

"Maya," called Kate from across the room, desperately trying to convey 'you're being adorable but also mortifying.'

"But I have IMPORTANT questions!" Maya protested, then looked at me with intense focus. "Do you want to marry Uncle Liam? Because I think you should. He's very nice and he knows how to fix things."

I looked at Liam, noting how he was covering his face with one hand while his shoulders shook with laughter.

"Your niece makes a compelling argument."

"She's very direct. Takes after her mother," he managed.

"I'm HELPFUL," Maya corrected. "Noah, tell her about Uncle Liam's good qualities!"

Noah pushed his glasses up with scientific precision. "He doesn't eat the last cookie without asking. And he knows the names of all the constellations. Also, he gave me a cool rock for my collection."

"See?" Maya beamed. "He'd be the BESTEST daddy!"

"I'm sure he will be," I said solemnly. "I'll add that to my pro/con list."

Maya clapped while Noah nodded approvingly, apparently satisfied that proper research protocols were being followed.

"Dinner!" Jo announced, and the chaos immediately reorganized itself around food and seating.

I ended up between Liam and Kate, which felt like careful planning or fortunate coincidence. The table was set with mismatched dishes that suggested functionality over presentation.

The conversation flowed with the rhythm of people who genuinely enjoyed each other's company. James's quiet humor, Sophie's thoughtful insights, Miguel's easy warmth, Abby's snarky opinions delivered despite obvious exhaustion.

Some families perform harmony for outsiders. This family actually liked each other.

It was weirdly refreshing. Also slightly intimidating.

My family gatherings involved seating arrangements to avoid academic feuds and topics selected to prevent extended lectures about research. The Westfields just... talked. About everything. Over each other. Occasionally at the same time.

As the evening wound down and family members began departing, I helped clear dishes. In the kitchen, Jo touched my arm gently.

"Thank you for joining us tonight," she said. "It means more than you might realize."

"Thank you for including me. Your family is wonderful."

Jo smiled with the particular satisfaction of a mother

watching her plans unfold. "They're pretty fond of you too. Especially Liam."

Before I could respond to that loaded statement, Liam appeared in the doorway, keys jingling. "Ready to head home?" he asked. "I'll walk you to your car."

"I'd like that," I said.

Standing in the driveway saying goodnight, I was reluctant to end the evening.

"Thank you," I said. "For including me."

"Thank you for coming. I know my family can be overwhelming, especially when you're not used to the chaos."

"It was good chaos," I said, surprising myself. "Your family is lovely."

"They loved you. They've already asked me to invite you again next time."

"Next time?" The assumption sent warmth through my chest.

"If you want there to be a next time."

I studied his face in the porch light, noting the careful expression, the way he was trying not to assume anything while hoping for everything.

"I want there to be a next time," I said.

His smile transformed his entire face. "Good."

Liam stepped closer, close enough to see the amber flecks in his brown eyes, the way his fingers flexed at his sides before he reached up to brush a strand of hair from my face.

I didn't bother with words. Instead, I rose up on my toes and kissed him.

Unlike our first kiss, there was nothing hesitant about this one. His response was immediate, his mouth moving against mine with an urgency that surprised us both. I threaded my fingers through his hair and pulled him closer, earning a low sound from his throat that made my stomach flip.

This was what I'd been trying not to think about since that first kiss at the cottage. The way his hands settled on my waist like they belonged there. The scratch of his stubble against my skin.

My back met the cool metal of my car as he pressed closer, his body solid against mine. His thumb traced along my jaw, then down the column of my throat, and suddenly I couldn't remember why I'd ever thought this wasn't a good idea.

"Gemma," he said against my mouth, sending a shiver down my spine.

When we finally broke apart, we were both breathing hard. The porch light cast everything in a soft glow. His forehead rested against mine. His hands trembled where they still held my face.

"That was..." he started.

"Better than the first time," I finished.

His laugh was low and slightly wrecked. "Much better."

My hands still fisted in his shirt. I made no move to let go. Neither did he, his thumbs still tracing gentle patterns along my cheekbones.

"I should let you get home," he said, though his body language suggested the opposite.

"You should," I agreed, making no effort to step away.

We stood there for another moment, the night air settling around us, the space between us charged with everything we weren't saying.

When he finally moved toward his truck, I was sorry to see him go.

Well. That was new.

Chapter 9

Liam

"That's definitely not what I was expecting to find," James said, which in fisherman speak translated roughly to 'holy hell.'

Two weeks into this renovation, it was becoming clear that Gemma's grandmother had possessed either supreme optimism or a wicked sense of humor. Every layer we peeled back revealed another surprise, and not the pleasant kind.

Rodriguez Plumbing had finished the rough-in yesterday, and James was checking their work before we started on the finish work. I stood in what used to be a bathroom, staring at damaged drywall where water stains spread across the pale surface.

The musty smell of old moisture hung in the air, mixing with exposed copper pipes. James traced a section with his finger, and the drywall crumbled like stale cake.

"Older cottages always need some extra attention," I said. The polite way of saying we're going to need a bigger budget.

"At least the main line to the street is intact," James grunted.

I was figuring out how to break this news to Gemma when my phone rang. As if summoned by plumbing-related anxiety, her name appeared on the screen.

"Let me guess... bad news?" she said the moment I picked up.

The woman had developed an almost supernatural ability to sense renovation disasters. Years of managing events where Murphy's Law was practically a business partner.

"How did you know?"

"The renovation gods demand their sacrifices," she replied with dry resignation. "What did you find?"

I explained the situation, trying to strike that balance between honesty and not sending her into a panic-induced home sale. Gemma listened with the focused attention of a surgeon receiving case notes, asking questions that revealed she'd been researching plumbing terminology.

"Bottom line: how much longer will this delay the bathroom being functional?"

Pure Gemma. Cut through the technical explanations and land on the one detail that affected her daily reality. A cottage without a proper bathroom wasn't just inconvenient when you were managing chronic pain.

"An additional week or two," I admitted, bracing for frustration.

Instead, I got a simple "What do you need from me?"

No complaints about hidden costs or timeline failures. Immediate problem-solving mode.

I smiled despite standing ankle-deep in renovation debris.

"Do what needs to be done," she continued. "I'd rather fix it properly than band-aid it."

Most people panic when the budget doubles. She was already reorganizing the timeline.

"I'll be there in twenty minutes," she added. "I want to see this for myself."

Of course she did. Gemma wasn't the type to delegate problems she could understand firsthand.

The crunch of gravel announced her arrival twenty-one minutes later. She appeared wearing jeans that had seen actual labor and a flannel shirt that looked familiar. Had I left that here last weekend? The possibility that she was wearing my shirt created an entirely inappropriate flutter of satisfaction that I firmly suppressed.

Professional boundaries, Westfield.

"Show me what we're dealing with," she said, stepping carefully over tools and debris.

She examined the exposed studs with the same intensity she'd brought to reviewing vendor contracts. Questions that proved she'd been doing homework.

"So the water damage was worse than it initially appeared," she concluded, studying the wall cavity.

"Water problems are like chronic injuries," I said. "By the time you notice the symptoms, the damage has been spreading for months."

Her fingers stilled on the damaged wood. Shoulders drew inward for just a moment before straightening again.

We weren't just talking about copper pipes anymore.

"What materials do you need that you don't have?" she asked James, pivoting back to practical matters.

After she catalogued the supply list, she declared, "Henderson's might have some of this in stock. I can go check while you continue working."

"You don't have to..."

"I'm already cleaned up, and you two are elbow-deep in my bathroom," she countered. "Besides, I need to feel useful. Demolition was satisfying, but I'm not much help with actual renovation."

Her hands flexed once before she shoved them into her pockets. For someone accustomed to orchestrating complex events where every detail responded to her direction, being sidelined by technical skill gaps had to sting.

After she left, James turned to me with an expression I'd learned to dread over four decades of brotherhood.

"She's not what I expected."

I focused intently on a pipe joint that didn't require nearly as much attention. "What do you mean?"

"Kate described her as this high-powered Boston event planner," James explained, reaching for a pipe cutter. "I was expecting someone more..."

"Demanding?"

James made one of those noncommittal sounds that somehow contained a lifetime of brotherly observations. "You're putting a lot of extra work into this place."

He wasn't wrong. I spent more time here than I did at my own house these days.

"It's interesting work," I said, aiming for casual and completely failing to fool anyone.

"Interesting how?"

"She approaches renovation like I approach patient care," I finally said. "She sees systems, not just symptoms."

James made another eloquent sound, this one translating to 'uh-huh, sure.'

The front door banged open, saving me from further interrogation.

"Success!" Gemma's voice carried triumph. She appeared holding a bag from Henderson's like it contained the crown jewels. "Ben had most of what we needed and says he can deliver this afternoon. Though I had to endure a lecture on the superior craftsmanship of pre-1950s homes."

"You got the full Ben Henderson experience," James observed. "Did he throw in the story about the blizzard of '78?"

"Complete with dramatic hand gestures," Gemma confirmed, producing a small paper bag. "He also sent this along, claiming it's essential for any proper renovation job."

Needhams. Ben believed chocolate covered potato and coconut was a legitimate tool. The man wasn't wrong. The candy had been fueling Mainers since the 19th century.

James snatched one and pure bliss overtook his normally stoic expression.

***

Fifteen minutes later, Gemma had transformed the disaster zone of a kitchen into a functional lunch area. Sandwiches and drinks appeared on a makeshift table of plywood and sawhorses. The scent of fresh bread and turkey drifted through the air, still thick with dust and old wood.

She chatted with James about his fishing operation with genuine interest. Her fork scraped against the paper plate as she listened, green eyes fixed on his words.

"So you're the third generation running the family boat?" she asked.

"Fourth, actually. Took it over from our uncle." James launched into the family history.

I'd heard this story countless times, but Gemma's attention made it fresh somehow.

"That's amazing," she said. Her fingers traced the edge of her sandwich wrapper. "That kind of continuity is so rare these days."

The child of academic parents. Her nomadic childhood, with its constant relocations and lack of roots, naturally drew her to this restoration. She was creating permanence from impermanence.

"Like Liam taking over your father's practice?" she asked, and I braced for what was coming.

James's eyes took on the dangerous gleam of sibling mischief. "That was less about tradition and more about guilt after Dad's heart attack. Mr. Boston Medical Center was all set for his fancy research position when duty called him home."

I shot him a look that roughly translated to 'abandon this topic immediately or find yourself short one brother.'

"It was more complicated than that," I hedged.

"Always is," James agreed, but gentled his tone. "But you stayed, even after Dad recovered. Waverly Cove has a way of reclaiming its own."

Gemma's coffee cup paused halfway to her lips. "My grandmother used to say the same thing," she said. "That Waverly Cove was like the tide. It always brought things back, eventually."

The town had indeed pulled me back, reshaping my career plans into a future I couldn't have imagined but now couldn't abandon. And here was Gemma, caught in the same pull, though whether temporarily or permanently remained unclear.

As we cleaned up, her presence filled the small space. I noted the careful way she bent, the brief pause before reaching overhead. Her pain management techniques integrated seamlessly unless you knew the signs.

"I got a call this morning," Gemma said suddenly. Her voice

carried a note I couldn't quite identify. "A former colleague floated the idea of me doing event planning consultancy in the area while I'm here. Expanding our clients to the Maine coast."

I looked up, catching the hint of excitement she was trying to modulate. Her cheeks had flushed pink.

"That sounds perfect for you."

"It's just exploratory," she cautioned, though her eyes held more investment than she was admitting. "But yes, it would be... convenient, location-wise, if it works out."

The implication of longer-term roots in Waverly Cove allowed an entirely unprofessional flutter of hope.

"The cottage renovation would be a higher priority when that happens," Gemma continued. "I'd need a functional home office sooner rather than later."

The shift from "if" to "when," and the use of "home office," did not escape my attention.

"We can adjust the schedule," I offered immediately, catching James's carefully neutral expression. "Once we stabilize the plumbing, we can shift focus to the second bedroom for office space."

Her face brightened. "That would be perfect. Thank you."

James cleared his throat with brotherly precision. "Not to interrupt this renovation planning, but we should get back to that bathroom if we want to patch that drywall today."

Heat crawled up Gemma's neck. "Of course. I'll clean this all up while you get back to it."

As we returned to work, the afternoon settled into a comfortable rhythm. But Gemma's presence remained throughout the cottage. The methodical click of her camera documenting progress, the rustle of papers as she updated her notebook, the soft hum she made when concentrating.

"You know," James said quietly, adjusting a fitting, "most

people renovating want updates but not involvement. Gemma's not just investing money. She's investing herself." He paused, wiping his hands on a rag. "That's not temporary fix behavior, Liam. That's somebody making this place home."

James was right. This wasn't just renovation anymore. For both of us, it had become something deeper.

By evening, we'd accomplished more than expected. James packed his tools with the methodical care of a fisherman who knew sloppy maintenance meant expensive repairs.

"Sophie wants to know what you're bringing to dinner tomorrow," he said with forced casualness. "She's making pot roast."

"I should check with Gemma first," I replied without thinking. "We were talking about reviewing tile patterns tomorrow."

The words escaped before I could consider their implications.

James paused, toolbox in hand, eyebrows climbing. "Tile patterns," he repeated slowly. "On a Sunday. When Sophie's making pot roast."

Heat rose up my neck as the realization hit. I was prioritizing a neighbor's renovations over my sister's Sunday dinner.

"Tell Sophie I'll let her know in the morning," I said, trying to regain equilibrium.

"Sure thing," James agreed, his tone carrying decades of understanding. As he headed for the door, he paused. "Just remember, brother, that renovation projects have endpoints. People's lives... those are more complicated."

The cottage settled into quiet after he left. I found Gemma in the kitchen, laptop open on the salvaged table. Spreadsheets filled the screen, numbers marching in neat columns. The blue light cast shadows under her eyes.

"James headed out?" she asked without looking up.

"Just left. We made substantial progress." I leaned against the doorframe. "The rough plumbing is complete, water damage repaired. Should be ready for tile next weekend."

She nodded, making a note on her tablet with quick, precise strokes. "I've updated the budget for the additional supplies. Even with unexpected costs, we're still within the contingency allowance."

Of course, she had contingency allowances. The woman probably had contingency plans for her contingency plans, each one color-coded and cross-referenced.

"What?" she asked, catching my expression.

"Nothing. Just appreciating thorough planning."

Her eyes narrowed, determining whether I was teasing, but whatever she saw must have reassured her. She relaxed, closing the laptop. The small click echoed in the quiet kitchen.

"Thank you," she said, her voice softening. "For today. For staying calm when everyone else would have panicked."

The specific gratitude caught me off-guard. "Panic is rarely productive in renovation. Or medicine. Both require steady progress and adaptation when complications arise."

"Is that your professional philosophy, Dr. Westfield?" A hint of playfulness entered her tone.

"It's my life philosophy."

She searched my face with the same attention she'd given the damaged walls. Her fingers drummed once against the laptop lid, then stilled.

"I'm learning that," she admitted. "The hard way."

The admission opened a door I hadn't expected. I remained

still, sensing she needed space to continue rather than reassurance.

"I've always been the person with the perfect plan," she continued, her gaze drifting toward the window where the harbor was visible through the trees. "Event planning rewards that thinking. You have to anticipate everything, prepare for more, leave nothing to chance." She paused, fingers tracing the laptop's edge. "And then my body decided it had its own agenda. Completely separate from my plans."

The simple admission lacked her usual careful filtering.

"The doctors gave me options, but none fit my plan. Surgery that might help the pain but could affect my ability to have children. Hormone treatments with side effects that would impact my work. Or continuing as I was, managing increasing pain while my condition worsened."

She turned back to me, green eyes clear and direct. "I came here because I needed space to think. To figure out which compromise I could live with. But I'm wondering if it's not a compromise at all. Maybe it's charting a different course entirely."

"Different courses can lead to unexpected destinations," I offered carefully. "Sometimes better ones than originally planned."

"That's what I'm considering." She gestured around the half-demolished cottage. "This place was never in my plan. Supposed to fix up my grandmother's cottage while I handle a condition that's rewritten everything? Definitely not on any timeline I mapped out."

"And yet?"

"And yet it feels right. Being here. In this space that needs restoration just when I do." She glanced down at her hands, then back up with surprising vulnerability.

"I understand better than you might think. I had everything planned. My dream research position at Mass General, slated to be the next department head. Boston apartment, conferences, publications." The memory was like looking at photographs of someone who resembled me but lived a different life. "Then Dad had his heart attack, and suddenly I was back in Waverly Cove 'temporarily.'"

"But you stayed," Gemma observed. "Even after he recovered."

"I stayed. Because the life I'd planned wasn't necessarily the one that would fulfill me. Knowing your neighbors' children and grandchildren, seeing patients through years of challenges, becoming part of a community rather than just working within it... those things mattered more than I'd expected."

Gemma absorbed this in silence. The cottage kitchen held us in its warm circle of lamplight.

"It's hard to let go of the plan," she said finally.

"The hardest part. But sometimes necessary."

Our eyes met across the kitchen, the space between us charged with recognition. We were both navigating reconstructed futures, though from different starting points.

The cottage creaked around us, wood settling as evening air cooled through the walls.

"I should go," I said, knowing she needed processing time. "It's getting late."

Gemma nodded, though her fingers tightened on the edge of the counter. "Thank you again for the plumbing situation. I appreciate having a partner who doesn't panic when things go sideways."

As I gathered tools, Gemma followed me to the door. Evening light caught in her copper hair, highlighting gold strands among the auburn. She looked more relaxed than I'd seen since her arrival.

"About those tile patterns," she said. "Were you serious about reviewing them tomorrow? Because I have ideas for the shower niche I'd like your opinion on."

"I'd like that. What time works?"

"Seven? I'm going to Maya's soccer game in the afternoon."

"Perfect. I'll bring wine."

I brushed a kiss against her cheek and turned to leave.

Her smile deepened, creating the faint dimple that appeared only with genuine delight. "I'll try to make something edible."

I drove away as the evening sky darkened over the harbor. My thoughts turned to courses and destinations. Today's conversation had clarified what I'd been reluctant to acknowledge. This project had become more than professional collaboration.

James's words echoed in my mind: *renovation projects have endpoints, people's lives are more complicated.*

True enough. But that's what made this different. Recognition of a kindred spirit navigating similar territories of reimagined possibilities.

My phone chimed with a text from Kate as I pulled into my driveway.

KATE

Still coming to Soph's for dinner tomorrow?

Family dinners were non-negotiable in the Westfield household. You showed up unless you were bleeding or had a fever over 101. But this thing with Gemma felt more important than keeping my streak intact.

I shook my head, smiling despite myself. My family had sensed whatever was happening between Gemma and me.

Maybe I'm reading too much into this. Gemma was still figuring out her health, her future, whether she'd even stay.

But today felt more like a partnership than a favor for a friend.

Tomorrow would bring tile patterns and wine. The rest could wait.

Chapter 10

Gemma

"Absolutely not." I spread the paint samples across Kate's kitchen table. "I have work to do."

Kate made a sound somewhere between a snort and a laugh. "It's the Harvest Festival, Gem. Town ordinance 47B: Mandatory attendance for anyone who's been here longer than six weeks."

"Pretty sure that's not a real ordinance." Sea Glass or Ocean Mist? The paint companies apparently believed there were fifty-seven distinct shades of "vaguely blue-green."

"And I'm not a resident. I'm a temporary cottage squatter."

"Your cottage. That you're gutting and rebuilding." Kate plucked the samples from my fingers. "People don't install heated bathroom floors in temporary housing."

The implication hung between us. Another gentle probe about my plans, my commitment, my postponed return to reality.

I reached for the samples, but Kate pulled them just out of reach.

"The bathroom will survive one afternoon of neglect. The festival happens once a year, and the children will stage a revolt if you don't see Maya's interpretive turkey dance."

Kate took on a posture I recognized with dread. The same stance that had convinced me to jump off quarry cliffs at age ten and ask Tommy Gillespie to the eighth-grade dance. Arms crossed, chin set at a determined angle.

"Fine." Resistance was futile. Kate possessed the negotiating skills of a seasoned diplomat crossed with a stubborn mule. "Two hours maximum. And I'm not volunteering for anything."

"Of course not," Kate agreed with wide-eyed innocence. "Just show up, consume questionable fried foods, absorb small-town charm. Maya has her dance, Noah has some pumpkin cannon demonstration that apparently requires advanced degrees in physics to appreciate."

The kids' enthusiasm was infectious. Maya had been campaigning for "Aunt Gemma" to witness her artistic interpretation of autumn, while Noah had explained the perfect pumpkin trajectory with scientific precision.

"Also," Kate added casually, "Liam will be there. First Responders dunk tank."

I rolled my eyes. "Subtle, Kate."

"I'm providing comprehensive festival information." She blinked with practiced innocence. "Would be irresponsible as your cultural liaison otherwise."

"The cultural liaison who's been scheming since I unpacked."

Kate didn't deny it. "You're both stubborn, soft-hearted workaholics. I'd be failing in my duty as best friend and sister if I didn't at least attempt to force you together."

Despite everything, I smiled. Kate's transparent scheming was comforting.

"These will survive twenty-four hours without your supervision." She swept the paint samples into a drawer. "Go change into something festive. The twins want to leave in thirty minutes, and Noah has already planned our route for maximum efficiency."

Defeated, I trudged upstairs. My wardrobe reflected poor planning—either Boston business attire or cottage demolition clothes. I settled on dark jeans, the emerald sweater Kate insisted brought out my eyes, and waterproof boots.

The mirror showed someone I didn't quite recognize. The hollow-cheeked, dark-circled woman who'd arrived in Waverly Cove had softened at the edges. Not my old self, but not nearly as haggard.

The realization was equal parts comforting and terrifying.

As if answering my burst of positivity, an ominous cramp twinged through my abdomen. I paused, fingers pressed against the dresser, breathing through the familiar warning. The targeted therapy had helped, but stress and weather changes still triggered reminders of my body's ongoing rebellion.

I dry-swallowed two ibuprofen and willed them to work faster than their usual twenty minutes. Just enough time to compose myself before facing crowds.

"AUNT GEMMA!" Maya's voice could shatter windows. "Noah says if we don't leave RIGHT NOW we'll miss everything and it will be CATASTROPHIC!"

"Coming, hurricane." I grabbed a jacket, slipping stronger medications into my pocket. "Tell Noah catastrophe waits for no one."

Maya appeared in the doorway, already bedazzled with festival pins and butterfly face paint. "He says that's EXACTLY why we have to go! And Daddy says all the best parking will be gone!"

"Can't have that." I forced brightness into my voice despite the deepening ache. "Let's save both science and parking in one heroic mission."

She beamed, grasping my hand with mysteriously sticky fingers. "You're going to LOVE everything! There's music and games and Uncle Liam might get dunked, which Daddy says is worth the price of admission."

"Is that so?"

She tugged me along, chattering about marvels awaiting us. Her enthusiasm became a shield against my body's insistent complaints.

October had turned Waverly Cove festive, and the common buzzed with community energy. The scent of cider donuts drifted from the Daily Knead's booth, mixing with salt air that carried laughter and the distant crash of waves.

Noah abandoned us immediately for the pumpkins. Maya lasted four minutes before spotting her dance troupe.

"And then there were two," Kate said, linking arms as Alex followed the twins into the fray.

"Let's walk first," I suggested, overwhelmed. The crowd pressed closer than I'd expected, voices layering over each other in that festival cacophony that made my shoulders creep toward my ears.

Kate understood without explanation that I needed time to acclimate. We moved along the booth perimeter while she provided commentary that required only nods.

The first cramp hit as we passed the pie judging station. I stopped, one hand finding Kate's arm for balance while I breathed through the tightening.

"Gem?" Kate's voice sharpened.

"Just settling in." I straightened, my hand dropping from my abdomen. "The ibuprofen needs time."

Her eyes narrowed, cataloguing my color and posture. "We could head back..."

"No." The word came out harder than intended. "I'm here for Maya's dance. Everything else is manageable."

Diane Westfield's approach interrupted the conversation, her flour-dusted apron somehow festive rather than work-worn. "Katie girl! And the lovely Gemma. How's the cottage project treating you?"

"Like an expensive, time-consuming education in century-old plumbing," I replied, surprised when genuine laughter escaped. Diane's warmth made honesty easier than performance.

The casual conversation created space between me and the building discomfort. Diane's cider donuts were worth the festival admission alone, still warm and dusted with cinnamon.

Until another cramp hit, this one sharp enough to steal my breath. I let out an involuntary gasp before I could stop it.

"Gemma?" Diane's voice carried immediate concern. "You've gone pale."

"Just tired," I managed, though the words came out tight. "Long week."

Kate stepped closer. "Why don't we find somewhere to sit for a few minutes?"

A familiar voice cut through the festival chatter before I could argue.

"Well, if it isn't Katherine Chen and our Boston visitor." Elena Orocho approached with measured stride. Her silver hair stayed perfectly styled despite the October breeze, and her smile held a particular quality of community authority I remembered from childhood encounters with teachers and principals.

"Elena," Kate replied, politeness wrapped in caution. "Have you officially met Gemma? Nancy Prescott's granddaughter."

"Of course, dear. We met briefly at Liam's lovely little clinic." Elena's handshake was firm, calculated. "How are you finding small-town life after Boston's sophisticated pace? It must be quite a change."

The pain medication hadn't kicked in yet, leaving me raw-edged. "I'm managing well, thank you."

"Such resilience," Elena continued. "Katherine was sharing how important proper support systems are during health transitions. Community care makes such a difference when dealing with... ongoing challenges."

The words hit like ice water. The careful pause, the meaningful look between Elena and Kate. My chest tightened.

Katherine was sharing.

The phrase echoed between my ears. My parents' voices materialized from memory: "We mentioned your condition to the Campbells—they have resources that might help." "Dr. Patterson's wife specializes in women's health issues. We shared your symptoms with her at the faculty dinner."

They presented this matter-of-factly, without asking, leaving me exposed in rooms full of colleagues and family friends who knew intimate details about my failing body. The academic world was small. Privacy was negotiable when framed as collaboration, as seeking resources, as building support networks.

My parents treated personal information like research data to be shared, discussed, analyzed with anyone who might have relevant expertise.

"My business partner is handling things beautifully in

Boston," I managed. "If you'll excuse me, I should check on the children."

My legs carried me on autopilot while another wave of cramping doubled me forward. The festival noise pressed against my ears, voices blending into meaningless sound while I found refuge under one of the ancient maples.

Katherine was sharing.

Maybe I'd misunderstood. Maybe Elena had twisted innocent concern into something more invasive. But the familiarity of casual mention of private medical information as community knowledge triggered responses built over twenty years of academic fishbowl living.

My parents had never seen medical information as private. Depression during graduate school became a dinner party conversation with psychology colleagues. Family friends in mental health fields heard about my brief therapy stint. Everything became case study material, discussed with clinical detachment and genuine desire to help, but always without considering that some things belonged to me alone.

"Aunt Gemma? Are you sick again?" Maya's voice carried that seriousness children reserve for adult distress. She'd appeared beside me with six-year-old stealth. The wings of her butterfly face paint were still vibrant, despite being smudged.

I straightened automatically, a smile sliding into place. "Just taking a little break, sweetheart. Lots of excitement to process."

Maya studied me with the unnerving perception kids possess when adults try to lie. "Mom says sometimes you need quiet when your tummy hurts. I can be quiet with you if you want."

The offer was so genuine, so uncomplicated by adult agendas, that my throat tightened. "That's very sweet. But I wouldn't want you to miss the festival."

"I already did face painting and cookie decorating. Noah's still doing boring science stuff." Without waiting for permission, she settled beside me, her small shoulder pressing against my arm. "I can stay until my dance starts."

For a moment, we sat in comfortable silence. Maya's presence was oddly soothing, her acceptance offering exactly what I hadn't known I needed.

"You know what's funny?" I said carefully. "Sometimes grown-ups share things about other people that aren't theirs to share."

Maya looked up, butterfly wings crinkling as she frowned. "Like secrets?"

"Not exactly secrets. More like... personal things. Private things."

She considered this with gravity that belied her young age. "Mom says everyone gets to choose who knows their private things. That's what makes them private."

I sat with that for a moment. "Your mom sounds very smart about that."

"She is. She says some people think they're helping but they're really just being nosy." Maya's matter-of-fact delivery carried the weight of overheard adult conversations. "Ms. Orocho talks about lots of people's private things. Daddy says she means well but doesn't understand boundaries."

A sharp intensification of cramping doubled me forward. This wasn't manageable discomfort. This was pain that stole breath and demanded immediate attention.

Maya's eyes widened. "Should I get Mom?"

"No, I'm okay. Just need to..." But the words died as another wave hit.

Maya was already moving. "I'll get Mom! And Uncle Liam! They'll fix it!"

Left alone with escalating pain, I fumbled for the stronger medication. My hands trembled as I removed lid from the prescription bottle. I swallowed the tablet dry, grimacing at the familiar bitter taste.

Thirty minutes minimum before it might help. Time I wasn't sure I had.

Standing, I tested my legs. Shaky but functional. The world tilted momentarily before stabilizing. The pain made everything distant, wrapped in cotton, thoughts moving slowly.

Katherine was sharing.

Physical distress had pushed the phrase to the background, but it hadn't disappeared. It lodged somewhere in my gut, waiting to be examined when I could think clearly again.

"Gem?" Kate's voice reached me first, concern clear. She appeared through the crowd with Maya trailing behind, Alex close behind them both.

"Maya says you're hurting," Kate continued, her practiced eye cataloguing my pallor and posture. "Bad one?"

Her face blurred slightly at the edges. "Getting there. I've taken the strong medication, but it needs time."

Kate's assessment was swift and decisive. "We're leaving. Alex can get the twins."

"No. Maya's dance..."

"Will be perfectly wonderful next year." Kate's tone brooked no argument. "You should be home."

Another wave of pain stole my breath before I could protest. Through the haze of medication and cramping, footsteps approached.

"How long has it been building?" Liam's voice broke through my gauzy thoughts, steady and professional.

Through the haze of pain, I registered that he was wearing

swim trunks and a Waverly Cove Fire Department t-shirt that looked hastily pulled on. His hair was damp.

"Did you just get dunked?"

"Twice. Henderson's kid has excellent aim." He crouched to my eye level, shifting seamlessly into assessment mode despite the ridiculous outfit. "How long?"

"About an hour. Got worse in the last few minutes." The admission came easier with him, because pretending was exhausting and medical personnel had seen worse.

"I'll drive," he offered immediately. "Kate can stay with the twins."

The simple offer was a relief. "Thank you. That would help."

Kate reached for my hand, and I let her take it, even though questions about boundaries and sharing and trust sat heavy between us, unspoken but present.

"We'll talk later, okay?" she promised. "About everything."

I nodded, not sure what everything included or whether I'd be ready for that conversation when later arrived.

Liam guided me through the crowd, his presence creating a buffer, his steady hand on my elbow keeping me upright when the world lurched. A few people called out jokes about his early escape from the dunk tank. He waved them off without breaking stride, his hand steady on my elbow, as if escorting a pain-addled woman through a festival while half-dressed was perfectly normal.

As we reached his truck, the festival seemed like a distant memory. The sounds of celebration faded as reality narrowed to the immediate challenge of managing pain and getting some-where safe.

"Thank you," I said as he helped me into the passenger seat, words coming out thick and slightly slurred. He paused before closing the door, one hand cupping my jaw. His lips pressed against my temple, lingering for a breath. "For rescuing me. Again."

"No rescue required," he replied, tone calm. "Just neighbors helping neighbors through rough patches. That's how community works."

As we pulled away from the festival chaos, the side mirror showed Kate's figure growing smaller in the distance. The hurt sat alongside the physical pain.

The questions would still be there when the medication wore off. The conversation with Kate would still need to happen.

But for now, I let myself sink into pharmaceutical cotton, trusting that some problems could wait until I was strong enough to hold their weight.

Chapter 11

Liam

My morning stop at Harbor Brew should have been straightforward: caffeine, maybe a cinnamon scone if my willpower crumbled. Instead, I ran straight into a room full of small-town intelligence gathering.

Elena sat in her usual corner with her "morning meditation group." The town's unofficial gossip network. Fresh coffee mixed with salt air from the open windows as they took notes in their color-coded notebooks. The scratch of pen on paper accompanied their whispered conversations.

"Liam, dear!" Elena's voice could carry across the harbor. "Just who I wanted to see!"

Years of Elena encounters had taught me to recognize these moments, but caffeine withdrawal made people do irrational things.

"Morning, Elena. Ladies." The polite but hurried nod that suggested Important Medical Professional Business, but Elena had already launched into her "concerned community member" voice.

"We were just discussing yesterday's festival. Poor Gemma was having such a difficult time. Margaret was saying at prayer circle how hard things must be with her endometriosis."

Cold flooded through me.

Margaret. At prayer circle. Discussing Gemma's specific diagnosis with Elena's distribution network.

"Margaret discussed a patient's medical information at prayer circle?" My voice went flat.

"Oh, not discussed exactly." Elena's fingers drummed against her notebook. "Just shared that we should keep poor Gemma in our prayers. Margaret's got such a heart for helping people understand how to be supportive."

Behind the counter, Diane's coffee grinder paused mid-motion. Mrs. Patterson looked up from her newspaper.

Margaret had turned confidential patient files into community service announcements, and Elena had no idea she'd just described a federal crime.

"Did Margaret mention how she knew these details?"

Elena's face brightened. "Oh, she knows everything about the patients! Always so well-informed about what everyone needs."

There it was. Confirmation that Margaret had been treating medical files like community newsletters for who knows how long.

"I should get to the clinic." I left without ordering coffee.

As I headed for the door, fragments of conversation followed about meal trains and "poor thing, dealing with all that pain."

Margaret sat at her desk when I arrived, organizing files. The familiar click of her keyboard filled the reception area. She looked up as I entered, face brightening.

"Morning, sweetie. You're in early."

The normalcy was jarring. This was Margaret, who'd bandaged my scraped knees and apparently spent twenty-five years treating patient confidentiality like community service.

"Margaret, I need to ask you a question. I ran into Elena this morning. She mentioned concerns about Gemma that you'd shared at prayer circle."

No surprise, no guilt crossed her features. "Oh yes. Poor thing, dealing with endometriosis at her age. I thought the prayer circle should know so they could include her in their intercessions."

My throat went dry at her casual confirmation.

"Margaret, patient medical information is confidential. You can't share details about someone's condition without their permission."

She waved dismissively. "Oh, Liam, that's for big hospitals where people don't know each other. This is Waverly Cove. We take care of our own here."

"Taking care of people doesn't include making decisions about their privacy without asking them first. How long has this been going on?"

"Oh, ages!" Her face lit up. "Your father understood how important it was for people to support each other. I've always made sure the right people knew what they needed to know."

Always. Twenty-five years of "the right people knowing what they needed to know."

"We need to talk about this more extensively. But immediately, from now on, patient information stays in this office. No exceptions."

She nodded agreeably, though her expression suggested her definition of "patient information" differed wildly from mine. "Of course, dear. I've always been careful about these things."

I spent the next three days investigating, uncovering layers of well-intentioned privacy violations. Every conversation revealed new depths to Margaret's community outreach program that was, legally speaking, indefensible.

The clinic emptied differently in the evenings. Quiet but heavy with antiseptic. Tonight involved explaining to someone who'd been family that her version of caring had crossed seventeen different legal lines.

"Margaret." My voice caught on her name. "We need to talk. In my office."

Her fingers froze over the keyboard. The shift in my tone penetrated her composure. She followed me with careful dignity, settling into the chair across from my desk.

"I need to discuss the extent of your information sharing," I began.

Her expression brightened with pride. "Oh, I've always made sure people knew how to help! Mrs. Casey during her back treatment, the Morrison boy's ACL, that young woman with the bladder issues..." She counted on her fingers, each name another violation.

Each example landed like a stone in my gut.

"Margaret, what you're describing are federal crimes."

Her laugh was soft, amused. "Crimes? That's for big city hospitals where people are strangers. I've been facilitating community support for twenty-five years."

"Did my father ever specifically tell you to share medical details with prayer circles?"

The pause stretched. Her fingers found her reading glasses chain.

"Not in... not in so many words. But the spirit of community care..."

"The spirit of community care doesn't override federal law. What you've been doing could cost us our license."

Her face went pale. The certainty crumbled, replaced by genuine fear. "You're really saying I've done wrong?"

"I'm saying you've violated the trust every patient places in us." The words burned in my throat. "Good intentions don't undo the harm."

Her face crumpled. "Twenty-five years, Liam. I was here when your father hung his first diploma. I bandaged your scraped knees, celebrated your graduation. And now you're treating me like some criminal?"

The words cut to my core. Family was everything to the Westfields, and after more than two decades with my father's practice, Margaret was as close to family as it got.

"This isn't about loyalty. This is about every person who trusts us deserving the right to control their own information."

Margaret sat in silence, shoulders slumping. The fight went out of her posture entirely.

"What happens now?"

"I have to let you go, Margaret."

She deflated. "Over helping people so they don't suffer alone?"

"You decided what level of privacy people deserve without asking them."

She pushed herself up with movements that had aged her years. "I'll clean out my desk."

As she reached the door, she paused without turning. "Your father would have fixed this without destroying everything good about it."

"Dad would have understood that patient trust isn't negotiable."

"He may have. Though I wonder if you'll feel the same when half the town stops speaking to you because you chose regulations over relationships."

After she left, I sank into my chair, watching Margaret pack twenty-five years into a cardboard box through my office window. Each item she removed, each photo frame, each personal mug—decades of loyalty reduced to cardboard.

My hands still trembled, not from anger, but from the certainty that I'd just broken something irreplaceable.

But the weight on my shoulders had lifted for the first time in days.

The hardest part wasn't the decision itself. It was knowing that protecting patient trust meant dismantling what I'd always taken for granted.

Patient trust wasn't just professional courtesy. It was the foundation.

Even when it cost everything.

Chapter 12

Gemma

Assumptions settle in without you noticing, like sediment in still water. Invisible until something disturbs them and clouds everything again.

I'd spent the week since the Harvest Festival nursing hurt, convinced that Kate had betrayed me to Elena's gossip network.

The sound of Liam's knock stopped my hands mid-motion over the dishwasher. The deliberate spacing of those three knocks meant my deflection tactics had finally met their match.

"We need to talk." He skipped pleasantries when I opened the door, his expression grave. "About what happened at the festival. About Elena."

My stomach dropped. "If this is about Kate—"

"It's not about Kate." Such certainty in his voice that I stepped back, allowing him entrance. "That's exactly what we need to discuss."

I perched on the edge of the couch while Liam chose the armchair across from me. Close enough for conversation but far enough to avoid crowding. Even now, he was calibrating his approach to my comfort level.

"Kate didn't share your medical information." He spoke clearly. "She never told Elena anything about your condition."

The statement took several seconds to penetrate the defensive narrative I'd built. "But Elena said—"

"Elena said Kate mentioned it, yes. But Elena has a talent for creative interpretation when it serves her purposes." Liam's jaw tightened. "The information came from our clinic. From Margaret, specifically."

Margaret. The name hit like a shock, followed by memory fragments: Margaret's warm welcome during my first appointment, her motherly fussing, the way she'd known details about my condition that I hadn't shared with anyone.

"HIPAA violation." The words came out flat. "She shared my medical information."

"With Elena's prayer circle. She thought she was providing community support." Liam's voice held exhaustion that suggested this conversation had cost him. "I had to let her go, Gemma. Twenty-five years of employment, but federal law doesn't make exceptions for good intentions."

The revelation rearranged the week. Kate hadn't betrayed me. My oldest friend hadn't weaponized my vulnerability. Instead, a woman I'd trusted with my most private medical details had transformed them into community talking points, no matter how well-intentioned.

Relief about Kate warred with fresh hurt about Margaret.

"Twenty-five years. You fired someone who's been with your family almost as long as I've been alive."

"I protected every patient who walks through that door." Liam's correction came gently but with underlying steel. "Including you. Especially you."

The fierceness in his voice made my throat tighten.

"Margaret doesn't see it as violation." Testing my understanding. "She sees it as caring."

"Exactly. Which makes it tragic rather than malicious, but doesn't change the legal or ethical reality." Liam leaned forward. "Your medical information belongs to you, Gemma. Not to the community, not to well-meaning church ladies, not to anyone who thinks they know how to help better than you do."

The validation landed somewhere deep. Years of dismissed pain had left me expecting my privacy to be treated as negotiable. He stated it as absolute principle, and suddenly the ground felt solid beneath my feet.

"That must have hurt Kate. Thinking I believed she'd betrayed me."

"Kate understands protective instincts better than most. She's not angry, just concerned about you carrying this alone." Liam's expression softened. "Though she mentioned your tendency to suffer in silence rather than ask for clarity."

The gentle accuracy made me wince. How many relationships had I damaged by assuming betrayal rather than seeking truth? How much pain had I created by defaulting to isolation instead of communication?

"I owe her an apology."

"You owe yourself some compassion." Liam's counter came swift. "You've spent years having your pain dismissed by medical professionals. Of course you'd be sensitive to having your struggles made public without consent."

I sank deeper into the couch cushions. It wasn't Kate. Her shocked expression, the way she'd stepped back when I'd accused her. Someone else had shared my information, wrapped their gossip in good intentions.

The hurt was still sharp and real, but I'd aimed it at the wrong person.

———

Guilt settled into my bones. Pervasive, bone-deep, impossible to ignore.

Three days of nurturing hurt over Kate's imagined betrayal, three days of careful distance and wounded silences, while my best friend had done nothing more than love me enough to be concerned.

I called her before I could talk myself out of it.

"Can you come over?" My voice came out small. "I need to... I owe you an apology. A real one."

"I'll be right there." Kate's response came without hesitation, without questions. Just the immediate answer of someone who'd been waiting for this call.

She arrived with coffee that steamed in the early November air and the particular expression of careful neutrality that meant she was giving me space to find my own words.

"I was wrong." The confession tumbled out before she'd even settled onto the couch. "About everything. About thinking you'd shared my medical information. About pulling away instead of just asking what happened. About—"

"Gemma." Kate's voice was gentle but firm. "Breathe first. Self-flagellation can wait until you've actually explained what changed."

The gentle humor in her tone almost broke me. After days of imagined betrayal, she was still so fundamentally Kate.

I settled beside her, hands wrapped around the coffee mug. "Liam came by yesterday. To explain what actually happened. It wasn't you. It was Margaret, sharing my information with Elena's prayer circle because she thought she was helping."

Kate's expression shifted through relief, anger on my behalf, and vindication. "How long have you been carrying this around, thinking I'd betrayed you?"

"Since the festival. Since Elena made her comment about knowing my medical situation through you." My stomach sank. "I should have asked. Should have trusted you enough to have an actual conversation instead of just... retreating."

"Why didn't you?" No accusation, just genuine curiosity.

The answer required digging into fears I'd barely admitted to myself. I set down my coffee. "Because I'm terrified." The words came out with force. "Because every medical appointment lately, I walk in with questions and walk out with prescriptions I never agreed to and referrals I didn't request. Because I'm losing control over everything that matters, one specialist consultation at a time."

Kate moved closer. "Keep going."

"Pushing you away was the only control I had left. The only territory still under my jurisdiction." Tears spilled over. "If I was angry at you, if I was protecting myself from betrayal, then at least I was making a choice instead of just... submitting to whatever medical consensus decided was best for my broken body."

The words came faster now. "Kate, I don't know who I am anymore. Every aspect of my identity is being redefined by this condition."

Kate's arms came around me then, and I collapsed into her embrace. Her hand found the back of my head, fingers threading through my hair.

"Oh, honey." Her voice cracked. She tightened her hold, and her chin came to rest on top of my head. "God, Gemma. You've been carrying all this by yourself, haven't you?"

I pressed my face deeper into her sweater, breathing in the familiar scent of her fabric softener and faint trace of paint. Her heartbeat drummed steady against my cheek.

"I didn't know how to..." I mumbled.

"I know." Kate's thumb traced small circles between my shoulder blades. "I know."

"Everyone looks at me differently now. Doctors who see my symptoms before they see me, family and friends who whisper about 'poor Gemma's female troubles.' Even I look at myself differently. Every decision gets filtered through this lens of limitation, every plan has to account for what my body might or might not be able to handle."

I pulled back, wiping my face. "And when I thought you'd turned my private struggle into community concern, it felt like you'd kicked down the last door I'd kept locked."

Kate's hands stilled against her coffee mug. "I hate sitting still when people are hurting." She traced the rim with her finger. "So I just... act. Plan things. Organize solutions. But that's not what you needed, was it? You needed someone to just be there without trying to fix everything."

"Kate, no." The words came out rough. "You've been—" I stopped, pressed my palms against the table. "You were patient when I was impossible. Present without making me feel like a specimen. Your help never made me feel broken. I'm the one who chose suspicion over trust."

"You assumed betrayal because you've been operating in survival mode for months." Kate corrected. "When you're constantly defending yourself against medical professionals who dismiss your pain, when you're navigating a system that treats your autonomy as optional, of course you'd be hypervigilant about protecting what privacy you have left."

My defensive responses might be reasonable adaptations. Not character flaws.

"Every choice carries weight I can't calculate. Stay in Boston or move to Waverly Cove. Surgery or continued management. Independence or accepting help. I keep second-guessing everything because I can't afford to get it wrong."

Kate was quiet for a moment. When she spoke, her words carried the weight of careful consideration. "Gemma, what if the goal isn't to reclaim the exact autonomy you had before? What if it's to build a different kind that includes acknowledging limitations while still making meaningful choices within them?"

The suggestion opened something in my mind. A path that had been there all along, but I'd been so focused on battering against the blocked route that I'd never noticed the alternative.

"You mean stop trying to be the person I was before and figure out who I can be now?"

"I mean recognizing that you're still you, just navigating different terrain. Your intelligence hasn't changed. Your creativity, your problem-solving abilities, your capacity for building beautiful things. None of that disappeared with your diagnosis." Kate turned to face me more directly. "But you might need to apply those skills differently than you used to."

The conversation settled into more comfortable rhythms after that. Kate helped me recognize patterns in my thinking that were creating unnecessary isolation, while I finally gave voice to fears I'd been carrying alone.

"I'm scared about the surgery." The admission came as afternoon light began to fade. "Not just the medical risks, but what it might mean for my future. For any chance at the kind of life I thought I wanted."

"What kind of life did you think you wanted?"

The question required more consideration than expected.

"I'm not even sure anymore. For so long, everything was about building my career, proving my competence, maintaining independence. A family was always something I might want eventually, when everything else was perfectly established."

"And now?"

"Now, it feels urgent. Not necessarily because I'm desperate to be a mother, but because I'm losing the option I've been keeping in reserve."

"Have you talked to anyone about preservation options? About what possibilities might still exist even if surgery is necessary?"

"The doctors in Boston mentioned some approaches, but they're all schedules and protocols and timed interventions. Nothing like the natural progression I'd imagined." I paused. "That's part of what I need to grieve."

"Grief makes sense. And so does taking time to figure out what you actually want rather than what you think you should want."

As evening approached and Kate prepared to leave, she paused at the door. "Gemma? For what it's worth, watching you navigate this has been incredible. Not the medical stuff, that's been heartbreaking. But watching you rebuild your entire life around new realities while still maintaining your essential self? That's inspiring in ways I'm not sure you recognize."

The compliment landed in an unexpectedly raw place. "I'm barely keeping my head above water most days."

"That's what courage looks like sometimes. Not fearlessness, but persistence in the face of uncertainty." Kate smiled, reaching out to squeeze my hand. "And for the record, you're going to be okay. Different than you planned, maybe, but okay. More than okay."

It was dark by the time Kate left. I sat on the porch swing in the cool evening air, processing the day's revelations.

The hurt I'd been nursing had transformed into understanding, relief, and a grudging recognition that my defensive responses had been both understandable and unnecessary.

Forgiveness wasn't just about pardoning others' mistakes. Sometimes it was about pardoning your own fear, your own imperfect responses to impossible circumstances. Sometimes it was about choosing connection over protection, trust over control.

Kate hadn't betrayed me. My fear had created enemies where none existed. But now, sitting in the space we'd created together, I could imagine building something more solid than the defensive walls that had kept me safe but also kept me isolated.

Chapter 13

Liam

In small towns, nothing escapes the gossip train for long. I arrived at Harbor Brew the next morning to discover that Waverly Cove knew everything about Margaret's firing. Half the town had convicted me in the court of public opinion, while the other half was reserving judgment.

Diane intercepted me before I'd taken three steps inside.

"Large coffee, extra shot, and a cinnamon roll for strength," she announced, sliding the order across the counter before I'd even opened my mouth. "You look like you wrestled with something bigger than yourself and lost."

"Word travels fast."

"Elena's prayer circle met here at six this morning," Diane replied, her tone dropping to a conspiratorial whisper. "She's been holding court like she's running for mayor on a platform of righteous indignation."

Translation: Elena was staging a campaign to restore Margaret to sainthood while casting me as the villain. Which meant Gemma would hear about this. The woman whose private medical information had been turned into prayer circle talking points would now watch the town debate whether protecting her privacy had been worth it.

The bell above the door chimed, admitting Ben Henderson with a purposeful stride.

"Liam." He nodded, measured and professional. "Heard about the situation at the clinic."

I gestured toward the empty chair across from me, recognizing that this conversation was happening whether I liked it or not.

"Margaret's been part of this community for twenty-five years," he began, calloused hands braced against the edge of the table, like he was ready for a fight. "Good woman. Heart's in the right place. Always been one to help folks out when they needed it."

"She is," I agreed, because arguing with Ben Henderson about community values was pointless. "But good intentions don't override federal law."

Ben's weathered face creased. "People are saying you fired her for caring too much about patients."

"People are getting their information from Elena's interpretation of events. Which is roughly as reliable as tea leaves."

That earned me a rusty chuckle from Ben, who'd lived in Waverly Cove long enough to understand Elena's particular relationship with objective truth.

"So what actually happened?" Diane asked, materializing beside our table. She'd been wiping the same counter for five minutes while eavesdropping.

I realized that conversations had dimmed to the specific frequency of people pretending not to listen. Mrs. Patterson rustled her newspaper with unusual vigor. Tom Bradley had abandoned all pretense of completing his crossword and was staring openly in my direction.

"Margaret was sharing patient medical information with people outside the practice," I said, loud enough for everyone to hear clearly. "Not because she was malicious, but because she genuinely believed she was helping. That doesn't make it legal."

"What kind of information?" Ben asked, his directness cutting through diplomatic niceties.

"The kind covered by federal privacy laws. The kind that could cost us our license." I drank deeply, needing significantly more caffeine to get through this morning. "I had a choice between protecting patient confidentiality or protecting Margaret from the consequences of violating it. I chose the patients."

Every patient who'd ever trusted us with something private. Including Gemma, who'd already spent years having her pain dismissed and her autonomy questioned. She didn't need her medical details discussed over coffee and prayer requests.

Ben's expression shifted, the skeptical furrow between his brows smoothing. He leaned back in his chair.

"Elena says you were looking for an excuse," Diane said quietly, glancing toward the window where Elena's distinctive silver sedan was visible in the parking lot. "That you wanted to bring in someone younger."

"Elena says many things," I replied, though I kept my tone neutral. "Most of them designed to position herself as the moral authority on situations she doesn't fully understand."

As if summoned by my words, Elena herself swept through the door. She'd definitely been monitoring the cafe from her car. She approached our table with confidence.

"Dr. Westfield," she said, her tone carrying enough chill to preserve seafood. "I suppose you're here to justify your treatment of poor Margaret."

"I'm here for coffee, Elena. Same as every morning." I gestured to the empty chair. "Though if you'd like to discuss the situation, I'm happy to explain the legal requirements that govern medical practices."

Elena settled into the chair with the deliberate grace of someone accepting a challenge. "Legal requirements? Margaret has been caring for this community since before you were out of high school. She knows every family's history, every child's allergies, every elder's concerns. That's not violation. That's dedication."

"It's also a federal crime." My voice stayed level. "Elena, I understand that Margaret's intentions were good. But sharing specific medical information without patient consent violates HIPAA regulations. Period."

"HIPAA," Elena repeated, scorn in her voice. Government interference in community care, her expression suggested.

Ben cleared his throat. "Elena, let me ask you..." He spoke with patient wisdom. "When you had that issue with your back garden last year, the one where the neighbor's drainage was causing problems, did you want me discussing your property situation with every customer who came into the store?"

The question landed with precision. Elena's expression flickered with uncertainty before her defensive walls snapped back into place.

"That's different," she said, though her voice lacked its earlier conviction.

"Is it?" Ben continued. "You came to me with a private concern, trusted me to help solve it discretely. Wouldn't you have been upset if I'd broadcast your business to the whole town, even with good intentions?"

Elena's mouth opened, then closed. Her fingers tightened around her purse strap.

"It's not the same thing at all," she protested, but the protest was weak.

Diane abandoned any pretense of working. "Elena, remember how concerned you were when people were talking about your nephew's troubles? You specifically asked folks to respect the family's privacy during a difficult time."

Elena's coffee cup clinked against the saucer. "That was family business."

"And medical information is personal business," Ben said. "Same principle, Elena. Sometimes caring for people means protecting their privacy, not sharing their troubles."

Elena's gaze moved from Ben to Diane, then finally to me. The cafe had stilled. The silence stretched.

"Easy enough to say," Elena replied finally, though her righteous indignation was deflating. "Margaret's the one who'll suffer for your principles."

"Margaret will be fine," Diane interjected. "She's got her pension, her health, and more casserole recipes than the rest of us combined. Plus, word is she's already talking to the library about part-time administrative work."

This was news to me, but I filed it away.

"The library?" Elena's eyebrows rose, her professional educator instincts intrigued despite her defensive posture.

"Makes perfect sense," Ben observed. "Place where she can help people, organize information, actually follow privacy rules since library records are stamped right in the back of the book anyway. Play to her strengths without the legal complications."

Elena was quiet for a long moment. Mental gears shifting.

"She'd be perfect," I said, meaning it. "Margaret's talents were never the issue. Just the venue where she applied them."

Elena assessed me with calculating intensity. When she spoke again, her voice had lost some of its sharp edges. "I suppose, if Ben thinks the decision was reasonable, there might be aspects I hadn't fully considered."

"I do," he confirmed. "Rules exist for a reason, Elena. Protecting people's private information, that's not government interference. That's basic decency."

Elena's nod was almost imperceptible, but it was there. A minor concession that cost her considerable pride.

The conversation dispersed after that, community members drifting back to their original tables. Elena departed with less theatrical indignation than her entrance, though her goodbye was still formal enough to preserve her dignity.

Ben traced one of the coffee rings with his finger before attacking it with his napkin. "That could've ended a lot worse."

"Margaret mentioned yesterday that she was starting to understand why the boundaries matter," I said. The tension in my shoulders was finally beginning to ease.

Ben nodded, then paused beside my chair. "For what it's worth, Liam, you did the right thing. Wasn't easy, but it was right. Sometimes protecting people means making decisions they don't understand at first."

The words settled something in my chest. It wasn't absolution—I didn't need that. But confirmation that standing up for patient privacy, for Gemma's privacy, had been worth the cost.

The morning proceeded with blessed normalcy. Word had spread that Ben had publicly supported the Margaret decision, which in small-town politics carried serious weight.

By lunchtime, Mrs. Peterson had stopped by to express

support. Mr. Johnson arrived with shoulder pain and a comment about "respecting protocols." Even Elena's closest allies seemed to have pivoted from outrage to acceptance.

Lisa appeared in my doorway at midday. "Well," she said with visible relief, "that could have gone much worse."

"Ben Henderson's support helped."

"Also helped that people like Margaret personally," Lisa observed. "Made it easier for them to separate the person from the professional mistake. Plus, the library thing gives everyone a happy ending to focus on instead of just the controversy."

The old leather of my chair creaked as I leaned back. Familiar. Comforting.

"Crisis management in small towns requires different skills than I learned in medical school."

"Probably why they don't teach courses in 'Therapeutic Communication with Church Ladies' or 'Advanced Techniques in Coffee Shop Diplomacy,'" Lisa replied with a grin. "Though they should."

By closing time, the Margaret situation felt genuinely resolved rather than simply postponed.

My phone buzzed as I walked to the truck.

MARGARET

Thank you for handling yesterday with discretion and professionalism. I've learned a great deal from this experience. I start at the library on Monday. I think it will be a good fit. Ben Henderson stopped by this afternoon to explain why the rules matter. I understand now.

The tension I'd been carrying loosened a notch. The library would be good for her.

Another buzz.

GEMMA

Kate told me what happened at Harbor Brew this morning. Thank you. For all of it.

I leaned against the truck and read the words twice. Then typed back before I could overthink it:

LIAM

Want company for dinner? I'll bring wine and takeout from that Italian place you mentioned.

GEMMA

Yes. Please.

I was already pulling up the restaurant's number when it registered how automatic that had been. A hard day, and my first impulse wasn't to go home and decompress alone. Wasn't the gym, or a beer with James.

It was Gemma.

I couldn't remember the last time I'd wanted that. The last time I'd let myself.

The engine turned over. Her cottage was starting to feel more like home than my own house, and I didn't let myself think too hard about what that meant.

Chapter 14

Gemma

The porcelain toilet was the only cool thing in a world of fire. My forehead pressed against it, knees aching against the floor, but that pain was nothing compared to the inferno raging through my pelvis. The bare overhead bulb cast harsh shadows across the walls, but I hardly noticed them. When your body stages a full rebellion, home improvement details fade into background noise.

My phone was ringing somewhere in the cottage. Kate's maternal radar pinging again. I'd made the strategic error of canceling on family dinner, citing "work commitments." Kate could probably smell my pathetic excuses from three blocks over.

Standing proved wildly optimistic. My legs buckled as the room spun. I grabbed the bathtub's edge, desperate for any sort of stability.

The pain had been building all day, but I'd been determined to ride it out alone.

A hesitant knock echoed through the cottage. Too patient to be Kate's impatient drumming.

"Gemma?" Liam's voice drifted through the windows, calm but edged with concern. "It's me."

Of course. Kate had deployed the nuclear option.

I opened my mouth to call out that I was fine, that he didn't need to worry. Instead, another wave crashed through my pelvis, stealing my breath and leaving me heaving into the porcelain.

"I'm using my key," he announced, and moments later, the front door opened with a whoosh of wind and rain before clicking shut.

His footsteps moved through the cottage with purpose. He knew where to find me. This wasn't his first rodeo.

I flushed and wiped my mouth, a futile gesture toward dignity.

"In here," I croaked.

The bathroom door opened and Liam appeared, hair dark with rain, canvas bag and thermos in hand. His gaze swept over me, huddled on the floor. For just a moment, his professional composure cracked. Raw worry flashed across his features before he composed himself.

"Hey." He set his things aside and crouched beside me. Rain and clean cedar scent. "How long?"

"Hour or two." The words scraped past my raw throat.

"Kate mentioned you might appreciate some company." He tested the air, noting the evidence without judgment. "But I was already planning to check on you after you canceled this morning."

His hand hovered near my wrist, a question in the gesture. "May I?"

I nodded. Too depleted for my usual boundaries, too tired to maintain walls.

His fingers found my pulse. Steady, practiced, but somehow more intimate than clinical, like he was checking on more than just my heart rate.

"Scale of one to ten?" His voice carried clinical calm while his eyes tracked every micro-expression.

"Six."

He raised an eyebrow.

"Fine. Eight," I amended, then squeezed my eyes shut as nausea surged again. "Maybe nine."

My honesty surprised us both.

"Medication?"

"Coffee table. But everything..." I gestured helplessly toward my stomach. "Express lane back up."

"When did you last eat?"

I tried to remember through the pain fog. "Breakfast?"

A cramp doubled me over, and I couldn't stop the whimper that escaped. His hand found my back, a steady pressure that made the pain less isolating.

"Let's get you more comfortable." Calm decisiveness. "A warm shower might help. Then we'll try some of Diane's broth before medication."

"Okay," I whispered.

He helped me stand, taking most of my weight when the world tilted. His movements were economical, turning on the shower with one hand while keeping me steady with the other.

"Think you can manage from here?"

"I think so." I gripped the sink, testing my legs. "Thank you."

"I'll be right outside." Liam stepped back, pulling the door mostly closed but leaving it slightly ajar. Close enough to hear if

I needed help, distant enough to preserve what dignity I had left.

I emerged a few minutes later to find clean pajamas draped on the door hook. Liam must have ventured into my bedroom. The thought should have been mortifying. Instead, warmth bloomed in my chest.

A soft knock interrupted my careful movements. "Would you like help with your hair? Wet hair won't help how you're feeling."

I hesitated. My hand moved toward my sopping waves, then stopped. The thought of detangling the inevitable mess after sleeping on them damp sent a preemptive ache through my shoulders.

"Actually... yes. That would help."

He waited in the living room with my hairdryer and brush, expression matter-of-fact rather than pitying. A chair sat positioned near an outlet.

"My sisters would murder me if I let you catch pneumonia," he said. "Mom considers wet hair during storms a cardinal sin."

I settled into the chair, cocooned in flannel that smelled like fabric softener. "Westfield family medical doctrine or legitimate concern?"

"Strongly held family belief supported by generations of anecdotal evidence." His smile warmed as he gathered my hair. "Temperature okay?"

Gentle heat replaced the day's accumulated stress. His hands moved with the same careful attention he brought to treating patients, never hurrying, never applying pressure beyond what was comfortable.

"You're suspiciously competent at this," I murmured, eyes drifting closed.

"Three sisters, four nieces." His hands remained steady, sectioning hair with precision. "I was conscripted early. Kate's ballerina phase required perfect buns for every recital."

The image of teenage Liam patiently styling his little sister's hair made something flutter beneath my ribs.

"Want a braid? Might be more comfortable."

"You braid too?"

"Man of many talents." He was already working, fingers weaving through my hair with surprising deftness. "French braids, sibling mediation, emergency formal-wear escort. I've been the backup date for two proms and several weddings."

The list delivered with such deadpan seriousness that I smiled despite everything.

"There." He secured the end. "Better?"

I reached back, tracing the neat plait. "Thank you."

He moved toward the kitchen, and I heard him rummaging through cabinets. "Now let's see about settling your stomach."

The broth he returned with was rich and salty, with that hint of ginger Diane always added. He'd arranged blankets on the couch, creating a nest of comfort.

"Small sips," he instructed, settling nearby with his own mug of tea.

The liquid coated my raw throat and settled my rebellious stomach. I managed several cautious sips without incident.

"Your bedside manner is annoyingly effective," I said, mustering a wan smile.

He moved through my kitchen with easy familiarity, preparing tea and cleaning up. The broth went down slowly, but it stayed down. Liam wasn't one to fill the silence with nervous chatter.

"Better?" he asked when he heard me spoon slurping the last bits of soup.

"Getting there." The pills and broth had finally worked their magic. "You didn't have to come. Especially in this weather."

"I know." He settled beside me, close but not crowding. "I wanted to."

Liam's calm understanding cut through every defense I'd constructed. The words escaped before I could stop them.

"I used to think pain made me weak."

Liam kept his gaze on the harbor, giving me space to speak without the weight of eye contact.

"That's the message, isn't it? Especially for women. That acknowledging pain is failure."

"My mother once told me successful women don't have time for 'female problems.'" I laughed, the sound hollow. "I spent years believing I could outwork this. Like it was a personal failing instead of biology."

"That's a heavy burden to carry. On top of everything else."

"I got very good at hiding it. But the isolation..." I traced patterns in the crushed velvet pillow. "Everyone else just continues with their lives. They can't see it, so they forget it exists."

Thunder rolled closer, and the lights flickered.

"I see it," Liam said quietly. A simple statement that landed harder than any grand declaration. "Even when you think you're hiding it."

The profound relief of being witnessed—not fixed, but understood—warmed my chest.

"Pain is like winter storms," he continued, voice low. "You can't control when they hit or how hard, but you can learn to weather them. And sometimes, you don't have to weather them alone."

The medication began softening the world's sharp edges. I leaned toward him, drawn to his steady presence like a magnet.

"Tell me something good," I murmured, needing an anchor beyond the pain and the medication and the fear. "Something completely unrelated to endometriosis or renovations or any of this."

He considered this, his profile thoughtful in the firelight. "When I was ten, James convinced me pirates had buried treasure on the western headland. Some elaborate story about shipwrecks during the Revolution that I believed completely."

Despite everything, I smiled. "Let me guess... you spent the summer looking for it."

"I spent an entire summer excavating that bluff." His mouth quirked. "Found so many rocks I probably altered the local geology. Dad kept finding them in my pockets during laundry."

"And?"

"Last day before school started, I found a wooden box."

"No way."

"Way." He grinned, the expression transforming his whole face. "James had planted it months earlier. Old cigar box with replica coins, a tarnished brass compass, and a hand-drawn 'treasure map' marking all the best fishing spots around the cove."

"That's... surprisingly sweet for a big brother prank."

"James has hidden depths." His arm brushed mine as he shifted. "I still have that compass. It sits on my clinic desk."

"The broken one?"

His gaze met mine, warm in the firelight. "Sometimes the things that don't work quite right are the ones worth keeping."

The double meaning hung between us, undeniable.

For once, I had no defensive retort. Instead, my head tipped sideways until it rested against his shoulder, my body making choices my brain was still too cautious to acknowledge.

His arm came around me, unhurried, careful. The question implicit in the gesture.

"Okay?" he asked quietly.

"Okay," I whispered, eyes closing as rain drummed against the windows.

My limbs grew heavy with the combination of medication, relief, and Liam's steady warmth. His hand traced gentle circles on my upper arm, and my breathing slowed to match his.

When his hand stilled and he shifted his weight slightly, reaching for something, the words escaped before I could think better of them.

"Stay." My voice was barely audible over the rain. "Until the storm passes completely. The forecast said it might circle back."

The excuse sounded thin even to my own ears, but exhaustion had stripped away my usual filters.

His movement paused. A beat of silence, then: "Okay."

He dimmed the lights, added another log to the fire, and settled more comfortably beside me. His body a solid line of warmth along my side.

I pulled my grandmother's quilt over both our legs, its familiar weight grounding me. His fingers found mine beneath the blanket, and I laced them together without hesitation.

I woke hours later to find myself stretched along the couch, head pillowed against a warm chest. Liam had shifted to accommodate me, one arm draped protectively around my shoulders, breathing deep and even in sleep. A book lay forgotten on his chest, rising and falling with each breath.

Pale moonlight filtered through the windows. The storm had passed, leaving only the gentle drip of water from the eaves.

I should move. Return to my bed, maintain the boundaries that had served me well for so long.

Instead, I nestled closer, drawn to his warmth and the steady rhythm beneath my ear. His heartbeat, constant and sure. His hand moved in his sleep, fingers spreading against my back, pulling me incrementally closer.

Tomorrow would bring complications, questions, and the reality of the chasm between my uncertain fertility and his dreams of family. The conversation we'd have to have eventually, about what futures we could or couldn't build together.

But tonight, in the storm's aftermath, I allowed myself this moment of connection. This feeling of being seen, understood, and held anyway.

His breathing shifted, consciousness returning. His hand stilled against my back, then resumed its gentle circles. Awake now, but making no move to pull away.

"Hi," I whispered into the dim evening light.

"Hi," he whispered back, his voice rough with sleep. His thumb traced a slow path along my spine. "How are you feeling?"

"Better." I pressed my palm flat against his chest, feeling his heart beat steady beneath my hand. "Thank you. For staying."

"Thank you for letting me."

Neither of us moved. The words we should probably say about boundaries and expectations and what this meant could wait. For now, there was just this: the quiet cottage, the rain-washed evening, and the simple comfort of not being alone.

Eventually, we'd have to get up. Eventually, reality would intrude. But not yet.

Not quite yet.

Chapter 15

Liam

Consciousness returned with the scent of lavender and vanilla. Gemma's shampoo. Awareness sharpened to the weight against my chest. During the night, she'd curled into me, face pressed to the hollow of my throat.

I should move. Extract myself before she woke and found us tangled together. But her breathing had finally evened out, no longer the shallow pants of someone negotiating with pain, and I couldn't bring myself to disturb the first proper rest she'd had in days.

The cottage held us in morning quiet, salt air drifting through windows I'd cracked before settling beside her last night. Golden light painted the worn pine floors, catching copper highlights in her hair where it had escaped its braid.

Beautiful.

Professional boundaries, Westfield.

Except those boundaries had eroded since the day she'd walked into my practice. They'd been obliterated since that first kiss.

Gemma stirred, her fingers tightening in my shirt before she registered where she was. The change in her breathing rhythm, the subtle shift from relaxed sleep to guarded awareness.

"Good morning," I whispered, not moving. Letting her decide how to handle waking up in my arms.

She lifted her head, green eyes still heavy with sleep. "Hi." The word came out rough, intimate in a way that made my chest tighten.

I was close enough to count the faint freckles across her nose.

"How do you feel?" I asked, though what I really wanted to know was whether she regretted this.

"Better." She didn't pull away immediately. "Like a car has run me over instead of a truck."

"Progress," I managed, hyperaware of her weight against me, the way her thumb traced absent patterns on my chest through my shirt.

"Liam," she began, then stopped. Her gaze dropped to where her hand rested against my ribs. "Last night..."

"Was whatever you need it to have been," I said quickly. "No pressure. No expectations."

She started to speak before pressing her lips together. The pulse at her throat quickened before she pulled back, cool air rushing between us.

"I should make coffee," she said, sitting up and immediately wincing as movement reminded her body of yesterday's rebellion.

"I'll do it." I stood, muscles protesting a night on the couch. "You rest."

But she followed me to the kitchen anyway, stocking feet silent on the cold floor.

"Kate stocked real food," she observed, gesturing to supplies that definitely hadn't been here before. "Your sister has strong opinions about my nutritional choices."

"Kate has strong opinions about everything," I replied, pulling out the carton of eggs and bottle of milk. "It's her most endearing and infuriating quality."

Gemma's laugh was hoarser than usual, still touched by sleep. "She mentioned you've been checking on me. More than medical protocol requires."

I paused, setting the ingredients down on the counter. "Is that a problem?"

"No." The word came quickly. "I just... I'm not used to people staying."

I turned to face her fully. She studied her hands instead of meeting my eyes. Walls I'd watched her build beginning to rise again.

"Gemma," I said, stepping closer. Close enough to catch that floral scent again. "Look at me."

She lifted her eyes reluctantly. Her breathing had gone shallow, the way it did when she was bracing for bad news.

"I'm not going anywhere," I said simply. "Whatever this is, whatever it becomes... I'm not going anywhere."

Her breath hitched. For a moment, her gaze dropped to my mouth before snapping back up, color flooding her cheeks.

"You don't know what you're saying," she whispered. "You don't know what being with someone like me would mean."

"Someone like you?" I stepped closer, closing the distance between us. "You mean someone brilliant? Someone who's survived sixteen years of medical dismissal and built an incredible career while managing chronic pain? Someone brave enough to start over when everything fell apart?"

"Someone broken," she corrected, voice barely audible.

"You're not broken." The words came out fierce. "You're

dealing with impossible circumstances with more grace than anyone has a right to expect. That's not broken, Gemma. That's extraordinary."

Her eyebrows drew together as if she were trying to parse words that made little sense. One hand pressed against her chest.

"The doctors want to do surgery," she blurted. "Complete excision, possibly more. They're saying it's becoming less optional and more... inevitable."

I kept my expression steady, even as the implications settled in my gut. "And how do you feel about that?"

"Terrified," she whispered. "Not just of the surgery itself, but of what it means. For my future. For any future I might want."

I touched her then, my hands finding her face. "What future do you want?"

"I don't know anymore." She blinked rapidly, tilting her face toward the ceiling. "Everything I thought I knew has changed. And I can't ask someone else to sign up for that uncertainty."

"What if someone wanted to sign up for it anyway?"

The kitchen filled with the soft tick of the wall clock and the distant cry of gulls. Her eyes searched mine.

"Liam," she breathed.

My body moved without permission, leaning closer, drawn by the way she said my name, by the want written clearly across her face despite her fear. Her hands came up, fingers curling into my shirt—

The front door burst open with a resounding bang.

"Emergency delivery!" Kate's voice rang through the cottage, followed by multiple footsteps. "Mom sent provisions and—oh."

Gemma and I sprang apart. Her hand flew to her hair while I turned toward the stove so fast I nearly knocked over the egg carton. Heat flooded my face.

Kate stood in the kitchen doorway, arms full of grocery bags, with Alex and the twins behind her. Maya peered around Kate's legs, bright eyes taking in everything.

"Uncle Liam, why is your hair doing that spiky thing? Did you stick your finger in a light socket like in cartoons?"

"Are we interrupting?" Kate asked with barely contained glee.

"Making breakfast," I said quickly, turning back to the stove.

"Uh-huh." Kate's eyebrow arched as she set down the bags. "That must be why you both look like you've been—"

"Coffee," Gemma interrupted loudly. "Who wants coffee?"

"Ooh, Gemma's face is all pink!" Maya stage-whispered to Noah. "Do you think she has a fever?"

"Uncle Liam, check her forehead like Daddy does when we're sick," Noah advised with scientific seriousness.

The moment was gone, dissolved into family chaos and knowing looks from my sister. But as the cottage filled with conversation and laughter, I caught Gemma's eye across the crowded kitchen.

Whatever had almost happened between us wasn't an accident or a moment of vulnerability. It was the beginning of something neither of us had planned, but both of us wanted.

The question was whether she'd be brave enough to let it unfold.

What followed was the kind of impromptu family invasion that Kate specialized in. Within minutes, she'd unpacked enough groceries to feed a small army, Alex had the twins settled at the kitchen table with coloring books, and proper coffee was brewing.

"Mom sent her emergency provisions," Kate explained, pulling containers from bags. "Diane's blueberry muffins, that soup you liked from last week, and enough frozen meals to get you through whatever this is." She gestured between Gemma and me.

"This?" Gemma's voice climbed slightly.

"Oh, you know." Kate waved a hand. "The inevitable thing that everyone except you two has seen coming for weeks."

Alex cleared his throat, not looking up from where he was helping Emma with her crayons. "Kate."

"What? I'm just saying—"

"You're making them uncomfortable," he said mildly, but there was steel beneath the quiet words.

I shot him a grateful look, then busied myself finishing the breakfast I'd abandoned.

Behind me, Kate's voice dropped to what she thought was a whisper. "Gemma, how are you feeling? Really feeling?"

"Better," Gemma replied. "Yesterday was... rough."

"Pain?" Kate's nursing instincts had kicked in, professional concern replacing her earlier teasing.

"Among other things."

I turned from the stove in time to catch the look that passed between them: understanding that went deeper than words.

"Well," Kate said finally, "that's why we're here. Emergency sister duty."

"I'm not your sister," Gemma protested, but there was no heat in it.

"You are in every way that counts," Kate replied, already moving toward the living room. "Alex, can you help me move this table? The kids need more space, and Gemma needs to rest without six-year-olds using her as a jungle gym."

The day unfolded in comfortable waves. Kate directed operations, organizing craft projects and snacks, while Alex provided steady support. I stayed, initially to help, but increasingly because leaving felt impossible.

Gemma settled on the couch with a book, but the kids were captivated by her calm presence and her genuine interest in their observations about crayon colors and butterfly wings.

"Uncle Liam," Maya announced around noon, holding up a drawing that might have been a house or possibly a purple dinosaur, "Gemma says you fixed her house. Did you use magic?"

"Just tools," I replied, settling beside Gemma on the couch as Maya climbed into my lap. "And a lot of patience."

"And coffee," Gemma added, her shoulder brushing mine. "So much coffee."

"Coffee is magic," Noah declared, which made Alex laugh from the kitchen where he was assembling sandwiches.

The afternoon passed in comfortable chaos. Kate regaled us with updates from town: Margaret's attempts to reorganize the library's collection, the harbormaster's mysterious girlfriend, Alex's ongoing feud with the pharmacy's new system.

I helped the twins build a fort out of couch cushions, hyperaware of Gemma's presence just feet away, the way she smiled at their architectural debates. When Noah declared the fort needed a password, Maya suggested "Gemma's house," which became "Gemma-Liam's house" in rapid-fire negotiation.

Neither Gemma nor I corrected them.

As afternoon stretched toward evening, Kate began gathering scattered toys and restoring order. The twins protested, but Alex distracted them with promises of ice cream.

"We should head home," Kate said finally, her gaze moving between Gemma and me. "Let you two have some peace."

"Thank you," Gemma said. "For today."

Kate's smile was gentler than usual. "That's what family does."

After they left, the cottage felt emptier and more intimate at once. Gemma stood at the kitchen window, watching their station wagon disappear down the drive.

"Your family is wonderful," she said without turning around.

"They adopted you pretty thoroughly today."

"Is that what happened?" She turned. "It felt like..."

"Like what?"

"Like belonging somewhere." The words were almost lost in the evening air. "I haven't felt that in a long time."

I moved closer. "Gemma, about this morning..."

"I know." She held up a hand, but it was trembling slightly. "We need to talk about it. About everything."

"The surgery?"

She nodded, then moved to the couch. I followed, leaving careful space between us but close enough to feel the nervous energy radiating from her.

"The doctors want to schedule it soon," she said, staring at her hands. "They're saying the endometriosis is getting more aggressive, that waiting might make things worse."

I was quiet for a moment. "Would you be open to getting a second opinion?"

"I've had multiple opinions. They all say the same thing."

"Not here in Maine," I said slowly. "I have a colleague in Portland. Someone who specializes in exactly what you're dealing with."

Her head tilted. "Someone you know?"

"Taylor's sister, actually. Dr. Sarah Jordan. She's one of the leading endometriosis specialists in New England, focuses on fertility-preserving treatments." I paused. "She might have options your Boston doctors haven't considered."

"Taylor never mentioned..."

"She probably doesn't even know you're dealing with this. Patient confidentiality works both ways." I leaned forward. "But I know Sarah's work, and I know she's helped women in situations similar to yours find alternatives to immediate surgery."

Gemma processed this for a long moment. When she finally spoke, her voice was steady but small. "Would you... would you come with me? If I decided to go?"

"Of course." The answer came without hesitation. "Whatever you need."

She nodded once, decisive. "Okay. Can you reach out to her?"

"I'll call tomorrow."

"Thank you." She shifted on the couch, turning to face me more fully. "Liam, about this morning..."

"You don't have to..."

"Yes, I do." Her voice was firmer now. "What almost happened... I wanted it to happen."

The words landed like a physical thing. "Gemma."

"I know the timing is terrible. I know I'm dealing with medical issues and uncertainty about my future. I know it's complicated." She took a shaky breath. "But I need you to know that whatever this is between us, it's not because I'm vulnerable or confused or grateful for your help."

"Then what is it?"

Her lips curved in the smallest smile. "It's because somewhere between your terrible coffee and your patient explanations of load-bearing walls, I started falling for you." She laughed, the sound catching. "And that terrifies me almost as much as the surgery."

My hands found her face, thumbs brushing across her cheekbones. "Can I tell you something?"

She nodded, eyes locked on mine.

"I started falling the day you walked into that first family dinner at Kate's and immediately took charge of the entire evening like you'd been doing it for years."

"That's just stubbornness."

"That's strength." I leaned my forehead against hers. "And I've been wanting to kiss you again for days."

"What's stopping you?"

"Nothing," I realized, and closed the distance between us.

Her lips were soft, warm, tasting of the coffee we'd shared throughout the day. The kiss started gentle, exploratory, but deepened when her hands fisted in my shirt the way they had when she was sleeping. My fingers threaded through her hair, careful of the braid, and she made a small sound against my mouth that made my heart stutter.

When we finally broke apart, both breathing unsteadily, she rested her forehead against my shoulder.

"So," she said eventually. "What happens now?"

"Now we take it one day at a time," I replied, my thumb tracing the line of her jaw. "Starting with Portland, and seeing what options you actually have."

"And after that?"

"After that, we figure it out together."

She pulled back enough to meet my eyes. Hope, fragile and new, bloomed across her face. "Together," she repeated, testing the word. "If you're sure that's what you want."

"I'm sure." I pressed a kiss to her temple. "Even if neither of us knows exactly what it looks like yet."

"That's okay," she said, her smile tentative but real. "We have time to figure it out."

Outside, the evening deepened toward night. But inside, everything had changed. The careful distance we'd maintained, the walls she'd built to protect herself—all of it had shifted to make room for what we were becoming.

Her hand found mine, fingers lacing together with easy certainty.

Whatever came next, we'd face it together.

Chapter 16

Gemma

The tile crew Liam had called in as a special favor had outdone themselves. Perfectly straight subway tiles. Every hexagon aligned in the accent border exactly as we'd sketched. The vintage clawfoot tub sat in the middle of the room, waiting for refinishing. Cans of enamel lined up against the wall.

Thanksgiving had come and gone. Over two weeks had passed since I'd woken in Liam's arms on my grandmother's couch, and my hand still remembered the feeling of his heartbeat steady under my palm.

LIAM

Just checking if we're still on for this weekend? James says he can help Saturday morning before his fishing run. I can bring breakfast from Daily Knead.

I smiled. His texts had evolved from functional renovation updates to these small acts of care woven through the mundane.

The cottage renovation had evolved from emergency repair to comprehensive improvement. Paint colors for the guest bedroom. A garden plan for next spring. Internet installation for a home office.

The truth hit with sudden clarity: I wasn't planning to leave.

My breathing deepened instead of quickening, like my body had been waiting for my mind to catch up.

A knock interrupted my thoughts. I ran fingers through my hair before catching myself in the gesture. Since when did I primp for unexpected visitors?

Kate stood on the porch with party supplies and wine.

"Emergency baby shower planning session," she announced. "Abby's nursery theme changed for the third time this week, and now all our previous ideas are worthless."

I stepped back, an automatic smile in place while my stomach dropped. "What happened to the woodland creatures?"

"Miguel's mother sent a handmade quilt with an ocean theme. Now my sister thinks the universe is telling them to go nautical." Kate rolled her eyes affectionately while uncorking the wine. "She's texted me fourteen times in an hour about the cultural significance of whales versus narwhals."

"Narwhals," I said immediately. "Obviously superior. Whales are majestic, but narwhals are majestic with built-in weaponry."

Kate's laugh was warm as she poured two generous glasses. "See? This is why I need you. Professional decisiveness through emotional chaos."

As she handed me wine, she studied my face. Both comforting and unnerving.

"So," Kate said, settling onto the couch. "You and my brother."

I took a long sip of wine. "What about me and your brother?"

"Oh, nothing much. Just that he spent the night here during the storm. The looks you gave each other over turkey last week. That I haven't seen him this happy since he was sixteen." Kate paused. "You know, minor details."

"He helped me through a bad episode. That's what physical therapists do."

Kate's expression said she wasn't buying it. "Mmhmm. And I'm the Queen of England."

"It's complicated."

"The best things usually are." Her voice gentled. "But since you're clearly not ready to dissect my brother's many virtues, let's tackle nautical baby shower plans instead."

For the next hour, we debated anchor centerpieces versus net backdrops, created a menu around artichoke dip "tide pools," and compiled a guest list that seemed to include every woman in Waverly Cove under seventy. Kate approached party planning with the same intensity she approached her paintings, and the familiar rhythm of event coordination settled into my bones.

"We'll host at my house," Kate decided, making notes. "More space for the chaos. Plus my pergola makes everything look more intentional when Alex strings fairy lights through it."

"When?" I asked, though part of me didn't want to know. My fingers were already reaching for my phone to check calendar availability.

"Two weeks from Saturday. Gives us enough time to execute a beautiful celebration without cutting it too close to her due date."

Two weeks. I nodded professionally while mentally calculating how many pain management strategies I'd need for an event filled with pregnancy talk, baby gifts, and enthusiastic discussions about family planning.

"Don't co-host if it's too much," Kate said suddenly, her gaze catching what I thought I'd hidden. "We can figure it out another way."

The acknowledgment landed somewhere tender. "I want to help," I managed. "It's what I'm good at. And I'm genuinely happy for them."

"I know you are," Kate said quietly. "But being happy for someone doesn't erase your own complicated feelings. They can coexist."

"When did you become so wise?"

"Around the time I became responsible for two humans whose emotional intelligence consists of 'happy,' 'mad,' 'hungry,' and 'why can't I wear my Halloween costume to school in February?'" Kate smiled. "Speaking of which—you'll be wonderful with kids someday, Gem. Whatever path takes you there."

Unexpected tears stung my eyes. I blinked them back, focusing on the color samples scattered across my coffee table. "Navy and aqua," I blurted. "With coral accents for a pop of color."

Kate allowed the redirect, and we continued planning until footsteps sounded on the porch.

"That's my cue," Kate said, gathering her materials. "I'm terrified to see the state of my house after the twins' latest art project."

"You don't have to leave just because Liam's here."

"Oh, I absolutely do." Kate grinned. "Mission accomplished. Event planned, wine consumed, subtle interrogation about your feelings for my brother successfully conducted."

"Kate!"

"What? Sisterly intelligence gathering is a sacred duty." She was already tucking papers into her bag as a knock sounded. "Come in, Liam. I was just leaving."

Liam appeared in the doorway, his gaze flicking between us. He looked bone-deep exhausted.

"Kate." His tone held familiar suspicion. "This is unexpected."

"Just some quick shower coordination," Kate breezed. "Naval theme. Very sophisticated."

"Nautical," I corrected. "Not naval warfare."

"That would be a very different shower," Liam observed, and that small half-smile appeared. "Though possibly more entertaining."

Kate headed for the door, squeezing Liam's arm. "You look exhausted, little brother. Don't let this one feed you restaurant leftovers. Make her cook real food."

"I cook," I protested, though we all knew my definition of "cooking" was flexible.

"Reheating Diane's casseroles doesn't count." Kate kissed my cheek, her voice dropping. "But honestly? He looks happy when he talks about you. Just thought you should know."

Then louder: "I'll text you about decorations tomorrow."

After she left, Liam sagged against the doorframe.

"Long day?" I asked, noting how he held his shoulders. My

stomach twisted. He'd already spent hours here this week, time he could have used for rest.

"Longer than expected." He rubbed the back of his neck. "Five walk-ins with various autumn mishaps, including Mrs. Peters, who decided today was the perfect day to clean gutters despite her inner ear issues."

"Is she okay?"

"Bruised dignity and a sprained wrist. Could have been much worse." Liam glanced toward the bathroom, then back at me. "We could postpone the planning session. I'm probably not at my most coherent right now."

"We could," I agreed. "Or we could just have dinner. I've got Diane's latest casserole delivery and I'm an expert microwave-er. I won't tell Kate if you don't."

The offer hung between us. Not renovation partners consulting over contractor schedules, but two people planning dinner like it was the most natural thing in the world.

His shoulders relaxed. "That sounds perfect, actually."

"Good." Oddly pleased. "Tuna noodle with some kind of breadcrumb topping situation. Very fancy for a Monday."

We moved to the kitchen naturally. Liam reached for plates while I preheated the oven, working around each other without collision or awkwardness. The domesticity of it struck me—how easily we'd learned each other's rhythms.

"Kate was interrogating you," he said.

"Was I that obvious?"

"No, but she's that predictable." Liam's smile was rueful. "She's been dropping hints about us at every family gathering for weeks."

The casual way he said "us" sent warmth through my chest. "What kind of hints?"

"Let's see. 'Did you know Gemma loves sailing? You should

take her out on the harbor.' And my personal favorite: 'Isn't it interesting how Gemma's favorite color is exactly the same shade as your eyes?'"

I choked on my water. "I never said your eye color was my favorite."

"But it is?" His voice was light, but his gaze had sharpened.

I was caught in that exact shade of honeyed brown. "Top five," I managed.

"I'll take it." His smile created those lines around his eyes that I'd stopped pretending not to notice.

We settled at the small table by the window, the cottage's pine walls still holding the day's warmth. Beyond the glass, late afternoon light spilled across the cove. The silence between us felt comfortable.

"Kate mentioned the baby shower," Liam said carefully.

"Yeah." I set down my fork. "It might be... challenging."

"Want to talk about it?"

The simple offer was free of pressure or judgment.

"I keep thinking I should be nothing but happy for them," I admitted. "It's selfish to have complicated feelings about someone else's joy."

"Feelings aren't selfish," Liam said quietly. "They just are."

"I've never been sure I wanted children," I continued, surprised by how easily the words came. "My career always came first, and my parents weren't exactly nurturing role models. They were more like academic advisors who occasionally remembered to feed me." I paused. "But now that the choice might be taken away..."

"It's different when it's not your choice anymore."

"Exactly." Grateful for the understanding that required no explanation. "Everyone keeps mentioning alternatives like adoption, surrogacy, fostering. And they're right, of course. But that doesn't make the potential loss easier to process."

We finished dinner in companionable silence. As we cleared the table, Liam's hands handled dishes with that steady competence I'd come to rely on.

"I got another call from my business partner today," I said, then wondered why I'd chosen this moment. Confessions were becoming easier in his presence. "The Coastal Maine Tourism Board is still looking for an event planning consultant for their off-season strategy. Waverly Cove is one of the target communities."

Liam looked up from loading the dishwasher, genuine delight in his expression. "I remember you mentioning it a few weeks back."

"It's just a preliminary meeting," I cautioned. "But yes, the location would be... convenient."

We both understood the implication. That I was considering staying. That this conversation was as much about us as it was about career opportunities.

"The town would be lucky to have your expertise," he said, but the warmth in his voice suggested he meant more than professional benefit.

At the door, as Liam prepared to leave, the space between us seemed to shrink. I was acutely aware of how close we stood, of the way his eyes kept dropping to my lips before returning to meet my gaze.

"I'm sorry we didn't get any planning done," I said, though neither of us seemed disappointed.

"Next time." His voice had dropped slightly, taking on that rough edge that made my pulse quicken. "Saturday still works? I'm sure I can round up some extra Westfield hands."

"Saturday's perfect." I stepped closer without conscious decision. "Eight o'clock?"

"Mmhmm." He wasn't looking at my eyes anymore.

My phone rang, shattering the moment.

"I should—" I started, torn between irritation and relief.

Liam stepped back, and I immediately missed his proximity. "Of course. I'll see you Saturday."

At the threshold, he paused. "About Abby's shower... If you need someone to create a diversion or provide emergency backup... just say the word."

"Thank you. I may need to call in that favor."

"I hope you do." His smile held promises of protection and understanding. "Bathroom renovation and special event extraction. I'm a man of many talents."

"I noticed."

After he left, I let the phone go to voicemail, standing in the doorway until his taillights disappeared around the bend. My hand came up to touch my lips, remembering what almost happened.

The cottage felt emptier without him. But also full of possibility for a future I was finally brave enough to imagine.

Chapter 17

Liam

Days later, I stood in Gemma's cottage kitchen, tools spread across her grandmother's refinished table, trying to focus on cabinet hardware instead of the memory of her skin warming under my hands. We'd stopped pretending the professional boundaries weren't dissolving.

"The hinges on the upper cabinet are still sticking," she said, stepping around the renovation chaos. Paint cans and drop cloths transformed the space into an obstacle course.

"I can adjust the tension." I reached for my screwdriver, hyperaware of how she tracked my movements. "Should only take a few minutes."

She settled at the table with her laptop, fingers flying over the keyboard with that focused intensity I'd learned to recognize. Work was her refuge when everything else felt out of control.

"Portland Museum of Art wants to discuss their spring fundraiser," she said without looking up. "If I can convince them I'm not a complete disaster hiding in rural Maine."

"You're not hiding. You're positioning yourself in a location with better lobster rolls and fewer pretentious art critics."

She laughed. The tight line of her shoulders dropped. It was the first time I'd seen her truly relax in this space in weeks.

"Spoken like someone who's never had to convince a board of trustees that your business can function from a cottage without a fully functioning bathroom."

I paused, wrench halfway to the cabinet. "About that. I actually finished installing the fixtures yesterday. It's not perfect, but it's usable. We could test the water pressure and the grab bars."

Her coffee mug stopped halfway to her lips. She blinked twice, that rapid flutter that meant her mind was racing through implications.

"Now?" Her voice was carefully neutral.

"Unless you'd prefer to wait." I set down my tools, meeting her gaze. "But the contractors will want you to verify everything's working before they start on the tile."

She closed her laptop with a decisive click. "Let's do it."

I turned on the shower, adjusting the temperature and pressure while she watched from the doorway. Steam filled the space, warm humidity carrying the scent of fresh grout and new beginnings.

"I positioned the bench for easy transfer," I explained, demonstrating the height and stability. "These grab bars can hold twice your body weight."

The silence stretched. Her fingers gripped the door frame, knuckles going white. She looked up, meeting my eyes in the worn mirror above the vanity. Her reflection wavered in the foggy glass.

"I should test the grab bars," she whispered. "Make sure they'll hold when I actually need them."

I nodded, stepping aside as she gripped the horizontal bar, testing its stability. Her movements were careful, measured—someone who'd learned not to trust automatic responses.

"Solid," she said, but her tone suggested she was testing more than hardware.

"They're anchored into the wall studs. Won't move." I moved closer as the steam enveloped us both. "Try the vertical one too."

She reached for the second bar, stretching up to test its mounting. The movement brought her close enough that the flutter of her pulse was visible in the hollow of her throat.

"This one's perfect height," she murmured, but her attention had shifted from the grab bar to my face.

The shower spray created white noise around us. The rest of the world fell away.

"Gemma," I said, voice rougher than intended.

She released the handle but didn't step back. She turned to face me, back against the unfinished wall, green eyes holding mine.

"I know this complicates things," she said. "But I can't pretend it isn't there anymore. This. Whatever's happening between us."

I moved closer, bracing one hand against the wall beside her head. Steam curled between us.

"What are we doing?" I asked, though my body already knew the answer.

"I don't know," she admitted, but her hands came up to rest against my chest, fingers curling into the fabric of my shirt. "I just know I'm tired of pretending I don't want this."

I leaned closer, forehead almost touching hers, breathing the same warm air.

"This could change everything," I warned. My hands trembled against the tile wall. Fifteen years of clinical training hadn't prepared me for this.

"Change can be good," she whispered, and then she rose on her toes, closing the distance between us.

Her lips met mine soft at first, questioning, then deeper as I responded with everything I'd been holding back for weeks. My free hand found her waist, pulling her closer as her back pressed against the warm tile. The shower created a curtain of sound around us, the outside world distant and irrelevant.

She made a small sound against my mouth, her fingers threading through my hair, and I deepened the kiss. Steam dampened our skin, made everything slick and close. When her tongue touched mine, tentative then bolder, my control fractured. I pressed closer, feeling her heartbeat racing against my chest, matching my own.

When we finally broke apart, both breathing hard, she looked up at me with eyes that held wonder and uncertainty in equal measure.

"We should probably turn off the water," she said, but made no move to step away.

"Probably," I agreed, but instead of moving toward the controls, I traced my thumb along her cheek, catching a droplet of moisture that might have been steam or might have been something else.

Then her phone rang from the kitchen, shrill and insistent.

We stepped apart like teenagers caught by parents, both breathing too hard. I found sudden interest in the shower controls while she studied the ceiling tiles.

"I should..." she gestured vaguely toward the sound.

"Yeah. And I should..." I reached for the dial, turning off the spray.

She paused in the doorway, turning back. "Liam?"

"Yeah?"

"Thank you. For making this space beautiful. For making it mine."

Then she was gone, leaving me alone in the bathroom where every sound now echoed off bare walls. The silence was broken only by final drips from the showerhead and my pulse still racing.

Everything had changed in the space of a kiss. The question was what we were going to do about it.

I washed up while she took the call, soap bubbles coating my forearms as her voice rose and fell in the next room. Twenty minutes of hold music punctuated by transferred calls about coverage for consultations. The same circular conversations, the same interdepartmental buck-passing.

By the time she hung up, I'd moved outside to the back deck. The harbor breeze helped clear my head.

"Sorry about that." She stepped outside, phone still clutched in her hand. "Insurance companies have turned medical care into a game show where nobody wins."

I turned from the railing. Late afternoon light turned her auburn hair copper where it escaped her ponytail. "Everything sorted?"

"They want to review my records before covering the appointment with Dr. Jordan." She moved beside me, setting the phone on the deck rail with more force than necessary. "Same story, different day."

"I can write letters if you need them," I said. "Or walk you through appealing their decision. Whatever helps."

"Thank you." She studied my profile while I watched the harbor. "Can I ask you something?"

"Always."

"What keeps you in Waverly Cove? Really?" She'd heard the standard answer about family practice and being needed. "You could have built a practice anywhere."

I gripped the railing, watching a small blue sailboat ride the swells. "You see that boat out there? The one with white trim?"

"Yeah."

The boat's sail caught the light as it came about. "My grandfather taught me to sail on a boat just like that when I was eight. Every Sunday after church, he'd drag me down to the dock despite my grandmother's protests about good clothes and salt water."

Gemma moved closer to the railing, her elbow brushing mine.

"He used to say sailing taught you everything about life. Patience. Respect for weather bigger than you. How to adjust course when conditions change." I glanced at her. "Most important: how to trust you can handle whatever blows in."

"Sounds like a wise man."

"He was. When I was in Boston, pulling sixteen-hour shifts in that sterile clinic, I realized I'd forgotten how to read the wind. Everything felt like swimming upstream, forcing solutions instead of finding them."

Gemma nodded slowly. That exhaustion lived in the way her mouth tightened.

"So you came home to remember," she said.

"I came home to remember who I was before I decided who I thought I should be." I turned to face her. "But that's not the whole story."

Her eyebrows lifted.

"I want to teach my kids to sail someday." The words came out quieter than I'd intended, but no less certain.

The air between us shifted. Her breath caught, barely audible over the gulls.

"Summer mornings when the water's glass," I continued, looking back at the harbor. My hands moved unconsciously, demonstrating the motion of cleating a line. "Teaching them to tie bowlines and read cloud formations. Watching them figure out how wind fills the sail, that moment when they realize they're actually moving the boat themselves."

I could see it so clearly. Tiny hands learning the ropes, the look of concentration followed by pure joy when they felt the boat respond. The kind of moment that becomes a core memory.

"I want to give them what my grandfather gave me. Confidence that comes from knowing you can navigate whatever weather rolls in."

Gemma's throat moved as she swallowed. She had a death grip on the railing, like it was the only thing keeping her upright.

"My grandfather always said the harbor would teach them about home," I added. "How to leave when you need to explore, and how to find your way back when you're ready."

"Roots and wings," she murmured, something wistful and painful crossing her face.

"Exactly." I met her eyes. "I want them to grow up knowing they belong somewhere, that they have people who'll be here no matter what. But also knowing they're strong enough to chase whatever dreams call to them."

Her hands tightened on the railing until her fingers trembled.

"That sounds beautiful," she managed, but the words came out fractured. Like something was breaking inside her.

The question hung unspoken in the salt air between us. What I wanted. What she might not be able to give me.

"What about you?" I asked, even though I could see the answer was complicated. "Do you want kids?"

Her knuckles went bone-white against the weathered wood.

"I did. I mean, I do. It's just...complicated." She admitted, jaw working.

I didn't push. Instead, I covered her hand with mine, thumb tracing across her knuckles.

"Complicated doesn't mean impossible," I said.

She stared at our joined hands, at the gentle pattern my thumb traced across her skin. Something cautious but hopeful flickered across her expression, fighting against something that looked like resignation.

"Would you teach me to sail?" she asked suddenly, voice barely above a whisper.

That caught me off guard. "You'd want to learn?"

"I want to understand what you see out there. I want to know what it feels like to work with the current instead of fighting it." She turned to face me fully. "And I want to understand this part of you. The part that dreams about teaching your kids to read the wind."

Even if she might not be able to give me those kids. The unspoken words hung between us.

A grin spread across my face despite the weight of everything unsaid. "I'd love to teach you. Fair warning though... my grandfather's method involved lots of patient repetition and zero coddling."

"I think I can handle that," she said, and her voice had steel in it.

As we stood watching the little blue sailboat tack toward the harbor mouth, the space between us felt different. Not just the physical pull that had been building for weeks. Something deeper. Something that looked like a future.

But also the shadow of everything that future might require. Everything she was afraid she couldn't give me.

I pulled her closer, wrapping my arm around her shoulders, and she leaned into me. For now, this was enough. For now, we'd work with the wind we had.

The rest would come when it came.

Chapter 18

Gemma

The research folder on my lap had transformed from organized preparation into a damp testament to my anxiety as Liam navigated I-295 toward Portland. Every highlighted article, every sticky note marking relevant passages, every careful question. It all represented a fundamental shift in my approach to medical care.

For sixteen years, I'd been a passenger in my own medical story. Today, I was grabbing the wheel.

"Storm's building faster than the forecast predicted," Liam observed, nodding toward the wall of dark clouds assembling over Casco Bay. The first fat snowflakes were tentative, but they'd built to a steady flurry.

"We could reschedule if you're concerned about the drive back," I offered.

"I'm more concerned about you missing an appointment you've prepared for like it's a doctoral dissertation." His glance caught the folder's pages curling slightly from my death grip, yellow sticky notes protruding like flags. "You've done your homework. All of it. Twice."

The fact that he understood what this level of preparation meant made my throat tighten.

"I'm tired of sitting through appointments feeling like a passenger in my body. Like a bystander to decisions about my uterus." The irony struck me. I orchestrated every detail of others' significant moments throughout my career, but let medical professionals handle me like I wasn't even in the room.

Portland's Eastern Waterfront unfolded before us, a mix of brick buildings and working wharves that looked both authentically weathered and carefully curated. The Old Port's cobblestone streets gleamed white under the growing storm, while boats bobbed in the harbor.

When we reached Maine Medical Center's campus, the building rose before us with that blend of medical authority and brutalist architecture every major hospital seemed to embrace.

Liam pulled under the covered entrance, where a steady stream of people hurried through the increasing snow.

"I'll park in the garage and meet you inside," he said, then caught my expression stuck somewhere between determined and terrified. "Take whatever time you need. I'll be in the lobby, reading decade-old magazines and questioning their definition of 'current events.'"

<hr>

The third floor smelled like eucalyptus instead of antiseptic, the first surprise. Framed seascapes replaced the baby photos I'd dreaded: weathered dock pilings, salt marshes at low tide, storm clouds over calm water. Real plants, not plastic ones.

I approached the reception desk, grateful for whoever had chosen charcoal gray over baby blue and pink.

"Gemma Prescott," I announced, clutching my folder. "I have an appointment with Dr. Jordan at 10:30."

The receptionist glanced up from her computer. "Dr. Jordan is running right on schedule today." Her eyes shifted past me as Liam entered, shaking snow from his jacket. "Will your partner be joining you for the consultation?"

Partner. The word hung between us, heavy with assumptions I wasn't ready to address.

Before I could clarify our undefined relationship status, Liam stepped forward with the diplomatic grace that came from years of navigating small-town dynamics.

"I'll wait out here," he said simply, his tone carefully neutral but his eyes searching mine. "Unless... you'd prefer I join you?"

"I'll go alone first," I decided, then softened what might have sounded like rejection. "But thank you for offering."

The intake forms demanded different attention this time. Instead of rushing through with automated responses, I considered what they were really asking. When I reached "family planning goals," my pen hovered over neat checkboxes that couldn't capture the complexity of my uncertainty.

"Those forms never have enough boxes, do they?" Liam had claimed a chair close enough to observe my pen-hovering but far enough to avoid appearing clingy.

I glanced up, surprised. "This one's asking me to categorize my 'family planning goals' like I'm choosing an appetizer. As if the answer shouldn't depend on whether I survive the recommendation."

"Medical forms assume linear decision-making," he said, understanding threading through his voice. "Kate once wrote a three-paragraph essay in the margins about how fertility isn't a yes-or-no question."

Kate. Of course she'd been here before, navigating her own reproductive challenges before conceiving the twins. The subtle reminder that I wasn't alone was strangely reassuring.

I checked "Gathering Information/Exploring Options" and continued.

Dr. Sarah Jordan entered the consultation room with a presence that communicated competence without arrogance. Early forties, dark blonde ponytail, intelligent blue eyes behind glasses that were both professional and approachable. She looked like a doctor who might remember that her patients were people.

"Ms. Prescott, I'm Sarah Jordan," she said, extending her hand. Her grip was firm without being aggressive. "I'm sorry we're meeting under these circumstances."

"Thank you for fitting me in, Dr. Jordan. I know your schedule must be—"

"Sarah, please." She settled into her chair, her movements unhurried despite the packed waiting room. "And I want to start by acknowledging something that too many physicians skip. You dealt with this for sixteen years before anyone took your pain seriously enough to investigate properly. That shouldn't have happened."

The directness was novel. No diplomatic hedging. Just acknowledgment, clean and clear.

"I've reviewed all your records from Boston," Sarah continued, rotating her computer screen so I could see the images. "Your diagnostic laparoscopy from earlier this year showed stage III endometriosis, but these recent MRIs suggest progression to stage IV. This darker area here—" She pointed to a shadowy mass. "—is an endometrioma on your right ovary, approximately four centimeters."

I leaned forward, studying the screen. Weeks of obsessive research had taught me to read these images, to understand what I was seeing instead of simply nodding along.

"My OB/GYN mentioned it was growing, but he talked about it like it was a minor inconvenience. Like I should just add it to my list of things to monitor, right after checking tire pressure."

"Let me show you exactly what we're dealing with." Sarah pulled up two ultrasound images side by side. "Six months ago versus today. About a twenty percent increase in size. That's significant both for pain levels and ovarian function."

The visual evidence made abstract medical concepts concrete. My body's betrayal mapped in gray-scale.

"Your chart mentions you've researched treatments," Sarah commented approvingly. "I'd like to hear what you've learned and what questions that research has raised."

So this was proactive medical care. Being treated as a competent participant rather than a complicated piece of machinery that occasionally made troublesome noises.

"I've been reading about the difference between excision and ablation surgery," I began, consulting my notes. "And I'm confused. Several sources say hysterectomy doesn't cure endometriosis, but the doctors in Boston seemed to suggest it was the solution."

Dr. Jordan nodded approvingly. "You're absolutely right to question that. Hysterectomy alone can't cure endometriosis because the disease exists throughout the body, not just in reproductive organs."

She pulled up a different scan. "However, your symptoms

and these imaging results suggest you likely also have adenomyosis."

"Adenomyosis?"

"Unlike endometriosis, adenomyosis only affects the uterus. Your pattern of heavy bleeding, significant clotting, and the specific type of cramping you describe, plus this uterine enlargement visible on ultrasound, all point to adenomyosis as a secondary diagnosis."

Finally, proof I wasn't imagining things. Unfortunately, proof that things were more serious than I'd feared.

"And adenomyosis would require hysterectomy to treat completely?"

"For complete resolution, yes. Combined with excision surgery for the endometriosis." Sarah leaned back, her expression growing more grave. "But before we discuss surgical options, let's discuss the fertility preservation question you raised on your forms."

"What are my options?" I asked, proud that my voice remained steady.

"If that's a priority, egg retrieval and freezing should happen within the next month or two, followed by an excision surgery that attempts to preserve at least one ovary." Dr. Jordan's tone remained gentle but direct. "However, I'll be completely transparent about success rates given your specific situation."

"Tell me," I said, squaring my shoulders.

"With stage IV endometriosis and your current ovarian reserve, even with the most aggressive preservation approaches, pregnancy rates would be reduced. We're talking a less than five percent chance of live birth per frozen egg."

The folder pressed against my thighs. All my research had prepared me for bad news, but hearing the statistics applied to my specific case made it real.

"And if fertility preservation wasn't the priority?" I asked, the question feeling both terrifying and liberating.

"Then I'd recommend complete excision surgery, hysterectomy for the adenomyosis, and likely removal of both ovaries given the extent of damage." Sarah's expression remained compassionate but honest. "We remove the ovaries to eliminate the estrogen that can fuel endometriosis growth, but that means surgical menopause and hormone replacement therapy."

"How much time do I have to decide?" The question came out smaller than I'd intended.

"The sooner the better, medically speaking. This endometrioma shows increased vascularity, which raises rupture or torsion risk." She leaned forward, eyes soft with genuine compassion. "This is a decision that will shape the rest of your life. Take the time you need to be certain. I'd say a month or two at most, but don't rush a decision this profound because of medical timelines."

The careful composure I'd built for medical appointments cracked open. Someone was finally saying that my struggle had been real, that the dismissals had been wrong.

Sarah reached into her desk and pulled out a small box of dark chocolates, the kind with elegant packaging. "Would you like one? I find chocolate helps most situations. Dark chocolate even has anti-inflammatory properties. Not enough to treat endometriosis, but every little bit helps, right?"

Despite everything, I laughed. "Liam mentioned this. Your chocolate reputation."

"Ah, the Westfield intelligence network strikes again." Sarah smiled. "Sophie mentioned you're staying with family in Waverly Cove while you sort through treatment options."

"I'm renovating my grandmother's cottage. Liam—Dr. Westfield—has been..." I searched for words that could encapsulate our evolving relationship. "Helpful with the renovation. And other things."

"The Westfields are good people. Liam especially. He's got a reputation for going above and beyond, both professionally and personally."

Heat rose in my cheeks, but I didn't correct her assumption about Liam's involvement. Mainly because I wasn't entirely sure what that involvement was myself.

Sarah handed me a thick folder. "These include detailed explanations of all surgical options, hormone replacement protocols, and fertility preservation resources. I'm also including contact information for a reproductive psychiatrist who specializes in helping people navigate these decisions."

"Thank you." My voice caught. "For everything."

"For treating you like a competent adult capable of making informed decisions about your own body?" Sarah's smile held a hint of sadness. "That should be standard care, not worth thanking someone for."

As I stood to leave, Sarah added, "Whatever you decide, there are no wrong choices here. Only the ones that are right for you, in this moment, with the information you have now."

No pressure at all, I thought as I made my way back to the waiting area, fingers worrying the edge of my research folder.

Liam looked up as I emerged, his expression carefully neutral, but his attention focused entirely on me.

"How did it go?"

"It was..." I paused, searching for the right word. "Clarifying. Like getting a detailed map of a place you'd rather not visit but clearly need to understand."

"Do you want to talk about it over lunch, or do you need time to process?"

"Lunch sounds good. I could use a break from medical thoughts."

Portland's Old Port buzzed with the energy that only happens right before a storm. We walked to the restaurant, our hands brushing once, twice, then deliberately intertwining. When his fingers wrapped around mine, I didn't pull away.

The place Liam had chosen overlooked the harbor, providing front-row seats to the approaching storm. Dark clouds massed on the horizon while the water churned with whitecaps.

"Barometric pressure's dropping fast," Liam observed, following my gaze. "Might be a rough drive back."

"Does barometric pressure really affect endometriosis pain, or is that just what people say to make weather-related complaints sound more legitimate?" I asked.

"It's completely legitimate. Changes in barometric pressure affect tissue fluid dynamics and nerve sensitivity. Your body isn't imagining things."

The validation still surprised me after years of having my pain dismissed.

Our lobster rolls arrived quickly. Liam had been right about the quality, though he made me promise not to tell anyone in Waverly Cove he'd praised Portland seafood over local catches.

The conversation flowed easily. I shared more than I'd intended about my professional crossroads.

"I've been thinking about the event planning business," I admitted. "Not just the tourism board project, but... what comes next. How do I rebuild my career when my body might derail any timeline?"

"What if you didn't build around the assumption of derailment?" Liam suggested. "What if you built with flexibility as a feature, not a bug?"

My sandwich hovered halfway to my mouth. "That's... actually not a terrible way to look at it."

"Smart business planning accounts for variables. Your health is just one of many factors to consider." He shrugged. "You're better equipped than most to create sustainable work practices."

"Because I'm learning my own limitations," I said slowly. "And how to work within them instead of against them."

"Exactly. Plus, think about your target market. Other people planning important events might appreciate someone who understands that life doesn't always cooperate with schedules."

Eventually, the conversation turned to the consultation.

"She clarified my diagnosis. Turns out I probably have adenomyosis too, which is treated differently than endometriosis. Two different but related chronic conditions that require different approaches."

Liam nodded, his understanding drawn from medical training rather than empty sympathy. "Adenomyosis involves the uterine muscle wall itself. That's why hysterectomy is definitive for that condition, even though endometriosis requires excision surgery since it exists throughout the pelvic cavity."

I studied his face. "You know about the difference? Actually know, not just polite medical professional awareness?"

"I may have done some research." He shrugged, as though this was normal.

The wind gusted outside, vibrating through the building's bones. The heavy snow began in earnest, drumming against the windows.

"We should probably head out," Liam said, glancing at his watch. "Before this gets biblical."

We drove in silence for quite some time so Liam could focus on the increasing storm while my thoughts turned inward. When we reached a calmer section of the interstate, I spoke.

"You know what scares me most about today's consultation?"

"Tell me."

"That I might have to choose between pain relief and the possibility of children I'm not even sure I want." I paused, the confession spilling free. "And my career. I built everything around being the person who creates perfect moments for other people. The planner who controls every detail. But what happens when your body won't cooperate with your schedule? When pain makes you cancel on your biggest client and everyone questions whether you're reliable?"

"What happened in Boston wasn't your fault," Liam said firmly. "You built an impressive career while managing undiagnosed chronic pain. That takes extraordinary resilience."

The glow of the headlights caught the tension in his jaw.

"How do you always know what to say?"

"I don't, actually. I just... see you. All of you. Not just the composed professional version you show the world."

Headlights from a passing plow illuminated the truck, catching the silver threading through his dark hair and the steadiness in his eyes as they focused on the road ahead.

I moved without conscious decision, my hand reaching up to trace the line of his jaw, exploring unfamiliar territory with careful fingers.

Liam went perfectly still, his breath catching as I mapped the texture of his skin, the slight roughness where he'd shaved that morning.

"Gemma," he breathed, my name both question and warning.

"I'm tired of pushing away good things because I'm afraid they won't last," I whispered. "I'm tired of making every decision based on what might go wrong instead of what might go right."

Liam's hand came up to cover mine, where it rested against his cheek. His palm was warm, callused from renovation work. "What are you saying?"

"I don't know what happens next," I admitted. "With my health, the cottage, with this." I gestured vaguely between us with my free hand. "I can't offer certainty about anything right now."

"I'm not asking for certainty," Liam replied, his thumb tracing slow circles on the back of my hand. "Just permission to be part of whatever comes next, however it unfolds."

The truck cab felt smaller, more intimate. Outside, the world was white chaos. Inside, something had shifted into place.

"I'd like that," I whispered.

His fingers tightened around mine for just a moment before he had to return both hands to the wheel as the wind gusted again. But he didn't let go completely. His right hand found mine in the space between our seats, holding on.

Outside, the storm's fury ebbed. The spaces between wind gusts grew longer and the snow's intensity softened from assault to steady percussion against the truck windows.

Inside, something new had taken root between us.

For the first time in longer than I could remember, I allowed myself to accept care offered without strings attached, without timelines or expectations.

His hand warm in mine, solid and real, as we drove through the storm toward home.

Chapter 19

Liam

The storm wasn't finished with us yet. Wind slammed against the cottage windows the moment we crossed the threshold, rattling glass in its frames like a threat.

Gemma set her medical folder on the coffee table. Her shoulders had dropped two inches since this morning. The drive back from Portland had changed something. Her confession in the car, her fingertips tracing my jaw.

"Thank you." She turned from the table, wool socks silent on the worn pine boards. "For today. For driving, for waiting, for—" Her voice caught. "Everything."

"You don't need to thank me for that." The words came out low despite my intention for casual.

She stepped closer. "I meant what I said in the car. About being tired of pushing away good things."

The storm may be raging on outside the cottage, but inside we'd created our own shelter: just her voice, the radiator's steady rhythm, and the fragile thing taking shape between us. She'd admitted in the truck that she wanted me to be part of whatever came next. Now we were here, alone.

I settled on the sofa's far end, close enough to let her know I was there, far enough to let her choose. The cushions wheezed under my weight. I patted the space beside me.

She crossed the room and sank onto the cushions, close enough that her thigh brushed mine. She tucked herself against my ribs like she belonged there. Her body heat seeped through my clothes, and my breathing went shallow.

"It's special, you know." The words ghosted against my shoulder. "You staying. And not making me feel like a burden."

My fingers found her hair and worked gently through the tangles. "You're not a burden, Gemma."

She tilted her head back, green eyes searching my face. "I'm complicated. This is complicated. The endometriosis, the uncertainty about whether I can even—" Her throat worked.

"Hey." I cupped her cheek, thumb stroking the soft skin below her eye. "I'm not going anywhere."

Not when her bad days hit, not when her body betrayed her again. She was worth staying for.

"Liam." My name was barely a whisper, but I heard the question in it.

When I kissed her, I tried for gentle. Careful. But she tasted like mint and something sweet, and the soft sound she made when my tongue traced her lower lip made my pulse kick.

Her fingers curled into my shirt, pulling me closer. I let her set the pace, following her lead as she deepened the kiss. My hand stayed light in her hair while the other found her hip, thumb circling through soft cotton.

When she pulled back slightly, her breathing had changed. "I've been thinking about this," she admitted, voice rough.

"About you. Since the bathroom. Since before that, if I'm honest."

"Me too." I traced the curve of her jaw with my thumb. "But we don't have to—"

"I know we don't have to." She shifted, and suddenly she was straddling my lap, settling against me with deliberate intent. The weight of her, the heat of her through our clothes, sent my pulse hammering. "But I want to."

My hands found her waist, steadying her. "Gemma—"

"Tell me you want this too." Her hands framed my face, green eyes holding mine. "Tell me I'm not alone in this."

"You're not alone." The words came out rougher than I intended. "I want you. I've wanted you for weeks."

She kissed me then, hungrier now, and I let myself respond without holding back. My hands slid up her sides, feeling her shiver under my touch. When I pulled her closer, she rocked against me, and I couldn't stop the groan that escaped.

The small sound she made in response—half satisfaction, half need—nearly snapped my restraint.

"Tell me what you want," I murmured against her lips.

"You." No hesitation. "I want you. I want to stop being afraid of wanting you."

She kissed me again, hands sliding from my face to my shoulders, fingers digging in. She was trembling, but not from fear. When she caught my bottom lip between her teeth, gentle pressure that sent heat down my spine, I had to force myself to slow down.

"Gemma." Her name came out rough. "Are you sure? With everything today, with how you're feeling—"

"I'm sure." She pulled back enough to meet my eyes. "My body isn't cooperating with a lot of things right now, but it knows what it wants. And I want you."

My hands tightened on her waist before I forced them to relax. She was trusting me with this, with her body that had been through so much today. That made it precious. Made her precious.

"Slow?" I asked.

"Slow." Her smile was soft. "But not too slow."

I lifted her carefully, and she wrapped her legs around my waist, arms circling my neck. Her lips found the sensitive spot below my ear as I carried her toward the bedroom, and each kiss traveled straight down my spine.

The bedroom was cooler, afternoon light filtering through lace curtains her grandmother had hung decades ago. I set her down beside the quilt-covered bed, and she reached for me immediately.

"Come here," she said, voice low.

I went willingly, the mattress springs creaking as I settled beside her. My hand found her face, thumb tracing her cheekbone as I kissed her slowly, taking my time. This wasn't something to rush. This was something to remember.

Her hands explored my chest through my shirt, learning the shape of me. When she tugged at my sweater, I helped her pull it over my head. She paused, fingers tracing the lines of muscle across my shoulders, down my chest.

"You're beautiful," she said softly.

"That's my line." I reached for the hem of her shirt, pausing. "Okay?"

She nodded, lifting her arms. I pulled it off slowly, revealing soft skin and a simple bra. My palms skimmed her sides, and her breathing changed. The small laparoscopy scars near her navel caught the light. Her cheeks flushed and she tried to hide them, but I found them beautiful because they were part of her story.

"These too," I said, kissing each small mark. "Beautiful."

Her fingers threaded through my hair as I kissed the tender places on her abdomen where pain lived. Old tension lived in her muscles, the way she held herself guarded even now. My hands mapped her curves slowly, working to coax that tension free.

"Liam." Her voice was breathless.

"Still okay?"

"More than okay."

She pulled me up for another kiss, this one deeper, and her hands explored my chest, finding the scar on my shoulder from the boat accident when I was twelve. Her fingers traced it with careful attention.

"What happened here?"

"Boom caught me during a storm. Split the skin pretty good."

"Does it hurt?"

"Not anymore."

She kissed it, lips soft against the raised tissue. Then she found the spot at the base of my throat, and smiled against my skin when I inhaled sharply.

"Found something," she murmured.

"You're going to be trouble."

"Good."

We shed the rest of our clothes slowly, no rush, no awkwardness. Just the certainty of choosing each other. When she was bare before me, I took a moment to drink in the curve of her hips, the soft swell of her breasts, the way afternoon light caught in her hair.

"You're staring," she said, but she didn't sound self-conscious.

"You're worth staring at."

I kissed her again, skin against skin now, and the sensation made us both gasp. My hands learned the shape of her her waist, the curve of her hip, the soft skin of her inner thigh. She was responsive, arching into my touch, making small sounds that drove me crazy.

When my fingers found her center, she was already wet. I explored carefully, watching her face for every reaction. She guided my hand, showing me what she liked, unashamed in her need.

"Like that," she breathed when I found the right rhythm. "Just like that."

I watched her climb, fascinated by the way her breathing changed, how color flooded her chest and face, the way her fingers dug into my shoulders. When she came apart under my hand, crying out softly, I memorized every second.

"That was—" She couldn't seem to find the words.

"Beautiful. You're beautiful."

She pulled me down for a kiss, still breathing hard. "I want you inside me."

"Are you sure? We can wait, we don't have to—"

"Liam." She met my eyes. "I want this. I want you. Please."

I reached for my wallet, grateful I'd had the foresight to bring protection. She watched as I rolled on the condom, then opened her arms to me.

I settled between her thighs, taking my weight on my forearms. "Tell me if anything hurts. If you need me to stop—"

"I will." She wrapped her legs around my hips, pulling me closer. "But right now, I need you to start."

I pushed in slowly, watching her face. Her eyes went wide, lips parting as I filled her. She was tight and warm, and holding still took every ounce of control I had.

"Okay?" I managed.

"Perfect." Her hands slid up my back, nails dragging lightly. "You can move."

I started slow, pulling almost all the way out before sliding back in. She met each thrust, her hips rising to take me deeper. The angle was good, but I wanted it to be more than good for her.

"How does this feel?" I shifted slightly, changing the angle.

"Good. So good." Her voice was breathless. "But—can you—"

"What do you need?"

"Touch me. Please."

I braced myself on one arm and slid my other hand between us, finding her center. She moaned when my fingers found her clit, circling in time with my thrusts.

"Yes. Like that. Don't stop."

I set a rhythm—slow, deep thrusts matched with steady pressure from my fingers. She was making sounds now, unconscious and honest, and each one drove me closer to the edge.

"Gemma." Her name was half prayer, half warning. "I'm close."

"Me too. Don't stop. Please don't stop."

I didn't. I kept the rhythm steady even as my own pleasure built, even as every muscle screamed for release. Her nails dug into my back. Her breathing went ragged. She arched beneath me, tightening around me.

"Liam—I'm—"

She came with a cry, body clenching around me, and I followed her over, face buried in her neck, her name on my lips.

After, when the world stopped spinning, I carefully withdrew and dealt with the condom. When I returned to the bed, she reached for me immediately.

"Don't go far," she murmured.

"Not going anywhere."

She curled against my side, head on my chest, one leg thrown over mine. Her fingers traced lazy patterns on my skin, following the lines of muscle and bone. I pulled the quilt over us, cocooning us in warmth.

"I feel different now," she said softly.

My arm tightened around her. "In what way?"

"Like I finally stopped fighting something I wanted." Her fingers traced my collarbone. "Like I chose something good instead of just enduring something difficult."

"You did choose something good." I caught her hand, bringing it to my lips. "We both did."

She smiled, and it reached her eyes this time. "No regrets?"

"None. You?"

"None." She settled back against my chest. "I should probably feel more anxious about this. About what it means, about what happens next. But I just feel... peaceful."

"Peace is good."

"Peace is very good."

We lay there in comfortable silence, listening to the water drip from the eaves. Her breathing evened out, and I thought she might be falling asleep, but then she spoke.

"Liam?"

"Hmm?"

"When you said you've wanted this for weeks... how many weeks are we talking?"

I smiled against her hair. "You remember that day you came into the clinic? When Kate dragged you in for the initial consultation?"

"That was almost two months ago."

"I'm aware."

She lifted her head. "Two months? You wanted me two months ago?"

"Longer, actually. I noticed you at that first dinner at Kate's.

But the clinic visit was when I realized it was more than just noticing."

"What happened at the clinic visit?"

"You were wearing jeans and that green sweater that matches your eyes. You were trying to be professional, asking all these careful questions about physical therapy protocols. But you kept tucking your hair behind your ear when you got nervous, and I couldn't stop watching."

She was quiet for a moment. "I was nervous because you were so patient with me. So calm. Everyone else had treated my pain like an inconvenience or a puzzle to solve, but you just... listened."

"I wanted to listen."

She kissed my chest, right over my heart. "I'm glad I stopped fighting this. Stopped fighting us."

"Me too."

Outside, the worst of the storm had passed, leaving only the sound of freezing rain on the roof and waves against rocks. But here, in this bed that smelled like her grandmother's lavender sachets and us, holding this woman who had finally let me in, I knew we were both right where we belonged.

Her breathing evened out again, deeper this time. Her body went heavy against mine, trusting even in sleep. I pressed a kiss to the top of her head and let myself relax.

Whatever came next—whatever decisions she had to make about her health, whatever challenges we'd face—we'd face them together. She'd chosen to let me in, and I wasn't going to take that gift lightly.

I closed my eyes and let the sound of her breathing lull me toward sleep, one hand tangled in her hair, the other resting on her hip, keeping her close.

Tomorrow would bring its own complications. But tonight, we had this. And it was enough.

Chapter 20

Gemma

I showed up at Kate's house three hours early, arms loaded with bags full of baby shower decorations. My emergency medication sat in my pocket where I'd tucked it after the cramping and spotting started this morning. A familiar consequence I'd gladly accept. Last night with Liam had changed something fundamental between us, and I wouldn't trade that for all the pain-free days in the world.

"You're early!" Kate swung open the door. Her hair stuck out in a messy bun, and she wore a t-shirt that read: *Mom: Because 'Miracle Worker' Isn't an Official Job Title.*

"Event planner," I said, hefting my supplies. "Punctuality is a hazard of the job. Right alongside an unhealthy obsession with backup plans."

Kate practically dragged me to the dining room, which looked like a craft store had exploded in navy, teal, and coral. Sophie's version of "helping" apparently involved ordering mountains of supplies online and leaving Kate to wrestle with tissue paper and those paper straws that disintegrated on contact with liquid.

"When should we expect the guest of honor?" I started sorting supplies into piles. My hands moved on autopilot while my brain catalogued potential disasters. Balloon clusters by windows. Check light sources. Banner placement. Avoid high-traffic areas. Gift display. Maximize visibility without creating a bottleneck.

"Abby's under orders to rest until showtime. Miguel's keeping her occupied with name lists." Kate lowered her voice. "Blood pressure's been sketchy, so we're minimizing stress."

I nodded. The Westfields protected their own. Period.

"Alright, let's fix this chaos." I pulled out my planning notes. "Banner across the mantel, balloon clusters by the windows. Please tell me you have a helium tank because my lungs won't cut it."

"This is why you're the professional," Kate said. "I've been staring at this pile for an hour."

We worked in rhythm. Kate followed my directions while I turned Pinterest inspiration into reality. My hands shook as I tied the first balloon. A warning. I gripped the ribbon tighter, forcing control over whatever was building in my pelvis.

"Earth to Gemma." Kate's voice cut through my focus. "That balloon's about to explode."

I blinked. I'd been inflating the same teal balloon for too long. One more puff and it would've burst. "Sorry. Mental logistics. Calculating balloon-to-square-footage ratios."

Kate's look said she wasn't buying it, but she let it slide.

By the time the doorbell rang hours later, we'd completely transformed the space. Paper sea creatures hung from the chandelier, balloon clusters mimicked waves, and Kate's hand-painted banner proclaimed "Welcome Baby Morales" in script that had taken her three tries to perfect.

"It's gorgeous," Kate said. "Seriously, send me your invoice."

"Liam's taking it in trade for his work on the cottage project." I tucked a strand of hair behind my ear. The movement sent a spike down my spine.

The house filled with overlapping conversations, bright laughter, the rustle of gift bags. I positioned myself near the kitchen door. Close enough to appear engaged. Far enough to retreat if necessary.

Sophie arrived with Taylor and little Zack toddling between them. Elena followed with a gift wrapped so crisp it could probably cut glass. Abby's teaching colleagues clustered together, sharing pregnancy war stories that sounded like badges of honor.

When Abby entered with Miguel hovering beside her, the room went quiet. Every conversation paused. She pressed one hand to her protruding belly, and her face lit up.

"Oh my gosh! This is incredible!"

Miguel's arm found her back. "Nothing but the best for our little princesa. She's been doing gymnastics all morning."

"He's convinced it's a girl," Abby said. "Try telling him the odds are 50/50. He's already picked out quinceañera dresses."

Their shorthand came so easily—shared glances, gentle teasing, the easy choreography of partnership. It settled somewhere raw, that ache for a future I couldn't count on.

The next hour required precision. I excelled at the baby food identification game (professional palate from years of catering tastings), dominated the memory tray challenge (event planner's curse: remembering every detail), and guessed at belly circumference with appropriate enthusiasm.

But with each squeal over tiny socks and receiving blankets, each knowing exchange about sleepless nights and growth spurts, I drifted toward the room's edges. The periphery was safer.

"Time for gifts!" Kate announced. "Abby, your throne awaits."

I used the transition to slip toward the kitchen. Ostensibly for water, really for space to breathe. The kitchen was empty. I sagged against the granite counter, drawing in air that caught halfway down.

The cramping started low, then climbed. No fanfare. Just the familiar burn spreading outward.

"Are you sick?"

I turned. Maya stood there with solemn six-year-old eyes, half-eaten cupcake in hand and frosting on her chin.

"Just a headache." I tucked away my medication container. "Nothing serious."

Maya nodded with that grave acceptance children have about adult mysteries. "Mom gets those too. She says sometimes grown-up brains get too full."

"That's very true." I smiled. Genuinely, for the first time in an hour.

"Is it hard?" Maya asked, licking frosting thoughtfully. "Being at a baby party when you can't have babies?"

She couldn't breathe. Kids didn't know you weren't supposed to name the thing that was breaking you. "I... what makes you think that?"

Maya shrugged. "I heard Mom talking to Dad. She said you were brave to come even though it might be hard because of your sick parts."

Mortification warred with grudging appreciation. At least Kate understood what this afternoon cost.

"It's complicated," I said finally, kneeling to Maya's level despite my body's protest. "Sometimes grown-ups have health issues that make certain things difficult. But that doesn't mean we can't be happy for other people."

Maya tilted her head. "Like how Noah can't eat peanut butter but he doesn't get mad when I have jam sandwiches?"

"Exactly like that." I laughed, surprised.

"Well," Maya declared with six-year-old wisdom, "I think you're doing a good job pretending to have fun. But it's okay if you need to go to the quiet place sometimes."

The simple permission tugged at my careful composure. "Thank you, Maya. That means a lot."

"Can I have another cupcake?"

"Ask your mom."

"That always means no." Maya sighed dramatically before bouncing back to the party.

"There you are." Abby stood in the doorway, one hand supporting her back. "I was wondering where you'd disappeared to."

I gestured vaguely at the sink. "Hydration break. Event planning 101."

"Mind if I join you? I needed an escape from being on display." Abby lowered herself carefully into a kitchen chair. "Between you and me, opening gifts while everyone watches is getting old."

"How are you feeling? Really?"

Abby's practiced smile slipped. "Huge. Uncomfortable. Terrified. Excited. Sometimes all at once, which is exhausting." She shifted, searching for a position that probably didn't exist. "The blood pressure thing has everyone walking on eggshells."

"Kate mentioned." I settled across from her. "That must add stress."

"Kate told me about your condition," Abby confessed. "I hope that's okay. She thought I should know in case today was challenging."

My automatic deflection died before reaching my lips. I was too tired for pretense.

"I had trouble conceiving initially," Abby continued, matter-of-fact. "Different situation, but there were about eighteen months where every baby shower felt like personal torture. Every announcement was a reminder of failure."

"How did you handle it?"

"Not gracefully. Definitely some bathroom crying sessions. One memorable occasion where I fled so quickly I forgot my gift altogether."

"What happened?"

"The mother-to-be thought I'd stormed out in anger. Whole drama until Miguel explained I had 'food poisoning.'" Abby shook her head. "Easier than admitting I'd had an emotional breakdown over a diaper cake shaped like a train."

A startled laugh escaped. "That's oddly reassuring."

"My point is," Abby's expression grew serious, "it's okay to not be okay with all this. You can be genuinely happy for someone else while still grieving what you might not have. Both feelings can exist simultaneously."

Before I could absorb this, my body reminded me why I'd sought kitchen refuge. The burning intensified, radiating outward. I gasped and gripped the table's edge.

"Gemma?" Abby's voice went faint. "Are you alright?"

"Fine." Even I didn't believe it this time. The medication I'd taken earlier was proving useless.

"Kate," Abby called out, then lowered her voice. "I'll tell everyone you're both helping me."

Kate appeared instantly, assessing the situation. One arm slid around my waist. "I've got you," she murmured, guiding me toward the powder room.

Once behind closed doors, I leaned heavily against the sink, focusing on breathing through the wave. The medication wasn't touching it. The pills hadn't been reliably effective for weeks. A reality I'd been avoiding.

"Sorry." The word came out as a whisper. "Terrible timing. I'm supposed to be managing this event, not becoming the drama."

"Don't apologize." Kate dampened a hand towel and pressed it to my neck. "Do you have your medication?"

"Already took it earlier. It's about as effective as thoughts and prayers at this point." I closed my eyes, concentrating on breathing. "Perfect timing, as always."

Kate stayed quiet. She didn't push, didn't offer platitudes. She simply stayed, one hand rubbing gentle circles on my back while the other kept the cool cloth in place.

Gradually, the worst of it eased from unbearable to merely excruciating. I straightened, meeting my reflection. The woman staring back looked pale and strained, mascara smudged despite touch-up efforts.

"Better?" Kate asked.

"A bit." I attempted a smile. "Go back to the party. I'll be out in a few minutes. Can't leave them hanging."

"Gem—"

"Please, Kate." I interrupted softly. "I just need a moment to regroup. I promise I'll tell you if it gets worse."

Kate hesitated before nodding. "Ten minutes. But I'm sending backup if you're not out by then."

"Backup?"

"Liam just arrived with Mom's reading glasses. Dad texted that she forgot them." Kate was already moving toward the door. "'Ten minutes, Gemma. I mean it."

Alone, I let my expression crumble. I sank onto the closed toilet seat, arms wrapped around my middle. Desperately trying to contain what was happening inside. Hot tears spilled over my cheeks, less from the physical discomfort and more from the failure at the one thing I'd always controlled: my work.

This was supposed to be payment for Liam's labor. Instead, I was hiding in the bathroom while the event I'd planned continued without me.

A gentle knock interrupted. "Gemma?" Liam's voice was pitched low. "Kate asked me to check on you."

Ten minutes, my ass. Kate's concept of time operated on a flexible schedule.

"I'm fine," I called, hastily wiping my eyes.

"Are you sure?" A beat. "Because I'm standing here trying to decide if 'fine' means 'actually okay' or 'in agony but too proud to admit it.'"

Despite everything, I almost smiled. "Has anyone ever told you that you're annoyingly perceptive?"

"Only about once a week. Usually right before they admit I was right."

I sighed. I couldn't hide indefinitely. After splashing cool water on my face and blotting away mascara smudges, I opened the door.

Liam leaned against the opposite wall. The simple navy button-down made his eyes appear more amber than brown, and his hair was damp. He'd come straight from somewhere involving physical activity.

"Hi," I said, suddenly self-conscious about my disheveled state.

His eyes moved over my face, cataloguing details I couldn't hide. "Bad flare?"

I nodded, too worn down to pretend otherwise.

"Kate said you took medication?"

"Over an hour ago. It's not working anymore."

His expression shifted. "That's been happening more frequently?"

I looked away, unwilling to voice what we both knew. My treatment plan was crumbling.

"Gemma." Liam's voice dropped. "I'm not asking as Kate's brother or as... whatever we are to each other. I'm asking as someone who specializes in chronic pain management."

Drop the pretense. "Yes. It's getting worse. I've had to adjust the dosage twice in the past month, and it's still not touching the severe episodes."

"What would you normally do when this happens? At home?"

"Heating pad, dark room, cancel whatever plans I had and wait it out." I smiled, but it felt hollow. "Not exactly an option when you're hosting someone else's celebration."

Liam glanced toward the living room, where laughter continued. "It could be, actually. I'd be happy to drive you home."

The offer was tempting. But leaving would mean explanations, would mean becoming the center of attention in exactly the way I'd been trying to avoid. Worse, it would mean failing to pay Liam back for all his help with the cottage.

"I can't. This event is my professional contribution to our cottage arrangement. I can't just abandon it when things get difficult."

"You're overestimating your ability to hide how much pain

you're in," Liam countered gently. "And underestimating every-one's capacity for understanding."

Before I could respond, another sharp wave left me gasping, one hand flying to the wall for support. My knees buckled.

Liam was beside me instantly, one arm around my waist, solid and steadying.

"That's it." His voice was firm. "I'm taking you home. And before you argue, this isn't about the cottage or professional obligations. This is about your health."

"But the event—"

"Will be fine. Kate's handled bigger disasters than a missing event planner." His tone brooked no argument. "Getting you somewhere safe. That's what matters."

This time, I didn't have the strength to protest. This episode was rewriting my pain scale entirely. I gripped his arm with white knuckles, unable to stand fully upright, while my mind cataloged symptoms that had never appeared together before.

"Okay," I whispered, leaning into his support. "But please, can we slip out quietly?"

"Leave it to Kate." He was already texting with one hand. "She'll handle everything. Don't worry about anything except getting through this."

As we moved carefully toward the back door, I caught a glimpse of the living room. Abby sat surrounded by opened gifts, one hand resting on her belly as she laughed at something her mom was saying. Picture-perfect. Exactly the kind of moment I'd created for countless clients.

A moment I might never experience from her position.

I turned away, blinking back fresh tears as Liam helped me into his truck. The pain was becoming all-consuming, narrowing my world to the immediate reality of my body's rebellion.

"Just breathe." Liam's hand found mine across the console as he pulled out of the driveway. "I've got you."

Waverly Cove's familiar streets blurred past the window. I surrendered to the reality of my situation and the unexpected comfort of not facing it alone.

His hand warm and steady in mine. Anchoring me through the storm.

Chapter 21

Liam

I kept my eyes on the winding coastal road, but every ounce of my mental focus was on the woman beside me. Gemma sat with her eyes closed, one arm wrapped around her middle, breathing in that careful rhythm I'd learned to recognize. Someone negotiating with pain.

Pain was my profession. I'd catalogued its presentations, developed treatment protocols. But watching Gemma suffer cut through every clinical boundary I'd built.

"Almost there," I said. My voice came out steady despite the hammering in my chest.

The road curved toward her grandmother's cottage, the late afternoon sun throwing long shadows across weathered shingles and salt-stained cedar. Winter in Waverly Cove meant shorter days, and this one had shifted from celebration to crisis faster than the tide.

Gemma's nod was almost imperceptible, knuckles white against the door handle. When she spoke, each word was rationed. "Just need my other meds."

The truck barely stopped rolling before I was around to her side. Gemma sat staring at the cottage door like it was twenty miles away instead of twenty feet.

No lecture about independence. No reminder that she'd managed fine for thirty-one years without my help. She just looked at my outstretched hand and took it.

That was more terrifying than her ghostly pallor or the way she moved with such fragility.

"Lean on me," I said, feeling the tremor in her grip. Her weight shifted against my side, trusting me to be strong when she couldn't be. "We're almost there."

The cottage stood unlocked, as most places did in Waverly Cove. Inside, winter's chill settled between walls. I guided her to the couch, her movements like someone walking through broken glass.

"Let me get the heat going first."

She'd already curled onto her side, knees drawn up to contain what couldn't be contained.

I moved through her space with purpose, adjusting the thermostat, retrieving the heating pad. Evidence of her struggle covered every surface: prescription bottles lined up like soldiers; a hot water bottle worn smooth from use; lidocaine patches stacked beside over-the-counter remedies. A small pharmacy of inadequate solutions.

When I returned, she'd drawn herself smaller, pale face pressed against the cushion, lips compressed in concentration. The sound of waves against the rocks below the cottage provided a rhythm that seemed to mock her uneven breathing.

"Here," I said, kneeling beside the couch. "Where does it hurt most?"

The laugh that escaped her held no humor. "Everywhere. But mainly lower abdomen, radiating into my back."

I positioned the heating pad where she pointed, covered her with a throw blanket that smelled faintly of lavender and sea air.

"Which medication?"

"Small bottle, red label. Two pills."

The prescription label made my frown deepen. Break-through pain medication, meant for crises. The bottle, filled two weeks ago, was nearly empty.

I returned with water and pills and waited while she gulped them down.

"Few minutes," she said. "Should be quick. You don't have to stay."

"I'm staying." The words came out more forcefully than intended. "At least until I know the medication is helping."

She started to argue, then stopped as pain crossed her features. "Okay."

The easy surrender worried me more than any protest could have.

I settled into the armchair, close enough to help but allowing her the space she valued. The silence stretched, broken only by waves against rocks and the occasional catch in her breathing. The eastern headland's lighthouse began its evening rotation, painting brief swaths of light across the dark-ening water.

"You're staring," Gemma murmured, eyes still closed. "I can feel it."

"Force of habit."

We both knew that wasn't true anymore.

"How's the pain now? One to ten?"

She took inventory, breathing carefully. "Seven. Down from nine."

A seven on Gemma's recalibrated scale would flatten most people.

"The medication is helping, then."

"For now." She opened her eyes, meeting my gaze with a directness that stole my breath. "It won't last. It never does anymore."

The admission hung heavy between us, stripped of her usual deflections.

Outside, the wind picked up, rattling the cottage windows with the promise of a storm rolling in from the Atlantic.

"How long has that been happening?"

Gemma shifted, adjusting the heating pad. "A few months. Since before I came to Waverly Cove. The pain kept getting worse no matter what we tried. My doctor increased the dosage twice, but even that's not really working now."

"Gemma," I began carefully, "have you talked to your doctors about this?"

Guilt and resignation crossed her face. "Dr. Jordan gave me the same speech as my doctors in Boston. That we're running out of conservative options. That the endometriosis is likely continuing to spread. That surgery is becoming less of an option and more of..."

"An inevitability."

"It's not that simple." Her hand drifted to her abdomen, protective and possessive. "The surgery they're recommending would likely remove at least one ovary. Possibly both, given where the adhesions have spread. And my uterus, depending on what they find."

"A complete hysterectomy."

"Don't." She winced, whether from pain or the clinical term, I couldn't tell. "Don't make it sound so clinical. We're talking about the children I might never have." Her voice cracked on the last words.

I thought of the future I'd always assumed waited for me.

The house I'd built with extra bedrooms, the swing set plans I'd bookmarked, the family dinners I'd imagined hosting. Now, looking at Gemma curled on her grandmother's couch, that vision shifted. Transformed into something less defined but somehow more real.

"I understand," I said softly. "More than you might think."

She studied me with those green eyes that seemed to see everything. "Do you? Everyone in this town knows how much you want a family. Kate tells me you've built the perfect house for it. That you've turned down perfectly nice women because they didn't fit your exact picture of what a mother should be."

The assessment stung with its accuracy. "That's not..." I stopped, considering. "It's more complicated than that."

"Isn't it always?" A tired smile touched her lips. "Look at us. The man with the perfect family plan and the woman who can't have children. If this were one of Kate's romance novels, we'd be the setup for a tragic ending."

"Or the beginning of something better than we imagined."

Vulnerability replaced Gemma's usual guardedness. For a moment, not just the capable woman who'd captured my attention, but someone achingly human.

"Liam," she began, then her words fractured around a noise that was half gasp, half sob. Her body folded, knees drawing toward her chest.

The distance between us disappeared. One second I was across the room, the next I was down beside her, hands hovering near her shoulders.

"Stay with me. Breathe when you can." I kept my voice level, clinical. "Show me where."

Her hand trembled as she pressed it low on her left side. "Here. It's not like the others." Tears leaked from the corners of her eyes. "It feels different."

My throat went dry. In fifteen years of treating chronic pain patients, I'd learned to distinguish between flare-ups and emergencies. This was the latter.

"Different how?"

She squeezed her eyes shut. "Wrong. Like it's pulling inside."

"I think we should call Dr. Whitman or Dr. Jordan."

"No." The protest lacked conviction, barely more than a whisper. "It'll pass. It always..." She cut off, face draining of what little color remained.

"Gemma," I said, medical training taking over. "This doesn't sound like your typical flare. The location and quality you're describing could indicate a more acute problem."

She started to respond, then froze, hand flying to her mouth. "I think I'm going to be sick."

She barely made it to the bathroom before her body rebelled completely. I kneeled beside her on the cold tile, gathering her hair away from her face as wave after wave of nausea hit. Her sweater was damp with perspiration, her skin clammy under my palm.

Between episodes, she sagged against the toilet, breathing hard. "I'm sorry. This is humiliating."

Her hair fell forward as she bent over the toilet. My palm settled between her shoulder blades as her body convulsed. Not clinical anymore. This was Gemma, vulnerable and trusting me to hold her together when she couldn't hold herself.

When the worst passed, I dampened a washcloth with cold water and pressed it to the back of her neck.

"Sorry," she said. Mortification obvious despite her distress.

"Don't," I said firmly. "Can you stand?"

She nodded weakly, allowing me to help her back to the

couch. The careful way she moved, clearly favoring one side, made every instinct scream warnings.

"I'm calling Dr. Jordan," I asserted, tone making it clear this wasn't a suggestion.

To my surprise, Gemma didn't argue.

Sarah answered on the second ring. "Liam? Is something wrong?"

"I'm with Gemma Prescott," I explained, outlining her symptoms, careful to note the change in pain quality, specific location, and accompanying nausea.

Sarah's response was immediate. "Bring her in. That sounds like it could be a bowel obstruction. With advanced endometriosis, the adhesions can sometimes twist or pull on intestinal tissue. It's potentially serious, Liam."

"Understood. We'll head to Coastal Memorial right away."

"I'll call ahead."

I ended the call and turned to Gemma, who'd been watching my face with growing alarm. "We need to go to the emergency room. Dr. Jordan thinks you might have a bowel obstruction caused by adhesions."

Fear crossed her features, quickly masked. "Is that serious?"

"It can be, if left untreated. But the important thing is to get you evaluated right away."

She nodded, attempting to sit up straighter but wincing. "I need to change. I can't go to the hospital looking like this."

Under different circumstances, this glimpse of the event planner's priorities might have made me smile, but her pallor kept my focus elsewhere.

"Let me help you to your room. But be quick."

The bedroom was neat, organized like everything in Gemma's life. She moved to the closet and pulled out loose pajama bottoms and a sweatshirt.

"I can manage," she said, though the slight tremor in her hands suggested otherwise. "Just give me a minute."

I nodded and stepped into the hallway, leaving the door ajar. The rustle of fabric, followed by a small sound of pain she couldn't suppress.

"Liam?" Her voice came moments later, smaller than I'd ever heard it. "I think I need help after all."

She sat on the edge of the bed, half-dressed and ashen, the loose sweatshirt pulled over her head but her arms not quite managing the sleeves.

Without comment, I gently guided her arms through, then helped her stand to adjust the fabric.

"Thank you," she whispered, not meeting my eyes. "This isn't how I'd hoped we'd spend the evening half-dressed in my bedroom."

The comment was so contrary to her usual careful boundaries that it startled a small laugh from me. "You were only imagining us half-dressed?"

Her answering smile was faint, but real.

"Ready?" I asked, offering my arm.

She nodded, reaching for her purse. "As I'll ever be."

The drive to Coastal Memorial passed in tense silence, broken only by Gemma's occasional sharp intake of breath when we hit a bump. Through the windshield, storm clouds gathered over the Atlantic, the kind that would bring serious weather to Waverly Cove by tomorrow.

Her fingers occasionally brushed against mine where they rested on the console.

The emergency entrance was mercifully quiet. Dr. Jordan's call ahead worked; a nurse immediately ushered us to a triage station.

"Ms. Prescott has stage IV endometriosis," I explained to the nurse. "She's been experiencing escalating pain today. It's localized to the lower left quadrant, with nausea and vomiting."

Everything moved with controlled urgency. An orderly wheeled Gemma away for a CT scan, leaving me alone in the small curtained area. The antiseptic smell of the hospital stripped away the last vestiges of the peaceful afternoon we'd started with.

I paced the limited space, my mind spinning between professional assessment and unprofessional thoughts. Somewhere between her stubborn independence and the rare moments of vulnerability, Gemma Prescott had gotten past every defense I'd built. She'd challenged my assumptions about what I wanted, what I needed, what a future might look like.

The curtain parted as a doctor entered, his expression neutral but serious.

"Mr. Westfield? Dr. Levine, head of surgery here at Coastal Memorial. Ms. Prescott has asked that I include you in the discussion of her condition."

I straightened, surprised and touched by Gemma's request. "I'm a physical therapist. I've been consulting on her case."

The doctor nodded, though his expression suggested he understood there was more. "We've completed the CT scan. Ms. Prescott has a partial small bowel obstruction caused by endometrial adhesions. It doesn't appear to be complete, which is good news, but it requires immediate surgical intervention."

"Surgery."

"Yes. We'll remove any adhesions constricting the bowel and assess the extent of the damage. We've contacted her specialist in Portland. Dr. Jordan is driving up now and will scrub in as soon as she arrives."

What had been theoretical was now immediate, forcing the very decision she'd been avoiding.

"She's been hesitant about surgery because of fertility concerns," I explained.

Dr. Levine's expression softened. "That's a valid concern, and one we'll discuss thoroughly with her. But right now, this obstruction takes precedence. We need to prep her for surgery within the hour."

<hr>

The elevator to the surgical floor carried the scent of antiseptic and anxiety. Fluorescent lights hummed overhead as I followed directional signs, each step taking me away from familiar territory and into the space where patients became cases, where people became problems to solve.

The room smelled like industrial laundry detergent and the faint metallic tang of medical equipment. Gemma lay propped against pillows that dwarfed her shoulders, the hospital gown's faded blue pattern making her skin look almost translucent. The fiery red of her hair looked wrong against the bland beige sameness of the room. Machines beeped around her. Heart monitor, IV pump, blood pressure cuff that inflated automatically every fifteen minutes with a soft whoosh.

Her eyes tracked to mine the moment I appeared in the doorway, my uncertainty reflected there.

"Hey," I said softly, taking the chair beside her bed. "How are you feeling?"

"Like the universe decided for me," she replied, voice quavering. "They need to operate. Adhesions are apparently strangling part of my intestine. Quite the dramatic way to force my hand."

Despite everything, I smiled at her dry humor. "Leave it to you to turn a medical emergency into cosmic irony."

"It's a gift." Her attempt at a smile faltered. "They've explained that while they're in there, they'll need to assess everything. The surgeon will decide about what else needs to be removed based on what she finds."

The implications settled heavy between us.

"I'll be here," I said simply, reaching for her hand. "Whatever happens."

She looked at our joined hands, then up at my face, searching. "Why?"

I considered deflecting, offering generic reassurance. But the sterile hospital room and the knowledge of what she faced had stripped away my usual caution.

"Because I care about you," I said. "More than I expected to. More than makes sense."

Gemma's eyes widened. "Liam—"

"You don't have to say anything. This isn't the time or place for deep conversations or grand declarations. I just need you to know you're not alone. Whatever happens in that operating room, whatever decisions you make, you have people who care about you. Who will be here after."

Tears welled in her eyes, and she blinked rapidly. "I'm scared," she admitted, voice barely a whisper. "Not just of the surgery. Of what comes after. Of who I'll be."

"You'll still be you," I said firmly. "Still the stubborn, brilliant, frustratingly independent woman who's challenged every assumption I had about what I wanted in life."

A small laugh bubbled up, shaky but genuine. "I haven't challenged anything."

"You've completely disrupted my carefully ordered life. In the best possible way."

Her expression softened. She tugged at my hand, drawing

me closer until I was leaning over the hospital bed. Her free hand came up to touch my face, fingers cool against my skin.

Then she was kissing me, her lips soft and warm against mine. I responded instinctively, one hand coming up to cradle her cheek, mindful of the IV as I returned the kiss with gentle pressure. More intimate than any kiss I could remember. Vulnerability, fear, hope, and feelings neither of us had yet named.

When we parted, Gemma's eyes remained closed for a moment, as if savoring the sensation.

A nurse entering with a clipboard interrupted. "Ms. Prescott? We need to go over surgical consent forms. The OR is being prepped."

Reality snapped back. I straightened but kept hold of Gemma's hand as the nurse explained the procedure, risks, and outcomes. Gemma listened with focused attention, asking clear, practical questions that reminded me why I admired her so much.

"I need to make one phone call before we start," she said after signing the forms. "My emergency contact should know what's happening."

"Of course," the nurse replied. "But we'll need to move quickly after that."

When the nurse stepped out, I released Gemma's hand reluctantly. "Kate?"

She nodded. "Would you mind calling her for me? I'm not sure I can manage the conversation without falling apart, and she'll have questions I can't answer right now."

"Of course. What do you want me to tell her?"

"The truth. That I'm having emergency surgery for a bowel obstruction. That endometriosis adhesions are the cause. That they'll likely need to perform the excision and hysterectomy while they're in there." She paused, swallowing hard. "And that I'll need her when I wake up."

"I'll tell her. And I'll be here too. The whole time."

The nurse returned with an orderly and a wheelchair. "It's time, Ms. Prescott."

Gemma nodded, her expression shifting back to determined composure. "I'm ready."

I squeezed her hand one last time before stepping back. She looked back at me as they prepared to transfer her to the wheelchair.

"Liam?" Her gaze lingered on my face, as if memorizing my features.

"Yes?"

"I'll see you when I wake up."

I nodded, unable to speak past the sudden tightness in my throat.

As they wheeled her away, I remained frozen, watching until she disappeared through the swinging doors that led to the surgical suite.

I waited until then to call Kate. My mind raced, anticipating hours of waiting and the decisions that would be made while Gemma was unconscious, decisions that could drastically change her future.

As the phone rang, I stared at the empty hallway where Gemma had disappeared and finally admitted what I'd been too terrified to acknowledge.

I was in love with her.

And I might be too late to tell her.

Chapter 22

Gemma

The last thing I remembered was the gentle pressure of the anesthesia mask and Liam's promise that he'd be there when I woke up.

Consciousness returned in stages. First static, then fragments of sound that eventually coalesced into the steady beep of monitors and the distant murmur of institutional life. The antiseptic tang of hospital air hit my nostrils before I could even open my eyes, followed by the weight of blankets that were both protective and suffocating.

When I finally convinced my eyelids to cooperate, the golden afternoon light was doing its best to look cheerful through venetian blinds that had witnessed more medical drama than a dozen soap operas.

A familiar figure sat beside my bed, and for a moment, I thought the anesthesia might have given me hallucinations with a sense of irony. My mother sat in the bedside chair, reading glasses on, tablet in hand. I blinked, still fuzzy from anesthesia. Dr. Elaine Prescott didn't do hospital vigils. Didn't do waiting rooms or hand-holding or any of the soft maternal things other people's mothers seemed to manage without effort.

"Mom?" The word barely cleared my throat past the irritation left behind by the breathing tube.

She startled, and her tablet slid off her lap, the corner hitting the floor with a sharp crack. For a woman who treated her electronics like priceless artifacts, the careless accident spoke louder than any verbal reassurance could have.

Post-surgical awareness returned in waves: first pain, managed but present; then the strange internal geography where everything was different and wrong, like furniture moved in a familiar room; then the cognitive fog that made thinking feel like swimming through thick water.

But beyond the expected physical sensations, something had changed in the fundamental architecture of hope. The space where plans used to live was empty.

I attempted to shift position and immediately reconsidered that life choice.

"Don't strain yourself." Her hands moved with surprising gentleness as she helped adjust my pillows. These were the same fingers that had graded countless papers and typed endless research proposals, but they touched me like I was more precious than scholarly theories.

"Dr. Jordan said the surgery was... comprehensive." The careful pause told me everything.

Hysterectomy. Both ovaries. I wasn't just infertile. I was fundamentally changed.

"Where's Dad?" I asked, because easier questions were safer than the tsunami of grief currently building in my chest.

"Terrorizing the hotel's customer service department about their WiFi situation," she replied, and the ghost of a smile crossed her face. "He's been conducting what I can only

describe as aggressive research into hormone replacement thera-
pies since Kate called us in Paris."

"Paris." The word hit me like a small slap. "You left the
symposium The one you've been planning for two years."

My mother removed her reading glasses and cleaned them
with the methodical precision of someone buying time to
arrange thoughts.

"Of course we left," she said finally. "You're our daughter."

The matter-of-fact delivery was so quintessentially Mom
that I almost smiled. This was the woman who had explained
puberty like a biological research project and approached my
teenage heartbreaks with peer-reviewed studies on adolescent
emotional development. Love, in the Prescott household, had
always been expressed through practical solutions and intellectual engagement rather than hugs and heart-to-hearts.

Yet here she sat, her tablet full of medical research instead
of conference notes, having abandoned her career passion to be
present for a situation that couldn't be solved with superior
knowledge and strategic planning.

"You didn't have to—"

"Gemma." Her voice carried that gentle firmness I remembered from childhood attempts to prove I didn't need help with
math homework. "You had major surgery. Where else would
we be?"

The tears I'd been holding back since consciousness
returned decided they were done waiting for permission. Not
tears of gratitude or pain medication side effects. These were
grief, pure and devastating, for everything surgery had taken.

"Oh, darling," my mother said softly, and then she did what
would have stunned us both into temporary speechlessness just
months ago. She reached out and took my hand, not her usual
careful, measured way of offering comfort, but like she was

holding onto something precious that might drift away if she wasn't careful.

We sat in silence for several minutes, punctuated only by the soft sounds of medical equipment doing its job and my sobs gradually subsiding. My mother's thumb traced gentle circles on my knuckles in an unconscious gesture of worry worn smooth by repetition, like a stone polished by ocean waves.

A nurse appeared in the doorway with the practiced stealth of medical professionals everywhere, checking me over with efficient kindness. While she adjusted my IV, my mother launched into a series of precisely worded questions about medication schedules, recovery timelines, and potential complications. Her organizing information like a protective barrier between me and medical uncertainty was oddly comforting.

When we were alone again, I asked, "Has Liam been here?"

"Kate took him home around midnight." My mother's sharp eyes assessed me with clinical care. "He's been here since they brought you in. Kate said she practically had to drag him out for food and rest."

Of course he had. Liam had always been so patient, devoted, unwilling to leave me to face difficult things alone. This was the same man who'd spent hours learning exactly how to touch me when pain flared, who'd memorized which positions helped and which made things worse, who'd held me through countless nights when my body betrayed me.

"He's been... understanding through all of this," I said carefully, like I was navigating around broken glass. The word tasted wrong in my mouth, too small for what I was trying to describe. How could "understanding" capture the way he'd learned to read the tension in my shoulders before I knew a flare was coming? The mornings he'd appeared with tea when moving felt impossible, never making it seem like charity? The nights he'd touched me with such careful reverence, mapping my body's changing geography with infinite patience?

My throat tightened. Understanding was too clinical a word for what his presence had meant.

My mother's expression suggested she recognized the careful way I was avoiding the actual subject. "He cares for you deeply," she said diplomatically.

I looked at her sharply. "What do you mean?"

She fiddled with her reading glasses again, a tell that meant we were venturing into emotional territory she typically avoided with the dedication of someone dodging academic committee meetings.

"When you were first diagnosed, we watched you build walls around this condition. Understandable, given how long you'd been dismissed and misunderstood." She paused, and for a moment she looked less like the composed professor and more like someone who'd been watching her daughter suffer from a distance. "But then we got the call from Liam earlier today. He speaks about you like you are precious, not fragile."

The admission hung between us, heavy with months of unspoken observation.

Grief opened in my chest, not just for what I had already lost, but for recognition of how much I still had to lose.

"I always thought you and Dad wished I'd choose someone more... academic," I confessed. "Someone who shared your intellectual passions."

"We wanted you to find someone who saw your whole self," she corrected, her voice growing fiercer. "The way your father and I had to learn to see each other beyond our scholarly identities. Liam sees your intelligence, your creativity, and your strength. But more than that, he sees your pain and doesn't minimize it or solve it. He simply makes space for it."

Another crack in the ice sheet that had formed around my understanding of what I was giving up.

I squeezed her hand. "But he wants children, Mom. Biological children. We've talked about it." My voice broke on the words. "He lights up when he talks about watching his child take their first steps, about teaching them to sail in the harbor. How can I ask him to give that up?"

My mother leaned forward slightly. "Gemma, it's evident that man has been choosing you every day for months. Choosing you when you were in pain, when you were difficult, when you were terrified. He chose you knowing this surgery was a possibility. Do you really think a hysterectomy would change that?"

The conversation settled into a more comfortable rhythm as afternoon faded toward evening, but her words circled in my mind like water finding its level.

Lunch arrived with a tray of substances that bore only a passing resemblance to actual food. I managed a few bites while my mother watched with the same focused attention she once applied to my teenage attempts at calculus.

Medication tugged at my consciousness, but underneath the pharmaceutical haze, my thoughts were swirling together. Dr. Jordan's careful words about future fertility. Liam's face when he'd talked about teaching his kids to sail. The way he'd been building our life around my limitations while I'd been too sick to notice.

He deserved someone who could give him choices instead of complications.

"I think I'd like to write something," I said suddenly.

My mother produced paper and pen from her bag without question. She always came prepared with office supplies.

"Work-related?" she asked, though her tone suggested she already suspected otherwise.

"A letter." I couldn't meet her eyes. "To Liam."

Her eyebrows shot toward her hairline. She was, after all, someone who believed in addressing problems directly rather than letting them fester like untreated academic disputes. But she was also someone who recognized when her daughter was about to make a catastrophic mistake.

"Gemma," she said carefully, "are you ending things?"

"I'm setting him free." I sounded steadier than I felt. "He deserves someone who can give him the family he dreams about. Someone whole."

"You are whole," my mother said firmly. "Different, perhaps. But whole."

"Am I?" I gestured toward my bandaged abdomen. "I can't have his children, Mom. I'll be on hormone replacement for the rest of my life. My body will never respond to his touch the same way again. How is that whole?"

"Because love isn't just about biology, darling. It's about choice. Daily choice." She set down her reading glasses. "But if you're determined to write this letter, then write it. Sometimes we need to see our fears on paper to understand how unfounded they are."

She left after kissing my forehead in a gesture that would have shocked twelve-year-old me into complete silence.

I stared at the blank paper. My hand trembled as I picked up the pen, whether from medication or emotion impossible to determine.

What could I possibly say that would make sense of this? How could I explain that this wasn't about not loving him enough, but about loving him too much to trap him in a diminished version of what we'd had?

I read the letter I'd written three times, my hands trembling enough to make the paper rustle. The ink looked permanent against the hospital stationary, each word chosen for maximum impact and minimum ambiguity. Clean sentences about his deserving wholeness, clear paragraphs about my inability to provide it.

The paper felt heavier than it should, weighted with everything I was choosing to destroy.

A loaded gun aimed at my own happiness.

I folded the paper and slipped it into the bedside drawer just as Kate appeared in the doorway, arms loaded with supplies and wearing a bright expression that meant she was working very hard to keep her own emotions in check.

"Reinforcements," she announced, unpacking real pajamas, soap that didn't smell like industrial cleaning products, and several books. "Plus these." She held up fuzzy teal socks. "Hospital floors are basically petri dishes for every plague known to humanity."

"You think of everything," I managed, my cheeks aching with the effort of arranging my features into gratitude.

"Westfield training. Mom always said the things you need most are the ones you hope you'll never need." Kate's hands stilled on the items she was arranging, processing the fact that we'd needed these after all.

"Speaking of preparation, I met your parents in the parking lot. Your mom mentioned you wanted to write Liam a letter?"

Of course she had. Probably suspected what I was planning and hoped Kate could talk me out of it.

"I wrote one," I said carefully.

Kate's expression shifted from casual interest to sharp attention. She'd known me too long not to recognize the tone of someone who'd made a terrible decision and was committed to seeing it through.

"Gem," she said softly, abandoning her unpacking to sit on the edge of my bed. "What kind of letter?"

I looked away, focusing on the pattern of shadows the venetian blinds cast across the far wall. "The kind that's necessary."

"The kind that ends things," Kate pushed, not making it a question.

I nodded, not trusting my voice to remain steady.

"You're making a mistake," she said simply.

"I'm setting him free."

"You're running away." Kate's voice held the particular firmness of someone who'd watched her best friend make self-destructive choices before. "Liam doesn't need setting free, Gemma. He needs you to trust that he knows what he wants."

"What he wants is children. A family. Someone whose body works the way it's supposed to." The words came out harsh, hardened by the truth of them. "I can't give him any of that now."

"Did he tell you that?"

"He didn't have to. I've seen how he lights up around kids, Kate. I've heard him talk about wanting to be a father. Wanting to give them the same Waverly Cove upbringing you all had. This surgery didn't just take my uterus. It took our future too."

Kate studied my face with the intensity of someone trying to read a map in failing light. "You know what I think?" she said finally. "I think you're scared. Not for him, but for yourself. Scared that he might actually stay, and then you'd have to figure out how to believe you're worth staying for."

The words landed hard, accurate enough to steal my breath.

"That's not—"

"It is, though." Kate's voice gentled without losing its firm-ness. "Gemma, I've watched you two together. I've seen how he looks at you, how he touches you like you're precious. That man isn't with you because he's settling. He's with you because he can't imagine being anywhere else."

"But the children—"

"Can happen in other ways. Or maybe they won't happen at all, and he'll be okay with that because he has you." Kate reached for my hand. "But that's his choice to make, not yours to make for him."

As Kate continued unpacking, filling the sterile room with familiar objects and gentle argument, my perfectionist brain began picking apart the letter's logic like a flawed business plan. I'd written it from the assumption that love should be easy, that the right person wouldn't require sacrifice. But Kate arranging flowers she'd brought from home made me wonder if I'd confused difficulty with unworthiness.

The envelope in the drawer mocked my careful reasoning. What if I'd solved the wrong problem?

But doubt didn't change the fundamental facts. The woman he'd fallen in love with was gone. And Liam deserved better than a shadow wearing her face.

"The nurse wants to know what you'd like for dinner," Kate said, smoothly changing the topic. "I told her you have sophisti-cated tastes, so she probably shouldn't get her hopes up about whatever passed for today's entrée."

I nodded, pulling myself back to this moment, this room, this version of reality where I was protecting the man I loved by destroying us.

One breath at a time. First recovery. Then figuring out how to live without him. Then, learning to believe I'd done the right thing.

The letter sat in the drawer like a loaded gun, waiting to fire the shot that would end everything beautiful we'd built.

But sometimes love required destruction. Sometimes the kindest cut was the deepest one.

As Kate rearranged my pillows for the third time and coaxed me to try a few bites of aggressively beige hospital food, certainty settled inside me. Not peace—I might never feel that again. But the terrible, necessary kind that came from choosing someone else's happiness over your own.

Even if it destroyed mine in the process.

Chapter 23

Liam

Five hours had passed since they'd wheeled Gemma behind those double doors. Five hours of watching the wall clock, counting down minutes that felt like days.

The surgical waiting room operated on its own twisted physics. Time crawled while anxiety raced. I'd counted ceiling tiles (two hundred and forty), memorized the vending machine's rotation (B7 dispensed stale pretzels), and worn a path in the industrial carpeting between the chairs and the coffee station.

"Dr. Westfield?"

I shot up from my chair, knees protesting hours of hospital-grade plastic. The surgical nurse approached with that practiced neutral expression they must teach in Delivering Difficult News 101.

"Ms. Prescott is out of surgery. Dr. Levine is speaking with her medical proxy now."

Medical proxy. The connection we'd built over months together meant nothing against emergency contact forms and next-of-kin checkboxes.

"How is she?"

"Stable. That's all I can share."

After the nurse disappeared back through those impenetrable doors, my hands demanded attention. The same hands that had spent three months learning the exact pressure Gemma needed for her hip flexors were useless now, when it mattered most.

Kate appeared twenty minutes later, still wearing her baby shower dress under a hastily thrown on coat, mascara slightly smudged. Her face carried news that didn't require words.

She sank into the chair beside me in a heap of exhaustion.

"Complete hysterectomy. Both ovaries. The endometriosis had..." She paused, medical terminology failing her. "It was everywhere, Liam. Wrapped around her bowel, her bladder, diaphragm. Organs I didn't even know could be affected."

The air left my lungs in a slow leak. I'd read the studies and understood that this was a possibility. But knowing and experiencing were different things.

"Can I see her?"

Kate's hesitation stretched too long. "Neither of us can. They said she's in recovery. We can try tomorrow." Her tone suggested tomorrow was more optimism than medical timeline.

The next morning, I received a brief text update from Kate.

KATE

She's awake. Give her time to process.

And an even shorter update the next day.

By day three, the pattern was clearer to me than x-ray results. Gemma was conscious, stable, and not asking for me.

"She's being discharged today," Kate said during Thursday's call. "She'll recover at our place. And Liam..." Her voice caught. "She wrote you a letter."

The words hit my gut hard. No need to read it to understand its contents. Gemma was deciding for other people based on what she thought they should want, cutting off possibilities before anyone could disappoint her.

"I'll bring it by tomorrow. Sorry. She's clearly not thinking straight, but..."

"But she's decided." The harbor stretched beyond the window, where the tide was pulling away, revealing rocks that had been covered just hours before. "I understand."

After hanging up, I stood in the cottage kitchen, surrounded by three days of manic renovation energy. The bathroom gleamed with vintage fixtures hiding modern support features. Kitchen cabinets hung at the right height to minimize strain. Everything designed around her needs, her limitations, her life.

None of it guaranteed to matter now.

Logic suggested stopping. Why finish a renovation for someone composing goodbye letters? But as my palm ran along the refinished countertop, feeling the smooth grain I'd spent hours perfecting, logic wasn't driving this anymore.

This wasn't about changing her mind. This was about building shelter, even when she thought she needed distance.

Kate arrived on Friday afternoon while I was securing the light fixture in Gemma's office. Snow fell in fat flakes that turned the small driveway and yard into a Christmas card.

The frosted glass of the front door reflected dark stubble and hollow eyes.

"I brought lunch." Kate held up a brown bag from Harbor Brew, though her other hand clutched the white envelope that had occupied my thoughts for two days.

We ate in careful silence at the small dining room table, the turkey sandwich turning to dust in my mouth. Kate stood, kissed my cheek, and left the letter on the table as if it might detonate.

After her car disappeared, I settled into the window seat overlooking the harbor. Morning light painted the water silver.

Inside the envelope, Gemma's usually tidy handwriting looked shaky, post-surgical fatigue clear in every letter.

Liam,

By the time you read this, you'll know what the surgery took from us. Not just my ability to bear children, but the woman you fell in love with. The body you learned to touch with such careful reverence. The future we started planning in whispered conversations after making love.

I keep thinking about that Sunday morning when you made pancakes. How your hands felt on my skin when my body was still capable of responding the way it should. How you looked at me like I was someone worth building a future around.

The surgery was more complicated than expected. Recovery will be longer and more difficult than either of us planned. The hormone therapy may help, but there are no guarantees about timeline or effectiveness.

I can't ask you to wait for someone who might never return to what we had.

I know what you'll say. That there are ways around these things, solutions we can find together. But I've seen the research, talked to the doctors. This isn't a problem that love can solve, Liam. This is loss, permanent and complete. And I won't trap you in a relationship with a shadow of who I was.

You deserve someone who can give you the children you dream about. Someone whose body doesn't require constant medical intervention to approximate normal function. Someone who can make love to you without you having to navigate around surgical scars and pharmaceutical limitations.

Please don't think this is about not loving you. It's about loving you enough to give you back your future. You've spent months adapting your dreams to accommodate my limitations. Now I'm freeing you to find someone who won't require such accommodations.

I need you to promise me something. Don't try to convince me I'm wrong. Don't fight for a relationship that can only diminish what we had. Remember the woman who laughed in your kitchen while you made terrible coffee, not the broken one writing this letter. Remember us when we were possible, not now when we're not.

Thank you for loving me when I was worth loving. For seeing me as whole when I was broken. For making me believe, for a brief and beautiful time, that I could be someone's choice rather than their compromise.

Find someone worthy of all that love, Liam. Someone who can give you everything I can't.

-Gemma

I read it twice. Then a third time, searching for the woman I knew beneath the pain medication and surgical trauma.

The letter trembled in my hands. Not from weakness, but from the effort of not crumpling it into nothing.

She'd written me out of her life with the same meticulous planning she brought to every event she'd ever organized. Clean sentences. Clear reasoning. A perfect execution of pushing away everyone who tried to get close when she felt vulnerable.

The window seat's cushion compressed under my weight as I sank back, letter still clutched between fingers that had gone numb. Outside, snow continued its silent accumulation, each flake adding to drifts that would take days to melt.

When I was worth loving.

Those five words circled in my mind like gulls over the harbor. As if surgery had somehow diminished her value. As if loving someone meant loving only the easy parts, the uncomplicated moments, the version that fit neatly into predetermined plans.

I thought about the first time I'd watched her navigate a pain flare at Kate's dinner table. The way she'd excused herself with practiced ease, the careful breath control as she stood, the micro-pause before each movement. Most people wouldn't have noticed. I'd been trained to see it.

That night, I'd recognized someone who'd learned to carry weight alone because asking for help meant dismissal. Someone who'd built elaborate systems of self-sufficiency because relying on others felt dangerous.

The letter was just another system. Another way of controlling the narrative before it could spiral beyond her management.

My throat tightened. She was protecting herself the only way she knew how. By leaving first, before I could leave her. Before her body could disappoint me the way it had disappointed everyone else who'd minimized her pain, dismissed her symptoms, suggested she just needed to relax.

The brutal efficiency of it hit harder than any emotional plea would have. This wasn't a dramatic breakup. It was Gemma making what she believed was a logical decision based on incomplete data.

She'd decided what I wanted without asking. She'd determined my dreams without discussing them. She'd chosen my future while lying in a hospital bed, convinced she was doing me a favor.

I stood and paced the small living room, letter still in hand. The cottage renovation surrounded me. Evidence of every conversation we'd had about her needs, her limitations, her fears about being too much trouble.

Each grab bar I'd installed spoke to her worry about falling. Each counter height adjustment acknowledged her pain patterns. Each carefully chosen fixture balanced her grandmother's aesthetic with modern accessibility.

I'd spent three months learning the geography of her limitations, not to fix them but to build around them. To create space where she could exist without constantly accommodating a world designed for bodies that worked differently than hers.

And she thought surgery changed that?

The bathroom door stood open, revealing vintage subway tile and a walk-in shower with a built-in bench. Gemma had mentioned, almost casually, that standing for long showers was sometimes impossible. I'd designed the entire space around that single admission.

Not because I pitied her. Because I'd wanted her to have a place where her body's needs weren't an afterthought.

Someone who can make love to you without you having to navigate around surgical scars and pharmaceutical limitations.

The assumption in that line made my hands curl into fists.

As if intimacy was only physical. As if I'd spent those nights learning her body because I needed it to respond in specific ways. As if the careful attention I'd paid to her pleasure was contingent on organs she no longer had.

She'd reduced what we'd built to biology and mechanics, missing the entire point.

I'd fallen in love with the woman who argued about tile choices with passionate intensity. Who noticed the exact moment Maya's enthusiasm tipped into overtired chaos. Who built contingency plans for her contingency plans because life had taught her that hope without backup was dangerous.

The woman who'd let me see her pain without apologizing for it. Who'd trusted me enough to ask for help when her body betrayed her. Who'd laughed at my terrible coffee but drank it anyway because the gesture mattered more than the taste.

That woman was still there. Surgery hadn't erased her. It had just confirmed what she'd always feared. That her body would eventually demand too much accommodation, require too much patience, cost too much in dreams deferred.

But she'd gotten one critical thing wrong.

My dreams had already changed.

They'd been shifting since the day she'd walked into my clinic, evolving incrementally with every conversation about her grandmother's cottage, every discussion of pain management strategies, every quiet moment when she'd let her guard down enough to show me the fear beneath her careful competence.

I thought about Sophie and Taylor, about the choice they made to adopt Zack because two women couldn't have a child on their own. How Kate and Alex had gone through countless cycles of IVF before conceiving the twins. How I'd had the conventionally perfect partner in my ex-girlfriend Molly, but how her priorities and values were so misaligned with mine that I couldn't see a future with her.

Family was built from choice as much as biology. So many people I knew and loved found fulfillment in paths they'd never imagined when they were twenty-five and certain about their futures.

The letter wasn't wrong about everything. Recovery would be hard. Hormone therapy was unpredictable. The future we'd vaguely discussed would require different conversations now, different timelines, different possibilities.

But none of that changed the fundamental question: Did I want to build a life with Gemma?

The answer was the same as it had been three months ago, six months ago, the first time I'd really looked at her across Kate's dinner table and recognized something I'd been searching for without knowing it.

Yes.

The complications didn't erase that. They just changed the map we'd use to get there.

I refolded the letter, creasing it along the lines she'd made, and slipped it into my shirt pocket. It settled against my chest like a weight I'd carry until she was ready to hear what I needed to say.

That I saw her. All of her. The planning brain that created beautiful events and elaborate contingency plans. The careful competence that masked deep vulnerability. The perfectionist who'd learned to manage everyone's expectations except her own.

That surgery hadn't diminished her. It had just clarified what had always been true. Bodies were complicated, futures were uncertain, and love meant showing up anyway.

That I didn't need her to be easy. I needed her to be honest.

That I'd rather navigate stormy waters together than sail smooth seas alone.

But she wasn't ready to hear any of that yet. Pain medication, surgical trauma, fear. They'd all conspired to convince her that leaving was mercy.

So I'd wait. I'd finish the cottage. I'd give her space to heal and time to realize that I wasn't going anywhere.

And when she was ready, I'd tell her what she should have known all along.

That I'd chosen her. Complications included. Medical history and all. For exactly who she was, not some imagined version that fit more neatly into conventional plans.

That she'd never been my compromise. She'd always been my choice.

I turned back to the renovation, measuring twice before cutting the final piece of crown molding. The physical work grounded me, gave my hands something useful to do while my mind processed what came next.

Each measurement became a meditation. Each careful cut, a commitment.

The cottage would be ready whenever she was.

And so would I.

Chapter 24

Liam

The letter lived on my kitchen counter for three days. Gemma had cast herself as the villain instead of the heroine struggling with plot twists she hadn't written. The pages closed doors with her characteristic directness, but they also opened a window into fears I could address if she'd let me.

Morning light caught the grain of the wide-plank floors I'd sanded and refinished during the dark months after Molly left. Every corner of my house whispered of an imagined future. Breakfast conversations, homework scattered across the table, the ordinary chaos of family life.

Through the window, I could just make out the tips of the weathered cedar shakes of Gemma's cottage roof across the small stretch of harbor.

Her letter assumed she knew what I wanted better than I did. Either impressively presumptuous or depressingly accurate. Either way, words wouldn't reach her now. Not in her current fortress of medical statistics and worst-case scenarios.

Actions, however. Those I understood.

I called the clinic and moved my morning appointments to later in the week. Then I loaded my truck with tools that had been sitting idle since her surgery.

The cottage renovation had frozen in time. We'd gotten the major work completed to make it liveable for Gemma, but the finish work had stopped the day before her surgery. The space still felt more like a construction zone than a home.

I would finish what we'd started.

Detail work demands total attention. That focus was what I needed. The constant hum of worry that had become my baseline since her surgery faded. Hours passed in the ritual of careful construction. Measure, cut, place, check, adjust. Repeat until perfect.

Something I could control. Something I could complete. A promise made tangible in trim boards and caulking.

"Thought I might find you here."

James appeared in the doorway around noon, carrying what looked suspiciously like one of Mom's care packages wrapped in familiar wax paper. My older brother surveyed the half-finished office with the appreciative eye of someone who understood that sometimes men said things with hammers and saws that they couldn't say with words.

"Decent progress." He settled onto the one finished corner of the floor with the careful movements of someone whose knees had seen too many fishing trips. "Especially considering you're doing precision work instead of your usual 'make it functional and move on' approach."

We ate lunch in comfortable silence that only comes from

thirty-five years of shared experience. James had taught me everything I knew about working with my hands and the meditation of craftsmanship done right. Today I needed that grounding more than I'd realized.

"She's ending things," I said finally. "Because she thinks she can't give me what I want."

James nodded, savoring his last bites of Mom's famous turkey sandwich. "And can she?"

The directness was pure James. No cushioning, no deflection. Just the uncomfortable question nobody else would ask.

"I thought I wanted kids. Biological kids, following the whole traditional path." I picked at the wax paper. "But I've been watching Sophie and Taylor with Zack, thinking about all the ways family actually forms itself."

"Biology's just one option, man." James leaned against the doorframe. "Trust me. Diane and I had biology down. Got her pregnant at eighteen without a clue what we were doing. The family part? That we had to actually build. You adapt or you break. Something tells me that this cottage isn't the only thing you're committed to building."

The simple wisdom settled something restless in my chest. James understood about reimagined futures, about building life around what was possible instead of what you'd planned.

"She needs to heal first," I said. "But when she's ready to see possibilities instead of limitations, I want this place to reflect that."

"This cottage is your message to her, then."

"That broken things can be beautiful again. Different, but not less valuable." I picked up a piece of molding and checked my miter cut for fit. "That someone cares enough to finish what she started, even when she can't see the value in it herself."

James nodded. Understanding passed between us without further explanation.

"Need help with the heavy lifting?"

We worked together through the afternoon. His experience saved me hours of trial and error. By evening, the major work was complete, with a level of care that would last decades.

I fell into a rhythm over the following days. Mornings at the clinic, afternoons at the cottage. The work gave me the fundamental satisfaction of creating beauty with hands and tools. My grandfather had built fishing boats with the same attention and care. My father had approached physical therapy with identical patience. I was just continuing a family tradition of putting broken things back together, one careful piece at a time.

The renovation took months. Coordinating contractors, overseeing installations, handling the detailed finish work myself during evenings and weekends. The space transformed from gutted bones into the magazine-worthy sanctuary Gemma envisioned. More importantly, it had become a love letter written in fixtures and tile. *I see your vision. I believe in what you're building. I'm not going anywhere.*

A text from Kate came as I was installing the vintage medicine cabinet Gemma had special-ordered from some estate sale in Boston.

KATE

Emergency at the pharmacy. Alex needed there. I'm with the twins at a birthday party. No one to stay with Gemma for a few hours. Any chance you're free?

My heart kicked at the possibility of seeing her, followed by anxiety about facing her rejection in person rather than through carefully filtered updates from Kate.

LIAM

I can be there in 20

I replied before my nerves could construct reasons to refuse.

A week ago, I would have walked straight into Kate's house, announced my arrival from the hallway, helped myself to coffee from her kitchen. Now I stood at her door like a guest, unsure of protocols I'd never needed to consider.

I knocked and called out as I entered. "Gemma? It's Liam."

When the door opened, the sight of her stopped my breath.

Weeks indoors had made her pale. Shadows etched new hollows beneath her eyes. She wore an oversized hoodie over loose sweatpants that emphasized how much weight she'd lost. But more than the physical changes, it was the expression that hit hardest. Embarrassment warring with defiance. Exhaustion deeper than any sleep could cure.

"Kate didn't mention you were coming." Her tone achieved perfect neutrality.

I explained about the pharmacy emergency. She processed this information as she moved toward the couch.

She insisted she could handle being alone. Of course she did.

I reminded her about doctor's orders in my gentlest professional voice, the one that had convinced hundreds of patients to follow their treatment plans.

She sighed. "Fine. But I'm not good company right now."

I offered tea, grateful for something useful to do. In the kitchen, I took a moment to steady myself against the counter. The shock of seeing her so diminished had hit harder than expected, triggering every protective instinct I'd been containing for weeks.

Our fingers brushed as she accepted the tea. Familiar awareness hummed through me despite everything. Some things, apparently, surgery couldn't fix.

Minutes passed in painful silence. The grandfather clock marked time relentlessly.

"This is ridiculous." Gemma set down her book with more force than necessary. "We're acting like strangers."

"I'm trying to respect your wishes. Your letter was pretty clear about wanting space."

Regret and frustration flickered across her face. "I was on heavy medication when I wrote that. Not thinking about anything beyond making sure you wouldn't waste your time on someone who couldn't give you what you deserved."

My heart lifted despite my better judgment. "And now?"

She looked away, focusing on the steam rising from her tea. "Now I'm trying to figure out who I am with these new..." She paused. "Constraints."

The word came out bitter, weighted with grief still raw around the edges.

"They're not constraints, Gemma. They're just different paths."

"Easy for you to say." The anger that flashed gave me a glimpse of the fiery woman I'd fallen for. Her passionate direct challenges to comfortable assumptions. Even now, it made me want to smile despite the sting of her words.

"You're right." I set down my mug. "But I know a thing or

two about having to completely reimagine your future when life takes unexpected turns."

I told her about Boston. About the research position I'd turned down. About choosing to stay here and redefine what success meant. About my messy breakup with Molly.

"Not the future I'd mapped out at twenty-five, but eventually one I chose."

"That's different." Though with less conviction than before. "You could have left anytime. You stayed."

"I reimagined what fulfillment meant." I leaned forward. "What I'm saying is that sometimes when life forces a change of direction, we discover roads we never knew existed. Roads that might be even better than the original route."

Vulnerability crossed her face before she looked away. "I don't know how to find those roads yet. I'm still mourning the old map."

"That's okay. You're allowed to grieve. You're allowed to be angry and sad and whatever else you're feeling." I held her gaze. "I just want you to know that when you're ready to explore those new roads, you don't have to do it alone."

The promise hung in the air. No pressure, no timeline. Just truth offered without expectation of reciprocation.

Her phone chimed. She glanced at it with a small frown.

"Hormone therapy reminder." A bitter little laugh. "Everything's on a schedule now. Even my emotions need hormonal intervention."

When she struggled to stand, I offered help. Grateful when she accepted. I found her medication in the kitchen, returning to find her sitting again, pale from the minimal exertion.

"Thank you." She took the pills with her tea.

I asked her about the hormone therapy. She described the

side effects with a mix of medical detail and self-deprecating humor.

"Months of adjustments ahead while my body figures out its new normal. The doctors are optimistic about the results, but apparently optimism doesn't make the process any less miserable."

The careful, measured tone she'd developed for discussing her condition had faded away. Her voice caught on certain words instead of gliding over them.

"How's the cottage?" She asked, changing the subject with obvious intent.

I hesitated, unsure how much Kate had shared. "It's coming along well."

"Kate mentioned you've been working on it." She eyed me with uncomfortable intensity. "I'm sorry I can't do more to help."

"I'm just finishing what we'd started. Just a handful of details left."

"Why?"

The simple question deserved a simple answer. "You needed a home to come back to. A place that worked for you. That represented possibilities instead of limitations."

Her eyes widened. "I pushed you away, and you responded by finishing my cottage."

Put like that, it sounded a bit unhinged.

"I'm better with actions than words. Always have been."

"Clearly." For the first time since I'd arrived, a smile touched her lips.

The front door burst open then. The twins arrived in a tornado of voices and birthday party sugar crash, followed by an exhausted Kate whose expression shifted from surprise to understanding.

The moment between Gemma and me cracked open. Small, but definite.

"I should go." I stood. "Let you rest."

"Thank you. For the tea. And the medication. And..." She paused, meeting my eyes directly. "Everything."

"Anytime. I mean that."

The drive home felt different that evening. My future no longer seemed like something to endure. Not dramatic reconciliation or immediate resolution, but the possibility that she might eventually see what I was building. Both literally and figuratively.

Chapter 25

Gemma

Morning light crept through the guest room curtains. Two weeks post-surgery, and hormone fluctuations were like having someone else control my emotional settings. One moment I was fine, the next I was crying at coffee commercials featuring families.

I descended the stairs with the careful deliberation of someone who'd learned that surgical incisions had opinions about sudden movements. The pain wasn't severe anymore, more like my abdomen sent sharp reminders whenever I forgot to move slowly.

The kitchen scene that greeted me was pure chaos. Dr. Elaine Prescott, whose idea of cooking usually involved arguing with the microwave, stood at the stove wielding a wooden spoon. Her audience: six-year-old Noah, taking notes in his dinosaur journal with the solemnity of a peer reviewer.

"Omega-3 fatty acids promote neural plasticity." Mom sprinkled cinnamon into the pot with scientific precision. "Hence including ground flaxseed in your oatmeal."

Maya, who'd inherited her father's practical sensibilities, prodded her bowl with deep suspicion. "Does brain food have to taste like research?"

Mom paused. Long enough for uncertainty to show in her eyes. This woman who could debate the cultural implications of Bronze Age burial practices was genuinely worried about whether this child would eat breakfast.

"I added honey," she offered, like it was a research breakthrough.

The entire scene was so fundamentally Mom that I almost laughed. This was progress, not transformation. She was still Dr. Elaine Prescott. She'd just expanded her areas of expertise to include the feeding and care of temporarily broken daughters.

"Morning, breakfast science committee." I settled into my chair. The movement sent a familiar jolt through my middle. My body's way of saying *remember me? Still under construction down here.*

"Gemma, dear." Mom placed a bowl before me. "I've calculated the optimal protein-fiber ratio based on yesterday's energy assessment."

The twins launched into their daily chaos report. Soccer practice, a missing homework assignment, whether dragons counted as dinosaurs for show-and-tell. I absorbed the domestic chaos with unexpected hunger. Not for food, but for this messy, complicated sense of belonging.

Kate's entrance disrupted the peaceful noise. She dropped into the chair beside me. "Mom called. Abby's in labor."

The words created an odd stillness in the room. Like expecting a wave to knock you over and instead it just laps at your ankles. Not the blow I'd expected. More nuanced. A bittersweet recognition of joy that would never be mine in this form.

"How's she doing?" I asked, surprised to realize I genuinely wanted to know.

"Good. Early stages, but everything's normal. Miguel's apparently providing live commentary in two languages." Kate grinned.

The knowledge settled under my ribs. Tender but not sharp. Progress in learning to witness other people's happiness without making it about my own loss.

"I'd like to visit," I heard myself say.

Kate's eyebrows rose. "Really? I mean, that's wonderful, but are you sure?"

"I'm sure." And weirdly, I was. "Abby was kind when I needed it. Time to return the favor."

Mom had gone still. Observing this exchange with the clinical attention she usually reserved for interesting burial sites. Her expression held approval mixed with fascination. With Mom, it was sometimes hard to tell.

"I'll drive," she offered. "If that would be helpful."

Mom's preferred emotional language was small gestures wrapped in practicality. I recognized the offer for what it was.

"Thank you."

Kate left to grab supplies for Abby with the twins in tow, leaving just Mom and me in the sudden quiet. She began wiping the already-clean counters. A sure sign of nerves.

"You know those are spotless, right?" I pointed out.

"Routine provides structure during transition periods." She paused mid-wipe. "I'm still calibrating my approach to this caregiving role."

Dr. Elaine Prescott was admitting professional uncertainty. Signs of an impending apocalypse.

"You're doing fine." I meant it. "Different doesn't equal wrong."

She turned, dish towel clutched like a security blanket. "Your father and I have been consulting with the university regarding sabbatical extensions. They're amenable to another semester."

Richard and Elaine Prescott, rearranging their research calendar. For me. The woman who once scheduled childbirth around conference presentations was now treating her academic commitments as negotiable.

"You don't need to restructure your entire existence," I began.

"You're our daughter, Gemma." Simple words, weighted with decades of affection expressed through practical support rather than emotional declarations. "Some variables in the family equation take precedence over others."

Her academic metaphor for love. Two decades of her prioritizing research over me, and now this. It wasn't a dramatic emotional revelation. Just a calculated decision delivered in Mom's plain style.

Before I could figure out how to respond without crying, the doorbell intervened.

Mom returned with a package wrapped in brown paper and careful twine. "From Liam." She set it before me with careful neutrality.

My heart kicked. Nothing to do with caffeine and everything to do with neat handwriting and careful presentation.

"Planning to open it, or should I schedule an academic conference on package appreciation?" Mom asked. A faint glimmer of humor showed in her voice.

Handcrafted wood formed the box, its lid inlaid with a compass rose created from different wood tones. Inside, nestled in soft fabric, lay a vintage brass key attached to a carved wooden float.

The note was brief, written in Liam's careful script:

I traced the compass rose, feeling the precise joinery of the wood. Hours of work. Hours of thinking about me, about what I might need, about metaphors that would comfort rather than wound.

"Exceptional craftsmanship." Mom switched into evaluation mode. "Handmade?"

"The Westfields have a workshop." I closed the box but kept the key, its edges already warming to my palm. "Woodworking is apparently another hidden talent."

"Alongside physical therapy, construction, and..." Mom's delicate pause carried weight.

I met her gaze, recognizing the question she wasn't quite asking.

"He wants a family. Traditional. Children. The whole domestic architecture I can't exactly provide anymore."

"And you assume your surgery prevents that possibility entirely?" Her question carried the same weight she'd give a flawed research method.

"He's always talked about biological children. The whole traditional progression. I can't offer that anymore."

She was silent. Fingers smoothing the dish towel with unconscious precision. "When I discovered I was pregnant with you at forty-two, I had just received the most significant research grant of our careers. Three years documenting indigenous practices in locations entirely unsuitable for infants."

This story was new. Unlisted in the family archives.

"What did you do?"

"We adapted." Simple statement, complex implications. "Modified our methods, adjusted our timeline. Discovered that unplanned paths often yield more valuable data than original hypotheses."

Her comfort words, delivered with academic authority instead of emotional fumbling.

"But I was biologically yours," I pointed out. "Your genetics. It's different."

"Biology represents merely one variable in family forma-tion." Mom's voice was firm. "I've studied enough diverse kinship structures to know that genetic connection is perhaps the least significant factor in creating meaningful bonds."

"I don't want him to settle," I admitted. "To compromise his vision because he feels obligated."

"Has he indicated that alternative family structures repre-sent 'settling'?" Her question cut through my assumptions to examine actual evidence.

I considered Liam's matter-of-fact discussions about the different paths to parenthood his own family had taken.

"No," I admitted. "Actually, the opposite."

"Then perhaps the limitation exists in your analysis rather than his reality," she suggested with gentle accuracy.

Before I could unpack this uncomfortable insight, Kate returned with shopping bags and organized energy. "Hospital supply run complete. Abby's in active labor, but everything's progressing normally."

Birth. The word sent another ripple through me. Not the

devastating crack I'd expected, but curiosity mixed with achiness.

"When do we visit?" Mom asked.

"This afternoon, if Gemma's still interested." Kate glanced at me with careful attention. "No pressure if you've reconsidered."

"I haven't." The certainty was solid beneath everything else. "I want to meet her."

Relief brightened Kate's expression. "Perfect. I have time before soccer practice chaos."

As we prepared to leave, my fingers found the key in my pocket. Its wooden float smooth and warm. Designed to stay afloat. Just like I was learning to be.

***

Room 108 of the maternity ward at Coastal Memorial bore a hand-lettered sign: "¡Bienvenida, Pequeña Morales!"

Inside, Abby laid against pillows, looking drained but glowing. Miguel cradled a tiny bundle as if he were holding something infinitely precious.

"Perfect timing." Abby's voice carried the particular weariness of recent accomplishment. "Meet Mirabelle Sofia Morales, our impatient early arrival."

"Miguel was right all along," Kate observed, approaching the bed. "A baby girl."

"Never doubt papa intuition." Miguel's exhausted pride showed in every word. "But she has a flair for the dramatic, just like her mama."

I lingered near the doorway. Emotions tangling.

"Gemma." Abby's voice drew me forward. "Come meet her."

I approached, setting aside my gift bag, and looked down at

seven pounds of new life. Mirabelle was perfect in that utterly vulnerable, completely herself way all newborns manage. Dark hair like tiny brushstrokes. Ears and fingernails with that translucent quality that seemed to glow from within. A person, already distinct. Containing limitless futures in miniature form.

"She's beautiful," I said, meaning it completely.

"Would you like to hold her?" Miguel offered. The question was simple but weighted with understanding. Abby must have told him about my situation. His gentle approach suggested he had more than just a passing awareness of this moment's complexity for me.

I paused. Considering the magnitude of this moment, mere floors down from where my own ideas of motherhood had shifted just a few weeks ago.

"Yes. I'd love to."

The transfer involved careful instruction about supporting her head. Practiced precision from new parents already fluent in newborn handling. Mirabelle weighed almost nothing, yet contained all the hopes and dreams packaged in a new life.

Mom had stationed herself near the doorway, observing with quiet attention. Now she stepped forward, offering congratulations in her own unique way.

"New life transforms the perception of time." Her lecture voice. "Future becomes more vivid than present."

"Exactly." Abby brightened at this academic articulation of maternal instincts. "I look at her and see kindergarten, adolescence, and college all at once."

As conversation flowed around me, I remained focused on Mirabelle, who'd drifted into profound newborn sleep. The weight of complete trust. Perfect vulnerability. Creating calm amidst recent weeks' turmoil.

Understanding settled into place: someday, I might hold a

child like this and experience the same overwhelming love, the same sense of infinite possibility. Even if that child arrived through channels different from what I'd once imagined.

The realization didn't erase grief over lost biological futures, but created space alongside it for different kinds of hope.

When departure time came, I transferred the baby back to Abby's waiting arms.

"She's perfect," I said simply. "Thank you for letting me meet her."

"Thank you for coming." Abby's perceptive teacher's gaze saw beyond my words. "It means everything that you're here."

In the corridor, Kate linked arms with me. "Okay?" she asked with sisterly directness.

"Different than expected," I admitted, surprising myself with the honesty. "But okay. Actually okay."

"Different how?"

I considered while we walked toward the elevator. "I thought seeing a newborn would be like salt in a wound. And there is sadness. But also possibility. Like maybe there are different doors to the same destination."

Kate's smile held understanding without pity. "Life specializes in offering unexpected doors when others close."

"That sounds suspiciously like what Liam would say." I gave her a pointed look.

"Great minds." Kate's deliberate innocence. "Speaking of my philosophically inclined brother, did you open his gift?"

"I did." My fingers found the compass rose keychain, already smooth from handling. "It was thoughtful."

"He carved it himself in his workshop. After finishing your office renovation."

The image of Liam crafting this for me made something

cautious take root. Not just the time investment, but the attention to symbolic meaning.

The compass rose pressed against my palm. Its directional
points promising navigation yet to come. Fundamental bearings
by which sailors found their way home.

I was beginning to think I already had.

Chapter 26

Liam

Four AM in the captain's house and I couldn't remember the last time I'd slept here. Years of restoration work. Every floorboard hand-sanded, every window casing rebuilt, crown molding I'd installed piece by careful piece. I'd imagined kids running through these rooms. A dog. Chaos and noise and someone else's life crammed into all this perfect space.

The coffee maker sputtered in the silence.

The letter I'd left for Gemma yesterday looped through my thoughts on repeat. Had I said enough? Too much? Should I have been more direct?

Now I stood in the kitchen I'd designed for Sunday pancakes and homework spread across the island, and all I could think about was her cottage. The worn couch barely big enough for two. The guest bedroom where I had to duck under the sloped ceiling. Her books stacked on every surface, coffee rings on the side table, the salt crusted windows that still stuck some-times despite our best efforts.

Her Nan's life layered into every corner, and Gemma slowly making it her own. Somehow in just a few months, I'd found more room for myself in those 900 square feet than I had in years here.

The captain's house was everything I'd thought I wanted. Square footage and sight lines and space for a family.

But I'd bought it for someone who didn't exist.

I wanted Gemma. The complications. The endometriosis. The event planning career that came first. The way she hummed off-key while making tea. I wanted her cottage that smelled like cinnamon and books, where I had to stoop through the doorways and didn't care.

I'd poured years of my life into refinishing this house imagining it full.

It only took months in her space to realize I'd been building the wrong thing all along.

A text alert interrupted my thought spiral.

JAMES

> Diane says you're coming for family dinner on Sunday. Non-negotiable. Sophie has news.

James, cutting straight to the point as always. I typed back, grateful for the distraction.

LIAM

> Wouldn't miss it. Should I bring anything?

JAMES

> Just your renovation-obsessed self. Though some of those craft brews you fancy wouldn't go unappreciated.

The easy humor was typical of James. Support wrapped in teasing. He'd watched me throw myself into Gemma's cottage project with an intensity that raised questions, but he'd offered help without commentary. From my older brother, that meant everything.

The drive to the clinic traced the same coastal route I'd taken hundreds of times, but today morning light caught the harbor buoys differently. Small constants seemed more important when everything else was suspended in uncertainty.

Lisa was already at the staff entrance, coffee in hand with a knowing look in her eye.

"Fair warning. Elena moved her appointment to nine-thirty. She'll complain less about waiting if we get her in early."

"This is why I leave reception to the expert. I promise we'll hire Margaret's replacement soon."

She laughed, but the subtle way she watched for my reaction was unmistakable. "We have a meeting with Maine Med on Tuesday about expanding their chronic pain protocols. Dr. Jordan wants to implement the integrated care model we developed down in Portland as well."

"Good." I nodded automatically, but my attention had already wandered toward a cottage across town and the woman who might or might not have read my carefully chosen words.

"Oh." Lisa added with practiced casualness. "Kate mentioned Gemma did well at yesterday's follow-up. Doctors Whitten and Jordan cleared her for cottage return this week."

My pulse kicked. "That's excellent news."

"Mmm. Interesting how Kate's suddenly asking about grab

bar installation and vintage bathroom modifications. Very specific questions for someone 'just planning ahead.'"

I focused on my patient files, avoiding her perceptive gaze. "Must be concerned about accessibility."

"Right." Lisa's tone held barely concealed amusement. "Nothing to do with helping Gemma prepare to move back in, I'm sure."

My hands stilled on the paperwork. "This week?"

"Kate seemed to think any day now." Lisa's expression softened. "I assumed you knew the timeline."

She'd be seeing the renovations soon. Walking through spaces I'd designed specifically for her needs. Would she find the letter?

"I finished the major work," I managed. "Just a few details remaining."

Lisa regarded me with the same directness she used in clinical assessments. "Well, Kate seems impressed with whatever you did there. She kept using words like 'thoughtful' and 'surprisingly intuitive.' Couldn't get her to elaborate, though."

Before I could process that or hide my surge of hope, Mrs. Cooper arrived for her shoulder assessment. Lisa retreated with a final, knowing look.

Patient care provided refuge from my spiraling thoughts. Mrs. Cooper's mobility work, Ben Johnson's knee rehabilitation, Elena's perpetual resistance to proper form despite repeated instruction. Each case demanded complete focus, silencing the uncertainty that had become my constant companion.

The reprieve lasted until Sophie called during lunch.

"We got approved for another adoption, Liam." Her excitement was infectious.

"Already? That's incredible."

"Eighteen months old." Sophie's voice caught. "Her name is

Lucia. If the meeting goes well, she could be home by month's end."

"I'm so happy for you three. Soon to be four."

"That's what I wanted to talk about." Sophie paused. "Zack keeps asking when his 'baby' will arrive. He doesn't know or care about biology. She's just his sister. Kids understand family differently than we do, don't they?"

The observation resonated more than she realized. "They really do."

"Could I come for dinner tonight? I want to talk about family. About different paths forward. It can't wait for Sunday dinner."

"Gemma," she said. The name containing everything.

"Yes. I left her a letter."

"Come at six. We'll talk after Zack's bedtime."

By the end of my appointments, I'd made several a decision. I'd stop allowing Gemma's assumptions to go unchallenged. If we were going to make hard decisions, I wanted them based on actual communication, not guesswork.

Sailing into uncharted waters. No logical course, but at least moving forward instead of drifting.

Zack launched himself at me the moment I walked into Sophie and Taylor's house.

"Unca Yam! Baby Loo-see coming home!"

"I heard, buddy." I caught his sturdy weight, his enthusiasm impossible to resist. "You're going to be such a good big brother."

"Me share toys. Teach her walking," he announced with two-year-old seriousness.

The matter-of-fact way he'd incorporated this new sister

into his world struck me. No complicated analysis of genetics or legal processes. Just expanded love and shared toys.

Dinner buzzed with celebration and planning. Taylor sketched ideas for Lucia's room while Sophie tried to maintain token protests about premature preparation. Their easy partnership, the way they balanced each other's enthusiasms and concerns, radiated warmth.

After Zack's elaborate bedtime negotiations (three stories, detailed discussion of sister arrangements, and promises about morning activities), we settled in their living room with coffee.

"So." Sophie began with characteristic directness. "You left Gemma a letter."

"I did."

"Kate described the bathroom renovation as 'a love letter in tile form.' She mentioned medical accommodations that don't look medical."

My face warmed. "Practical adaptations. Gemma's condition means certain modifications help, but I wanted them integrated."

"And the hand-carved compass rose box containing her cottage key?" Taylor asked with gentle humor. "Also practical?"

"Kate talks too much," I muttered.

"Kate wants her best friend and favorite brother to figure things out," Sophie corrected. "You've been different since Gemma arrived. More present."

I considered deflecting, then abandoned the impulse. These were my people. Pretense wouldn't work.

"She makes me question assumptions I didn't know I held. About what I want versus what I think I should want."

Taylor nodded with the understanding of someone who'd traveled similar territory. "When Sophie and I got married, we already knew that biological kids were an impossibility for us.

We weren't sure which path would take us to parenthood, but we always knew we'd be here. When she first discussed adoption, I had to confront internalized expectations about family. About what makes someone a parent beyond biology."

"Watching you two with Zack has been educational," I admitted. "Seeing how completely he's yours, despite genetics. How family forms through commitment, not DNA."

"Which brings us to your letter," Sophie prompted. "What did you tell her?"

I set down my coffee, organizing thoughts that had been circling for days. "That my definition of family has evolved. That her assumptions about what I 'deserve' were just that. Assumptions, not my actual perspective."

Sophie and Taylor exchanged one of their wordless conversations.

"And if she disagrees?" Taylor pressed. "If she maintains you should find someone who can give you biological children? Or that she isn't open to adoption or surrogacy?"

The question prodded at fears I'd been avoiding. "Then I'll respect her choice. But I won't pretend it's what I want. She made a unilateral decision about my priorities without asking what they actually were."

"What are those priorities?" Sophie asked with gentle directness. "Beyond theoretical flexibility about family structure."

I ran a hand through my hair. "I want Gemma. With all her complexity and strength and stubborn independence. How and if we build a family together is secondary."

Sophie's expression warmed. "Have you told her that specifically?"

"Not so directly. I focused on challenging her assumptions instead of stating my feelings. Didn't want to overwhelm her while she's still recovering."

"Sometimes directness is exactly what's needed," Taylor observed. "People need unvarnished truth to break through protective barriers."

Taylor's words stuck with me. I had been too careful, too respectful of boundaries. The situation needed transparency, not more patience.

I slept better that night than I had in weeks.

The next day found me at the cottage before the sun had cleared the horizon. With the knowledge that Gemma was moving in soon, I wanted every last detail to be perfect. Each room received finishing touches. Vintage door handles from Ellsworth antique shops, last paint touch-ups, testing every system one final time. Each task grounded me, providing purpose while I waited for whatever response might come to my letter.

This cottage had become hope solidified.

I was securing the final cabinet base in the kitchen when gravel crunched outside. Through the window, an unfamiliar sedan.

When I opened the door, I faced a distinguished older couple who could only be Gemma's parents. Richard Prescott's distracted academic air and Elaine's assessing gaze reminded me of their daughter's analytical intelligence.

"Dr. and Dr. Prescott." I wiped my hands before extending one. "I'm Liam Westfield. I've been helping with the cottage renovation."

"So we understand." Elaine's handshake was precisely firm. "Gemma has mentioned your hard work. We thought a property assessment prudent before her return."

I recognized the formal language immediately. The same careful structure Gemma used when navigating emotional territory.

"Of course. Please, look around freely."

Richard wandered toward the preserved bookshelves, drawn by Nancy Prescott's collection. Elaine maintained focus on me, her gaze evaluative but not unkind.

"You're the physical therapist," she stated. "Chronic pain management specialist. Boston University, class of 2014."

The thoroughness of her research was impressive. "That's correct."

"Academic habit." She offered the hint of a smile. "When my daughter mentions someone's involvement in her recovery, I research appropriately. Your work on integrated chronic pain approaches is quite insightful."

That Gemma's mother had read my professional publications was both flattering and intimidating. "Thank you. That research came from observing limitations in traditional pain management."

"Indeed. Your emphasis on patient-directed care aligns with my work on agency in vulnerable populations." She gestured around the cottage. "May I ask about the adaptive elements? Gemma mentioned 'thoughtful accommodations' without elaboration."

I walked them through each modification. Kitchen counters at optimal height, bathroom features that offered support without medical appearance, furniture arrangement that created clear pathways and rest spots. I explained how each element served a practical purpose while maintaining the cottage's historical character.

"Impressive integration," Elaine observed. "You've balanced

historical preservation with modern necessities. Challenging work."

"Gemma's grandmother left detailed renovation notes. Many choices followed her vision."

"Nancy always had excellent taste," Richard added, rejoining us. "I'm particularly pleased about her botanical collection. Gemma spent hours with those books during childhood summers."

Richard and Elaine exchanged one of those loaded parental glances I recognized from growing up with my own communicative family.

"This space meets our criteria for Gemma's recovery environment," Richard concluded. "The modifications align with medical recommendations while maintaining psychological comfort."

"Agreed." Elaine fixed me with a direct look. "Liam, may I speak candidly?"

"Please."

"My daughter is experiencing profound transition. Physical, emotional, psychological. Her traditional response to disruption is isolation rather than seeking support."

I nodded. That pattern was familiar.

"What you may not have observed is the vulnerability beneath that self-protective behavior," she continued. "Gemma's independence developed as necessary response to certain parental limitations." Her voice faltered. "Richard and I prioritized academic achievement over emotional attentiveness. Our daughter learned to manage difficulties alone because we were often unavailable."

The unexpected candor caught me off-guard. "I think all parents do their best with available resources."

"Generous interpretation," Richard said with a sad smile.

"Though not entirely accurate. We chose intellectual development over emotional nurturing. The consequences became evident during her years of undiagnosed pain and medical dismissal."

The purpose of this conversation was clear now. Not just property inspection, but evaluation of my potential role in their daughter's vulnerable recovery.

"We observe considerable investment in creating an environment for her recovery," Elaine continued. "The time, expertise, and obvious consideration go beyond professional courtesy."

The implication was clear. I could deflect or offer honesty that matched theirs.

"You're right. My interest in Gemma's wellbeing is personal and professional."

They exchanged another loaded glance.

"Despite her insistence on self-sufficiency," Richard said, "Gemma responds positively to consistent, reliable support offered without expectation. A rare experience for her."

"What my husband means," Elaine translated, "is that patience may be necessary, but persistence equally important. Our daughter protects herself by anticipating rejection. She makes preemptive choices based on what she assumes others want."

The insight resonated with my observations about her post-surgery letter. "I've noticed that pattern. I'm working on addressing it directly rather than allowing her assumptions to stand."

"A sound approach," Elaine approved. "While I wouldn't offer relationship advice outside my expertise, I observe that unambiguous communication proves most effective with Gemma's self-protective barriers."

"What my wife means," Richard added with a look that conveyed infinite patience, "is that our daughter responds to people who say exactly what they mean. She's had enough uncertainty in her medical journey without adding relational ambiguity."

The straightforward advice, delivered with academic precision but genuine concern, moved me. "Thank you. For sharing that, and for trusting me enough to be direct."

"Our research indicates you're worthy of such trust," Elaine replied matter-of-factly. "Both professionally and through community consensus regarding character." Her expression softened marginally. "The cottage renovations reflect not only technical competence but emotional intelligence regarding Gemma's specific needs."

From Dr. Elaine Prescott, this was high praise. "I want her to have a space that works for her. A place she can call home."

"A laudable objective," Richard commented. "Nancy would have approved of preserving her vision while adapting to current needs. She insisted spaces should evolve with inhabitants."

They prepared to leave, and the weight of unspoken evaluation lifted.

"We appreciate your time." Elaine's handshake was as precise as her greeting.

"Oh." Richard paused at the door. "We're hosting dinner at our rental tomorrow evening. Nothing formal, just family. You're attending the Westfield gathering, but you'd be welcome afterward if your schedule permits. Around eight o'clock."

The invitation, delivered with casual academic detachment, wasn't just social courtesy. It clarified my place in Gemma's evolving life.

"I'd be honored."

After they left, I returned to my work with renewed purpose. That conversation had clarified something crucial. The need for absolute clarity with Gemma. A directness that left no room for misinterpretation.

The letter had been a beginning, but perhaps not explicit enough.

I rehearsed what I'd say when we finally spoke face-to-face as I completed the last cabinet details. Not just about possibilities, but about specific feelings and intentions.

By late afternoon, the cottage was complete. Every system functional, every space considered, every detail reflecting the care I'd wanted to put into this sanctuary for Gemma's recovery.

Standing in the living room center, sunlight streaming through windows that now opened and closed securely against coastal storms, the space hummed with potential.

Not just a finished renovation. Groundwork for Gemma's future here. Whether that included me remained uncertain, but I'd done everything possible to ensure the space offered the foundation she deserved.

I had just locked the cottage and reached my truck when my phone chimed with a text from Kate.

KATE

She's asking about you. Specifically, when you might be at the cottage next. Just FYI.

My chest loosened. Gemma was asking about me. Not maintaining careful distance, but wondering when our paths might cross.

I laughed despite myself and pulled onto the road home. Late afternoon sun warmed the dashboard, pine scent drifting through the cracked window. For the first time in weeks, tomorrow was something to anticipate rather than endure.

Gemma was coming home to her cottage. She was asking about seeing me.

***

Parking at my house later that evening, I stared at the captain's quarters I'd purchased with one specific vision in mind. The perfect family home, designed for children's laughter and growing families.

But looking at it now, my perception had fundamentally shifted.

Family wasn't a structure built to predetermined specifications. It grew from love, commitment, and shared experience. The house seemed to breathe around me as understanding settled.

Breaking free from previous expectations into a space to build something new.

That night, I slept eight straight hours.

Chapter 27

Gemma

The brass key was warm in my palm, attached to the wooden compass rose float Liam had carved. I stood on the front porch while December wind cut through my coat, staring at the door.

Four weeks. That's how long I'd been staying with Kate and Alex, recovering in their guest room while my body adjusted to surgical menopause and hormone therapy. Four weeks of being cared for, monitored, protected.

Four weeks of not being myself.

"You don't have to do this today." Mom set down a box labeled *Kitchen - Fragile*. "We can wait until you're ready."

"I've been ready for weeks." Kate's guest room had been comfortable, her family supportive, but I needed my own space. Needed to figure out who I was in this changed body without an audience watching my every move.

An entire month of knowing Liam was finishing renovations on my cottage while I recovered in his sister's house. Four weeks of careful avoidance at family dinners, of polite distance, of pretending we were strangers who happened to share a history.

Dad emerged from the rental car with my laptop bag and a determined expression. "Strategic approach: establish base camp in living room, expand operations systematically by room."

Only my father would treat moving day like a military operation.

I unlocked the door.

The scents of fresh paint and lemon oil filled my nostrils. Afternoon light through windows that opened smoothly, no longer swollen shut from coastal humidity. The hardwood floors gleamed, refinished to match Nan's original wide planks.

Everything was exactly as I remembered.

And completely different.

"Oh."

The furniture had been rearranged. The sofa faced the window seat now, creating unobstructed pathways. Side tables were positioned at perfect heights for setting down tea or medication. The coffee table had been replaced with an ottoman, comfortable seating without sharp corners.

"He did good work." Dad's observation carried the careful neutrality of someone determined not to interfere.

I moved through the living room in a daze. The kitchen revealed more thoughtful details. Cabinets at varied heights, the most-used items within easy reach. A pull-out cutting board that meant I wouldn't have to stand for extended prep work. Under-cabinet lighting that eliminated shadows.

The bathroom stopped me in my tracks.

Vintage subway tile in soft cream with the perfect hexagonal insets. The aesthetic I'd described once, months ago, in a casual conversation about Nan's taste. A walk-in shower with a built-in teak bench and grab bars that looked like intentional design elements. The toilet at a comfortable height. The vanity included a pull-out stool for days when standing to do makeup was impossible.

I sank onto that stool, fingers tracing the smooth wood.

He'd listened. To every offhand comment about standing too long, every casual mention of what made daily tasks harder, every fear I'd voiced about losing independence.

He'd built me a sanctuary.

"Gemma?" Mom's voice drifted from the hallway.

"I'm fine." Another lie. I wasn't fine. Each thoughtful detail hit harder than the last. Subway tile and cabinet placement and the realization that Liam had finished this work after receiving my letter. After I'd pushed him away.

After I'd told him to find someone else.

The bedroom revealed the same attention. Nan's iron bed frame with a new mattress at the optimal height for getting in and out. Bedside tables on both sides with outlets within easy reach. A comfortable reading chair positioned near the window with good natural light.

A folded piece of paper rested on the dresser.

I unfolded it with shaking hands.

Gemma,

The cottage is ready for you.

The heating system has been updated but maintains the original radiators (your grandmother would approve).

The pilot light instructions are taped inside the basement door. The bathroom plumbing occasionally makes noise when the outside temperature drops below twenty degrees - perfectly normal, just letting you know so you don't worry.

Welcome home.

-Liam

Professional. Courteous. Carefully impersonal.

The distance in those words hurt more than the letter I'd written him.

"Everything looks wonderful." Mom appeared in the doorway, tablet in hand. "I've been documenting the accessibility features for my research on adaptive living environments."

Of course she had. Mom processed emotions through academic frameworks.

"It's perfect." My voice came out rough.

"The attention to detail suggests significant time investment. And considerable understanding of your specific needs."

I met her eyes. "Don't."

"I'm simply noting objective facts."

"You're noting that I made a mistake."

Mom cleaned her glasses with methodical precision. "I'm noting that sometimes we make decisions based on fear rather than data. Both choices have consequences we must live with."

The grandfather clock in the hallway marked three in the

afternoon. Dad appeared with another load, Kate trailing behind with my favorite throw pillows.

"Everything's coming together." Kate's brightness had an edge. "This place is going to be perfect for you."

"It already is." I gestured at the modifications. "Liam made sure of that."

Kate's expression shifted to something careful. "He wanted you to have a home that worked for you."

"Even after I told him to leave."

"Especially then." Kate set down the pillows with unnecessary focus. "By the way, family dinner Sunday. Mom's making her famous pot roast. You should come."

My stomach tightened. "Will Liam be there?"

"It's family dinner. Of course Liam will be there." Kate's tone suggested this should be obvious. "But if you're not ready..."

"I'm ready." Third lie of the day. "What time?"

Sunday arrived too quickly.

I'd spent two days discovering more thoughtful details in the cottage. The kitchen step stool that folded flat. The programmable thermostat set to my preferred temperatures. The bookshelf organized exactly how Nan had kept it, with her sea glass collection at eye level.

Each discovery was a conversation I couldn't have.

I changed outfits three times before settling on jeans and a sweater. The same dance I'd done for the past few Sunday dinners at Kate's. Too dressed up looked desperate. Too casual looked like I didn't care. The mirror showed someone who'd lost weight and gained shadows under her eyes.

Tonight would be no different from the other awkward

family dinners. Except now I'd be returning to my own home afterward, not Kate's guest room.

Kate's house glowed with warm light when I arrived. Through the window, I could see everyone gathering. Diane helping with place settings. Alex corralling the twins. James gesturing while telling some story.

And Liam, standing near the fireplace with a beer, laughing at whatever his brother had said.

The same scene I'd witnessed for the past month. The same careful choreography we'd all perfected.

I froze with my hand on the car door.

I could leave. Text Kate that I wasn't feeling well. Nobody would question it. I was still recovering, still adjusting to medication, still learning hormone therapy side effects.

Still terrified of seeing the man I'd pushed away.

The front door opened. Kate stood silhouetted against the light.

"You coming in, or planning to sit in your car all evening?"

Caught.

I grabbed the wine I'd brought and headed up the walk. Kate pulled me into a hug that lasted too long.

"You look good," she whispered. "The cottage is working for you."

"It's perfect. Tell Liam thank you."

"Tell him yourself. He's right inside."

My stomach dropped. "Kate..."

"You're both adults. You can survive one family dinner." She tugged me through the door.

Warmth and noise enveloped me. Maya launched herself at my legs, chattering about her dance recital. Noah showed me his latest dinosaur drawing with serious pride. Diane kissed my cheek and pressed a wine glass into my hands.

And through it all, I felt Liam's awareness.

He stood across the room, beer halfway to his mouth, eyes meeting mine for two seconds before he looked away and rejoined his conversation with James.

"Gemma!" Alex appeared at my elbow. "How's the cottage? Kate said you moved in this week."

"It's wonderful. The renovations are incredible."

"Liam does amazing work. You should see what he did with..."

Alex continued talking about the historical preservation at the Captain's house. I nodded while tracking Liam's position.

He'd moved to the kitchen. Helping his mother. Not looking at me.

Dinner was careful choreography.

Kate had seated us at opposite ends of the table. Close enough for the same conversation, far enough to avoid direct interaction. We spoke around each other, through other people, in response to general questions.

"Liam, how's the clinic expansion coming?" James asked.

"Good. Lisa's implementing the new chronic pain protocols. Dr. Jordan's been supportive."

"Gemma, Kate mentioned you landed the Tourism Board contract?" Diane's smile was warm.

"Yes. Starting in March. It's exciting to build something focused on sustainable tourism."

We took turns filling the conversational space, never over-lapping, never connecting.

Maya, bless her six-year-old directness, finally broke the pattern.

"How come Uncle Liam and Aunt Gemma aren't sitting together? They always sit together."

The table went silent.

"Uncle Liam's helping me with homework tonight," James interjected smoothly. "Had to keep them separated or they'd ignore the rest of us."

Maya accepted this logic. The adults relaxed. Conversation resumed.

But I'd felt Liam tense at the question. Seen his jaw tighten before James's rescue.

After dinner, I helped Kate clear while the men handled dishes. Through the kitchen doorway, I watched Liam dry plates with methodical precision. His shoulders carried tension I recognized. The careful way he wasn't looking in my direction spoke volumes.

"This is ridiculous," Kate said quietly, loading the dishwasher.

"What is?"

"You two. The elaborate avoidance. The talking around each other."

"I don't know what you mean."

Kate fixed me with her most penetrating look. "You wrote him a letter ending things because you were scared. He finished your cottage anyway because that's who he is. Now you're both pretending the other doesn't exist. It's exhausting to watch."

"What do you want me to do, Kate? I told him to move on."

"And did you mean it?"

The question punched me in the gut. I focused on scraping plates.

"I thought I did. When I wrote it, it felt like the right thing."

"And now?"

"Now I live in a cottage he renovated for me. Every detail reminds me he paid attention to things I barely noticed myself. The bathroom bench is the right height. The kitchen layout minimizes standing time. He positioned the furniture to maximize natural light because I mentioned once that overcast days made me sad."

Kate waited.

"I pushed away someone who saw all of me and stayed anyway. Because I was terrified he'd leave eventually, so I left first." The admission tasted bitter. "And now I don't know how to undo it."

"Have you considered just talking to him?"

"And say what? Sorry I broke your heart, can we try again?"

"That would be a start."

Through the doorway, Liam laughed at something James said. The sound carried ease that had been missing during dinner. When he wasn't trying not to look at me, he could relax.

"He seems fine without me."

Kate made a sound of frustration. "Gemma. He's doing everything except dealing with the fact that you're not in his life."

"How do you know that?"

"Because I'm his sister and I pay attention." Kate dried her hands. "Look, I'm not going to push. You both need to figure this out on your own timeline. But for the record, you're both idiots."

"Noted."

"And if I have to sit through another dinner where you perform this avoidance theater, I'm going to lose my mind."

"Also noted."

The evening wound down with dessert and coffee. I made my excuses early, citing fatigue that wasn't entirely false. The hormone therapy created unpredictable exhaustion.

Liam was in the hallway, putting on his coat, when I emerged from the bathroom.

We both froze.

"Hi."

"Hey." His voice was carefully neutral. "How are you feeling?"

"Good. Better. The cottage is perfect. Thank you."

"I'm glad it works for you." Professional. Polite. Distant.

"Liam, I..."

"Gemma, I should..."

We'd spoken simultaneously.

A painful pause.

"You first," he said.

What could I say that wouldn't sound like taking back my letter while still being too scared to commit?

"The bathroom bench is exactly the right height. I don't know how you knew that."

Something flickered in his eyes. "You mentioned it once. During a pain flare at Kate's. You said standing for long showers was exhausting."

He'd remembered. A single comment made months ago, in passing, during a moment when I'd been trying to downplay my limitations.

He'd remembered and built me a bathroom around it.

"Thank you," I whispered. "For all of it."

"You're welcome." He finished buttoning his coat. "Take care of yourself, Gemma."

Then he was gone, the door closing quietly behind him.

I stood in the hallway, Kate's words echoing.

You're both idiots.

She wasn't wrong.

That night, I lay in Nan's bed, staring at the ceiling. The cottage settled around me with familiar sounds. Wind against windows. Radiators ticking. The distant rhythm of waves.

I'd asked for this. Pushed him away because I'd convinced myself it was merciful. Given him back his future because I couldn't bear to watch him realize, years from now, that he'd settled.

But lying here, surrounded by evidence of his care, I couldn't escape the truth.

He hadn't settled. He'd chosen.

And I'd been too scared to let him.

My phone glowed on the nightstand. I could text him. Call him. Show up at his house tomorrow.

But then what?

I was four weeks into learning how to live in a body that didn't work the way it used to. Still adjusting to hormone therapy that made my emotions unpredictable. Still figuring out what energy levels felt normal versus medication side effects. Still discovering which activities triggered pain and which ones I could sustain.

I didn't know who I was anymore.

The event planner who'd built a successful Boston business had disappeared along with my uterus. That version of Gemma had relied on her body performing predictably, on being able to push through discomfort, on never showing weakness to clients.

This new version needed grab bars and medication schedules and careful planning around energy limitations.

And she deserved better than to stumble into a relationship before she'd figured out how to stand on her own.

Liam deserved better too. He deserved someone who knew what she wanted, what she could offer, what kind of life she could build. Not someone still grieving what she'd lost while pretending to be fine.

The Tourism Board contract started in March. I needed to establish my business, prove I could handle the workload, build something authentic that didn't require pretending my body had no limitations.

I needed to discover who Gemma Prescott was now.

Maybe by March, I'd know if I had anything real to offer him. Or maybe I'd discover that being alone was actually what I needed.

Either way, I owed it to both of us to figure that out before attempting anything.

The questions that had circled earlier faded, replaced by something steadier. Not certainty, but direction.

I'd built a career on meticulous planning. Every event required knowing your venue before you could design the experience. Understanding your resources before you could create something meaningful.

This was no different.

I needed to know my venue. Understand my resources. Build something solid before inviting anyone else into it.

The cottage would be my foundation. The business would be my purpose. And the rest would come when I was ready.

If Liam was still available then, maybe we'd find our way back to each other. If not, at least I'd know I hadn't asked him to build a life with a version of me that was still under construction.

Chapter 28

Gemma

March arrived with the kind of reluctant thaw that forced a person to question every decision they'd ever made about living in Maine. Ice retreated in grudging increments. Morning frost gave way to afternoon mud. The sun appeared for an hour, then disappeared behind clouds the color of old dishwater.

I'd given myself until March.

The deadline lingered in the back of my mind every morning when I woke, every night before sleep. March first to figure out who I was in this changed body. To build something that felt like a future. To decide if pushing Liam away had been self-preservation or the worst mistake of my life.

March first was yesterday.

I stood at the cottage window, my coffee growing cold between my palms. The cove's surface rippled under wind that couldn't settle on a direction. The tourism board contract sat signed on my desk. My business plan had evolved from wishful thinking to actual billable hours. I'd survived winter in Waverly

Cove without running back to Boston or hiding under my parents' academic safety net.

Everything I'd promised myself I would do.

Everything except the one thing that mattered.

My phone lit up with a text from Kate.

KATE

Coffee at Harbor Brew in 20? Or are we still pretending you're not spiraling?

I stared at the message. Then at the last text thread with Liam from after that last awkward family dinner months ago.

LIAM

I'm here if you want to talk.

I'd never responded.

I could text Kate. Spend an hour getting a pep talk I didn't need. Or I could stop planning and just go.

I grabbed my jacket.

The walk to Westfield Physical Therapy took me past landmarks that had become routine. Henderson's Hardware where Ben probably already knew where I was heading. The Daily Knead where Diane would mention to James who would mention to Liam that I'd walked past at eleven-forty-three looking determined. The pharmacy where Alex had perfected the art of the knowing look.

Small-town living meant privacy was performance art.

The front door to Westfield PT stuck slightly from winter moisture. The waiting room was empty except for magazines from last month and a potted plant that looked healthier than anything I'd managed to keep alive.

My planning brain calculated exit routes, backup conversation starters, contingency plans for if—

Footsteps in the hallway.

"Sorry, I thought I heard the door, but we're actually closed for lunch—" Liam appeared in the doorway. Stopped.

He'd changed. Same broad shoulders, same careful way of moving. But thinner. Hair that needed cutting. His blue clinic polo had a small stain near the collar that the old Liam would have changed before opening the clinic.

Every month of our separation showed on his face.

"Gemma."

My name in his voice felt like coming home and falling off a cliff at the same time.

"I should have texted." The words tumbled out fast. "I know you're closed for lunch. I can come back. This is unprofessional, showing up without—"

"I was eating a sandwich in my office." He didn't move closer. Didn't retreat either. "You're not interrupting anything important."

The heating system kicked on. Outside, a truck rumbled past on Harbor Street.

He shoved his hands in his pockets. "How are you feeling?"

Such a Liam question. Practical. Concrete. Giving me space to answer however I needed.

"Physically? Better. The hormone therapy stabilized. I can work full days without needing to lie down." I let my hands fall to my sides. "Emotionally? More complicated."

"Yeah." He glanced at the waiting room chairs, then back at me. "Do you want to talk in my office?"

"Okay."

His office looked lived-in. Anatomical charts on the walls, shelves of medical texts with broken spines, patient files spread across his desk. But also a photo of his nieces, a coffee mug from The Daily Knead, winter boots kicked off in the corner.

Evidence of a life I'd removed myself from.

Liam cleared a chair stacked with continuing education materials and gestured for me to sit. I remained standing, leaning against his desk with careful distance.

"My letter was wrong." I gripped the edge of the desk. "Not the feelings in it. Those were real. But the conclusion. That we didn't make sense. That you'd be better off without me." I made myself look at him. "I convinced myself that pushing you away was protecting you when really I was protecting myself from the possibility that you'd eventually figure out I was too much work."

He crossed his arms. Uncrossed them. Shoved his hands back in his pockets.

"So I'm asking now." My voice came out steadier than I felt. "What do you want?"

"I want—" He stopped. Started again. "You sent me a letter explaining why we couldn't work. You didn't ask what I wanted then. Why does my answer matter now?"

The question landed like a punch.

"Because I was wrong. Because I spent the past few months learning that running away from hard things doesn't make them easier." I faltered.

"What changed, Gemma?" He pushed off the desk. "You're still going to have complicated health stuff. So what is so different now?"

"I am." I grabbed his wrists, held on. "I changed. I spent the last three months building a business while managing chronic pain. I proved I could do this alone. And then I realized I don't want to do it alone just because I can."

"That's not enough." He said it quietly. "I need more than 'I don't want to be alone.' I need you to actually want this. Want me. Not as the safe option because I've already seen you at your worst."

"I do want you. I have wanted you for months. I've just been too terrified of what it would mean to actually say it."

"What does it mean?"

"It means I'm choosing uncertainty. Choosing a future that includes chronic health management and possible complications and all the messy reality of bodies that don't cooperate with plans." I stood because sitting felt wrong. "It means I'm choosing you even though you've seen me at my worst and somehow still want this. It means I'm done protecting you from me."

His careful control cracked. Relief, want, hope visible in his loosened shoulders, the way his breath caught.

"I need you to understand what you're signing up for," I continued. "The endometriosis is gone, but surgical menopause has its own challenges. The scar tissue causes complications. My doctors think I might have POTS. Family planning would require conversations about adoption, fostering, or acceptance that children might not be part of our future. This isn't going to be simple."

"Gemma." He lifted one hand, hesitated, waited for permission.

I closed the remaining distance, gave him permission by stepping into his space.

His hand found my face, thumb tracing my cheekbone. "Family can form around choice instead of biology."

"But you wanted—"

"I wanted what I was raised to expect. But I need partnership with someone I actually want to build a life with." His other hand found my waist. "Your health complications aren't a dealbreaker. They're just part of the landscape we navigate together."

"You say that now—"

"I'm saying it after months of thinking about that and nothing else. I'm saying it knowing exactly what I'm choosing."

I should say something more about what he was signing up for, but what came out was: "I missed you."

"I missed you too." He leaned his forehead against mine. "So what happens now?"

"Now we stop pretending this isn't terrifying and just try. No promises about perfect futures. No guarantees. Just two people choosing to build something together."

"I can work with that."

"Yeah?" I tipped my face up, met his eyes. Found want there, and caution, and something that looked like relief.

"Yeah."

When he kissed me, it felt like no time had passed between us at all. I pressed closer, needed to feel him solid and real after months of distance. His hands tightened on my waist as he pulled me flush against him and deepened the kiss, months of restraint finally breaking.

My fingers found the collar of his shirt and twisted the fabric. He made a sound low in his throat that went straight through my core. His hands slid under my sweater, palms warm against skin that had forgotten what this felt like.

We broke apart barely, breathing hard, foreheads pressed together in the middle of his office where anyone could walk in.

"We should..." I started.

"Yeah." His voice had gone rough. "We should." But neither of us moved.

"Does your office door lock?"

"It does." His thumb traced my lower lip. "You planning to stay?"

"That depends. Are you going to make me spell out what I want, or can we skip the part where I'm articulate?"

He kissed me again before I could finish. Walked me backward until my shoulders hit the wall. His hands framed my face. I grabbed his shirt and pulled him against me.

"Gemma." My name against my mouth, rough and wanting. "Tell me if this is too much."

"I'm fine. Better than fine. Stop treating me like I'll break."

"I'm not treating you like you'll break. I'm checking in because I spent our time apart regretting that I didn't ask enough questions. Because your body's different now, and I don't want to assume I know what you need."

"I need you. Not being careful. Not holding back because you're worried about my limitations." I traced the line of his jaw. "I need you to trust that I'll tell you if something doesn't work."

His expression shifted. Relief bleeding through.

"Okay." He kissed me again, less gentle this time. "But we're not doing this against a wall in my office."

"No?"

"No." He stepped back, caught my hand. "I'm taking you home. Where I can actually take my time."

We barely made it down the hallway. Hands found zippers and buttons with urgent efficiency. My sweater hit the floor somewhere between the living room and the bedroom. His shirt followed. By the time we reached the bed, we were mostly undressed, breathing hard, three months of separation compressed into urgent need.

He lowered me onto sheets that smelled like lavender fabric softener. Settled above me with careful attention.

"Tell me if anything doesn't work." His voice had gone rough. "Your body's different now—"

"Liam." I pulled him closer. "Stop assessing me like a patient."

He kissed me hard enough to stop the words. His hand slid down my ribs, over my hip, found the places that made breath catch in my throat. I arched into his touch, months of want and restraint finally breaking into something that felt like relief and homecoming and heat compressed together.

We'd done this before. That night at the cottage, after Portland, before everything fell apart. But this felt different. Less tentative. More certain. Like we'd both stopped pretending this was casual or temporary.

His mouth traced patterns down my neck, across my collarbone. I gripped his shoulders, let myself feel without planning or overthinking. Just sensation. Just him. Just this moment I'd been too terrified to let myself want.

"Tell me what you need." His voice against my skin, rough and patient.

"You. Just you."

He settled between my thighs, careful despite urgency, still reading my body for signals. The first moment of connection pulled a gasp from both of us. He stilled, forehead pressed to mine, breathing hard.

"Okay?" he managed.

"Perfect. Don't stop."

We found rhythm together, months of separation dissolving

into physical conversation that needed no words. His hands found places that made me gasp. My fingers traced muscle and bone and skin I'd memorized before and was learning again. He knew my body better than he should after one previous time, the PT in him reading every response, adjusting angle and pressure and pace.

It built slowly, inevitably, toward a peak that felt less like release and more like recognition. When I came apart beneath him, his name escaped my lips and his hands anchored me and the absolute certainty that this was right in ways I'd been too afraid to acknowledge.

He followed seconds later, face buried against my neck, breathing my name like prayer and promise combined.

We lay tangled afterward. Heartbeats gradually slowing. March light filtering through curtains. The world outside reduced to irrelevant noise beyond this small space we'd created.

"I should probably ask," Liam said eventually, fingers tracing idle patterns on my shoulder, "whether you actually have plans this afternoon, or if I just derailed your schedule."

"I had a color-coded timeline." I shifted closer, tucked myself against his side. "Kate was expecting me for coffee an hour ago. My phone is definitely full of increasingly concerned messages."

"Should you text her?"

"Probably." I made no move toward my phone. "But that would require being able to stand upright."

His quiet laugh vibrated through his chest. "POTS acting up?"

"Maybe. Or maybe I'm just boneless from being thoroughly distracted." I tilted my head to look at him. "You're very distracting."

"I'll add it to my resume." He pressed a kiss to my forehead.

"But seriously. How are you feeling? Any pain? Nausea? Dizziness?"

There it was. The doctor brain kicking back in.

"I'm fine. Good, actually." I traced the line of his collarbone. "Tired, but in that good way. Not the 'my body is staging a revolt' way."

"You'll tell me if that changes?"

"Yes." I caught his hand, threaded our fingers together. "I promise to communicate clearly about my symptoms instead of pretending everything's fine until I collapse. It's a new habit I'm working on."

"It's good to have goals." He squeezed my fingers. "And for the record? You don't have to perform okay-ness for me. If you need to rest, or take medication, or just lie here for three hours, that's fine."

The absolute sincerity in that statement tightened my throat. Made three months of separation feel simultaneously too long and completely necessary. I'd needed that time to learn I was worth choosing. He'd needed it to prove he was choosing anyway.

"I should probably text Kate," I said eventually. "She's probably convinced I've murdered you."

I finally reached for my phone, found exactly the messages I'd expected.

KATE

Okay so you've gone radio silent

Which I'm guessing means either you're having an actual conversation with my brother or you've murdered him and are disposing of the evidence

> If it's murder please use the industrial trash bags, the regular ones are too thin

> Gemma I swear if you don't text me back I'm coming over there

I chuckled as I put her out of her misery. Thankfully the last text had only come through a few minutes ago.

GEMMA

> Still alive. Liam says hi.

Her response was immediate.

KATE

> FINALLY. Don't do anything I wouldn't do.

> Actually scratch that, definitely do things I wouldn't do.

I showed Liam the messages. He smiled, that private smile I'd missed more than I'd realized.

"So." He shifted slightly, propped himself on one elbow. "What now?" His thumb traced circles on my hip.

I caught his hand. "We should probably also have a conversation. About what this actually looks like going forward."

"Okay." He settled back, pulled me against his chest. "What do you need to feel secure in this?"

"Honesty. About health stuff, about when things are hard, about what we're both actually feeling." I paused. "And patience. Because I'm going to spiral sometimes. I'm going to overthink and create contingency plans for contingency plans."

"I can work with that." His fingers combed through my hair. "What else?"

"Regular check-ins. So I know if your feelings change, or if the reality of my health stuff becomes more than you signed up for."

"I'm not going anywhere. But yes, we can do regular check-ins if that helps you feel secure."

"What do you need?" I asked.

He was quiet for a moment. "Communication when you're struggling. Not just physically, but emotionally. I need you to not disappear into that place where you've decided you're handling everything alone." He paused. "And I need you to believe that I actually want this. That I'm choosing you, not settling."

"That might take practice."

"That's fine. We'll practice." He kissed the top of my head.

"Good." He pulled me closer. "Because I'm not letting you leave."

"Bossy."

"Practical." He kissed the top of my head. "We have three months to make up for."

I'd given myself until March to figure out who I was.

Turned out, I was someone brave enough to choose uncertainty with the right person. Someone who could want without apologizing. Someone who'd learned that the best plans were just starting points anyway.

Epilogue

I checked my watch. 5:45. Low tide at 6:47 AM meant we had about an hour before the hidden beach disappeared beneath the rising Atlantic.

The path down to the western headland's secret cove required careful footwork. Liam's hand found my elbow as the breeze carried the scent of exposed rockweed and distant beach roses. My compression socks helped with the early morning circulation issues, and I'd timed my medication so the worst symptoms would stay calm during the ceremony.

"You sure about the stairs?" Liam asked, scanning the uneven stone steps. His hand stayed at my elbow, ready to catch me but not hovering.

"I'm sure about everything." My voice came out clear. None of the shakiness that had plagued me during months of traditional wedding planning. The knot in my stomach that had appeared at every venue tour and vendor meeting was gone.

This felt right.

Cathedral aisles and reception halls had never felt right for us. Our love had been anything but conventional.

The Justice of the Peace waited at the water's edge, gray hair whipping in the coastal breeze. She'd tucked her official paperwork into a waterproof folder marked with salt stains and sand from other beach ceremonies. Behind her, my cottage's weathered shingles caught the light.

I breathed easier looking at the view that had sheltered my recovery and watched us fall in love.

"Ready?" she asked. Her hands stayed steady on the paperwork despite the wind tugging at everything else. She treated our dawn ceremony like any other wedding. No raised eyebrows at the timing or location.

Liam reached into his pocket and pulled out something that caught my breath.

James's compass. Brass gleaming, worn smooth from decades of handling.

"I realized this was the only wedding gift that mattered." Liam held it out to me. The metal was warm from his palm. "A reminder that the best things in life take work. That battered doesn't mean broken."

I remembered the story. Ten-year-old Liam digging for pirate treasure, finding the planted cigar box, keeping this compass on his desk all these years.

Now it would guide us into marriage.

The ceremony unfolded with the tide's rhythm. No processional music. Just waves against rocks and gulls crying overhead.

I'd chosen a comfortable cotton dress that moved with the ocean breeze. No restrictive fabric that might trigger pain symptoms, no complicated undergarments that would make breathing harder. Liam wore a simple button-down, sleeves rolled up, looking more himself than any tuxedo could make him.

Our vows were brief. Promises we'd already been keeping for months.

When I talked about choosing each other over what other people expected, Liam's thumb traced the compass. When he promised to navigate whatever came together, I squeezed his hand three times. Our code for "I love you."

The Justice pronounced us married.

We kissed while seagulls called overhead and waves whispered against the rocks.

"You eloped."

Kate set down her fork too hard. Metal clinked against ceramic. Her eyebrows shot up while her mouth opened and closed without sound.

"You actually eloped."

I'd made the announcement during Sunday dinner at Liam's parents' house. Just held up my left hand between bites of Diane's potato salad, let the vintage ring catch the afternoon light streaming through the dining room windows.

"Last Tuesday," Liam added. His arm found its usual spot around my waist. "Low tide ceremony."

"I can't believe you didn't tell us." Sophie's words tumbled out fast, but she was leaning forward. Curiosity, not anger.

"Can't believe you pulled off a secret wedding in Waverly Cove," James said, raising his beer. "That takes skill."

My shoulders dropped from where they'd hunched near my ears. I sank deeper into my chair.

"Turns out the event planner who creates fairy tale weddings wanted something different for herself."

"Like what?" Maya asked from her spot at the kids' table.

I knelt down at Maya's eye level. The movement pulled at my surgical scars, but I ignored it.

"Something real instead of perfect."

"But why?" Maya looked up from arranging her carrot sticks into an intricate log cabin formation. "Don't you like parties?"

"I love parties. But sometimes the most special things happen when it's just the people who matter most."

"Like when Mama reads me extra stories but only when Noah's asleep?"

"Exactly like that."

Mom cleared her throat. I straightened, bracing for the inevitable academic analysis of our choice.

Instead, a smile curved upward as she cleaned her reading glasses with unusual care.

"Optimal return on investment," she announced. "Maximum emotional impact with minimal stress variables."

Dad nodded. "Excellent problem-solving approach. We've been observing the correlation between event size and stress indicators in your health data."

"Wait," Alex said, grinning. "Now I owe Kate twenty dollars."

"You bet on our wedding?" Liam asked.

"I bet on Gemma's common sense," Kate corrected. "After years fighting for the right to make her own medical decisions, I figured she'd eventually apply that logic to her wedding."

306

That evening, I stood in the cottage kitchen watching the fog roll in while Liam showered. Cool evening air filtered through windows that opened now, thanks to his restoration work. The space hummed with the satisfaction of a house that was lived in and loved.

"Wine?" Liam appeared in the doorway, hair still damp, wearing gym shorts and a well-loved Northeastern sweatshirt.

"Already on it." I poured two glasses. "Fair warning though, your brother texted that he needs help at six AM with some truck emergency."

"Right. Truck emergency." Liam accepted his glass, his fingers brushing mine. "Probably needs help loading lobster traps again."

We settled into the window seat, our favorite evening spot. From here, we could watch the town wind down. Fishing boats puttered past, heading home. A family walked their golden retriever along the shore.

"The Art Museum emailed today," I said, leaning against Liam's shoulder. "They want to discuss a year-round contract."

"That's incredible." His free hand found mine. "You'd be okay with that workload?"

His thumb made lazy circles on my knuckles. As always, his partnership made room for my health needs without making them the center of every decision.

"I think so. Especially if it means we can afford to keep the Captain's house."

Liam glanced toward the harbor, where his bigger house showed through the evening haze. "Still thinking about it?"

"Some days I question the logic of heating two homes through Maine winters." I followed his gaze. "Other days, when adoption brochures show up in the mailbox or we're researching surrogacy options, it feels like keeping a promise to ourselves."

"No rush," Liam said. Same words he'd used about surgery, career changes, every major decision. "We've got time to figure it out."

Through the window, Waverly Cove kept its ancient rhythm. Tides and seasons and daily life. Salt air drifted through screens that would soon need swapping for storm windows. Summer's end in Maine required preparation, but I'd learned the difference between planning for difficulties and being defeated by them.

My phone chirped with a text from Kate.

KATE

Coffee date. 9am tomorrow at the DK.
Bring wedding photos. Or else.

I smiled, already reaching for the calendar app to make a note.

This was home. Making plans with Liam steady beside me. A business that prioritized my values over my bank account. Love that made space for both of us.

The tide was turning outside our window, but we'd learned to work with rhythms rather than fighting them. Sure, we were heading into uncharted waters. But after everything we'd weathered to get here, I trusted our navigation skills.

Afterword

This story is based on my lived experience, but every woman's health journey is different. What remains consistent, however, is how our healthcare system continues to fail women. It took over a decade for me to receive an endometriosis diagnosis, and another decade before I found a doctor who believed that my quality of life mattered more than preserving my fertility. I am not alone in this struggle. Endometriosis affects roughly 10% (190 million) of reproductive age women and girls globally, yet on average it takes 9 years from the first GP visit to get a diagnosis.World Health Organization. "Endometriosis." *World Health Organization,* https://www.who.int/news-room/fact-sheets/detail/endometriosis.

I was tired of reading romance novels where everything magically worked out in the end. The ones where the heroine got married, had a baby, and lived happily ever after without acknowledging the very real health challenges that millions of women face. Gemma's story reflects the reality that sometimes "happily ever after" looks different than we imagined, and that's okay.

The statistics surrounding women's health research are staggering. As of 2020, only 10.8 percent of the National Institutes of Health (NIH) funding is allocated to women's research-Temkin, Sarah M., et al. "Perspectives From Advancing National Institutes of Health Research to Inform and Improve the Health of Women: A Conference Summary." *Obstetrics & Gynecology*, vol. 140, no. 1, 2022, pp. 10-19, https://doi.org/10.1097/AOG.0000000000004821. Even more shocking, less than 2% of medical research funding is spent on pregnancy, childbirth and female reproductive health.World Economic Forum. "Closing the Women's Healthcare Gap Could Be Worth $1 Trillion." *World Economic Forum*, Jan. 2024, https://www.weforum.org/stories/2024/01/women-healthcare-gap/. Endometriosis receives a fraction of the research funding that other conditions with similar prevalence receive, despite the profound impact it has on women's lives.

I want to thank my husband, Ryan, who not only gave me the support to take power over my own health and make the decisions I knew were right for me, but who encouraged me to share this story.

If you're struggling with endometriosis, adenomyosis, or other reproductive health issues, please know you're not alone. Organizations like The Endo Co, Adenomyosis Awareness Network, and Endofound.org provide valuable resources and community. I also recommend watching the documentary "Below the Belt," which exposes the systemic issues in women's healthcare.

Every woman deserves to be believed, to be heard, and to receive quality care. Until that becomes reality, we must continue sharing our stories.

Acknowledgments

Writing a novel is never a solitary endeavor, and bringing Gemma and Liam's story to life wouldn't have been possible without the incredible support system that surrounds me.

To my family—your unwavering support means everything. Ryan, thank you for never questioning why I was glued to my laptop, for listening to me talk through plot problems during dinner, and for believing in my dreams even when I doubted them myself.

To my friends who've become chosen family—thank you for celebrating every milestone, for understanding when I disappeared into revision caves, and for reminding me that there's a world outside my laptop screen.

To my beta readers and critique partners—DR, RE, and AC— you are absolute treasures. Thank you for your honest feedback, for catching my plot holes, and for cheering me on through every draft.

To the readers, bloggers, and reviewers who champion romance novels—thank you for understanding that love stories matter, that they provide hope and joy and comfort in ways that are both simple and profound. Your enthusiasm for the genre creates space for stories like this one to exist.

To the women who live with chronic illness and invisible disabilities—you inspired Gemma's strength, resilience, and determination to build a life that honors both your limitations and your dreams. Thank you for sharing your stories and for showing the world that health challenges don't diminish your capacity for love, adventure, and happiness.

Finally, to my readers—thank you for taking this journey to Waverly Cove with me. Thank you for believing in second chances, for cheering on slow-burn romance, and for understanding that sometimes the best love stories begin not with sparks, but with kindness, patience, and the courage to try again.

If you fell in love with this little Maine town and its residents, know that more Waverly Cove stories are coming. The Westfield family has more tales to tell, and I can't wait to share them with you.

About the Author

Angelica lives in Southern Maine with her husband Ryan, two step-sons, and a chaotic bunny who thinks he runs the household.

She started writing on a whim after years of complaining about unrealistic depictions of women's health in fiction. Finally fed up with yelling at books, she decided to write the story she wanted to read: one where women's experiences are portrayed with honesty, complexity, and respect.

With deep roots in Maine, Angelica draws inspiration from the tight-knit communities that define New England. This series allows Angelica to explore the rich tapestry of small-town life while celebrating authentic love stories. Learn more about the secrets and romances of Waverly Cove at www.angelicael-ing.com.